LAKOTA HONOR

BRANDED TRILOGY, BOOK 1

KAT FLANNERY

MW00748390

LAKOTA HONOR: BRANDED TRILOGY #1

www.katflannerybooks.com

SECOND EDITION Paperback
May 30, 2018

ISBN: 978-0-9811056-7-3

Cover designed by Carpe Librum Book Design

PRAISE FOR
LAKOTA HONOR

"For something different, transport back to the old west with this paranormal historical, and its alpha hero, and a heroine hiding her secret talents."

—Shannon Donnelly, author of the
Mackenzie Solomon Urban Fantasy series

"Ms. Flannery doesn't shy away from writing gritty scenes or about unpleasant topics. In this book, she deals with child labor and abuse, as well as animal abuse, and I simply wanted to reach through the computer screen and kill the awful villain myself, I got so angry. That's what good writing is all about—bringing out strong emotions in a reader. Congratulations on a job well done!"

—Peggy L. Henderson, bestselling author
of the Yellowstone Romance Series

"Talented, Kat Flannery knows her Native American history and those who relish the conflict of a heroic half-breed trapped between the white man's world and the Indian will fall in love with *LAKOTA HONOR*."

—Cindy Nord, award-winning author of *No Greater Glory*

"Kat Flannery's, *LAKOTA HONOR*, weaves a fast paced and beautiful prose that lures you through every chapter and leaves you wanting more. The struggles of the main characters break your heart and leave you rooting for them, for their struggles—although different—are similar at the core."

—Erika Knudsen, paranormal author of *Monarchy of Blood*

"*LAKOTA HONOR* by Kat Flannery will hold your attention from beginning to end. Her ability to intertwine good and evil within the confines of the Indian and white worlds is nothing less than inspired. Nora and Hawk come together in a very different, magical way; she as a healer and he as a killer. The ancillary characters are well drawn. You either like them or hate them. You might also wonder about some of them as the story progresses."

—Katherine Boyer, romance reviewer

"*LAKOTA HONOR* is a book that leads readers back in time and then invites them to question just how much has really changed. Get comfortable—you're not going to want to put this one down."

—Leanne Myggland-Carter, operations manager
at Canadian Authors Association-Alberta

ACKNOWLEDGEMENTS

Writing this book was so much fun. I'd like to thank my publisher and friend Cheryl Tardif for planting the seed of a paranormal western in my head. I never would've thought to go there.

Rhonda, my editor, bless you for your patience. Carrie, for the millions of titles you shot my way until we decided on one. Mom and Dad, for letting me bounce ideas around and being my sounding board.

My husband and three sons for again allowing me to work many hours researching and writing this book; I love you.

To my readers, thank you for all your support.

Love,
Kat

NOVELS BY KAT FLANNERY

Chasing Clovers

The Branded Trilogy
Lakota Honor (Book 1)
Blood Curse (Book 2)
Sacred Legacy (Book 3)

Hazardous Unions:
Two Tales of a Civil War Christmas
(*by Alison Bruce & Kat Flannery*)

The Montgomery Sisters Trilogy
FERN (Book 1)
POPPY (Book 2)

For my brother, Joe.

"Each man is good in the sight of the Great Spirit"
—Chief Sitting Bull

PROLOGUE

Colorado Mountains, 1880

The blade slicing his throat made no sound, but the dead body hitting the ground did. With no time to stop, he hurried through the dark tunnel until he reached the ladder leading out of the shaft.

He'd been two hundred feet below ground for ten days, with no food and little water. Weak and woozy, he stared up the ladder. He'd have to climb it and it wasn't going to be easy. He wiped the bloody blade on his torn pants and placed it between his teeth. Scraped knuckles and unwashed hands gripped the wooden rung.

The earth swayed. He closed his eyes and forced the spinning in his head to cease. One thin bronzed leg lifted and came down wobbly. He waited until his leg stopped shaking before he climbed another rung. Each step caused pain, but was paired with determination. He made it to the top faster than he'd thought he would. The sky was black and the air was cool, but fresh. Thank goodness it was fresh.

He took two long breaths before he emerged from the hole. The smell from below ground still lingered in his nostrils; unwashed bodies, feces and mangy rats. His stomach pitched. He tugged at the rope around his hands. There had been no time to chew the thick bands around his wrists when he'd planned his escape. It was better to run than crawl, and he chewed through the strips that bound his feet instead. There would be time to free his wrists later.

He pressed his body against the mountain and inched toward the shack. He frowned. A guard stood at the entrance to where they were. The blade from the knife pinched his lip, cutting the thin skin and he tasted blood. He needed to get in there. He needed to say goodbye. He needed to make a promise.

The tower bell rang mercilessly. There was no time left. He pushed away from the rocky wall, dropped the knife from his mouth into his bound hands, aimed and threw it. The dagger dug into the man's chest. He ran over, pulled the blade from the guard and quickly slid it across his throat. The guard bled out in seconds.

He tapped the barred window on the north side of the dilapidated shack. The time seemed to stretch. He glanced at the large house not fifty yards from where he stood. He would come back, and he would kill the bastard inside.

He tapped again, harder this time, and heard the weak steps of those like him shuffling from inside. The window slid open, and a small hand slipped out.

"Toksha ake—I shall see you again," he whispered in Lakota.

The hand squeezed his once, twice and on the third time held tight before it let go and disappeared inside the room.

A tear slipped from his dark eyes, and his hand, still on the window sill, balled into a fist. He swallowed past the sob and felt the burn in his throat. His chest ached for what he was leaving behind. He would survive, and he would return.

Men shouted to his right, and he crouched down low. He took one last look around and fled into the cover of the forest.

CHAPTER ONE

1888, Willow Creek, Colorado

Nora Rushton scanned the hillside before glancing back at the woman on the ground. She could be dead, or worse yet, someone from town. She flexed her hands. The woman's blue skirt ruffled in the wind, and a tattered brown Stetson sat beside her head. Nora assessed the rest of her attire. A faded yellow blouse stained from the grass and dirt, leather gloves and a red bandana tied loosely around her neck. She resembled a ranch hand in a skirt.

There was no one else around, and the woman needed her help. She chewed on her lip, and her fingers twitched. *I have to help her.* She sucked in a deep breath, held it, and walked the remaining few feet that stood between her and the injured woman.

The woman's horse picked up Nora's scent, trotted over and pushed his nose into her chest.

"It's okay, boy," she said, smoothing back the red-brown mane. "Why don't you let me have a look at your owner?"

She knelt down beside the woman and realized she was old enough to be her grandmother. Gray hair with subtle blonde streaks lay messed and pulled from the bun she was wearing. Why was she on a horse in the middle of the valley without a chaperone?

She licked her finger and placed it under the woman's nose. A cool sensation skittered across her wet finger, and she sighed.

The woman's left leg bent inward and laid uncomfortably to the side. She lifted the skirt for a closer look. Her stomach rolled, and bile crawled up the back of her throat. The thigh bone protruded, stretching the skin bright white, but didn't break through. Nora's hands grew warm, the sensation she felt so many times before.

The woman moaned and reached for her leg.

"No, please don't touch your leg. It's broken." She held the woman's hand.

Ice blue eyes stared back at her, showing pain mingled with relief.

"My name is Nora," she said with a smile. "I am going to get help."

The wrinkled hand squeezed hers, and the woman shook her head. "No, child, my heart can't take the pain much longer." Creased lips pressed together as she closed her eyes and took two deep breaths. "Please, just sit here with me." Her voice was husky and weak.

She scanned the rolling hills for any sign of help, but there was no one. She studied the woman again. Her skin had a blue tinge to it, and her breathing became forced. *I promised Pa.* But how was she supposed to walk away from this woman who so desperately needed her help? She took another look around. Green grass waved in the wind. *Please, someone, anyone come over the hill.*

White daisies mingled within the grass, and had the woman not been injured, she would've plucked a few for her hair. She waited a few minutes longer. No one came. Her hands started their restless shaking. She clasped them together, trying to stop the tremors. *It would only take a few minutes. I can help her. No one would see.* She stared at the old woman, *except her.* If she helped her, would she tell everyone about Nora's secret? Would she ask any questions? *There were always questions.*

Nora's resolve was weakening. She ran her hot hands along the woman's body to see if anything else was broken. Only the leg, thank goodness. Lifting the skirt once again, she laid her warm palms gently on the broken thigh bone. Her hands, bright red, itched with anticipation. The leg seemed worse without the cover of the skirt. One move and the bone would surely break through the skin. She inhaled groaning at the same time as she placed her hands on either side of the limb. In one swift movement, she squeezed the bone together.

The woman shot up from the grass yelling out in agony.

Nora squeezed harder until she felt the bone shift back into place. Jolts of pain raced up and down her arms as the woman's leg began to heal. Nora's own thigh burned and ached, as her bones and flesh cried out in distress. She held on until the pain seeped from her own body into nothingness, vanishing as if it were never there.

She removed her hands, now shaking and cold from the woman's healed limb, unaware of the blue eyes staring up at her. Her stomach lurched, like she knew it would—like it always did afterward. She rose on trembling legs and walked as far away as she could before vomiting onto the bright green grass. Not once, but twice. She waited until her strength returned before she stood and let the wind cool her heated cheeks. The bitter taste stayed in her mouth. If the woman hadn't been there she'd have spit the lingering bile onto the grass. She needed water and searched the area for a stream.

Her mouth felt full of cotton, and she smacked her tongue off of her dry lips. She was desperate for some water. Had she not wandered so far from the forest to set the baby hawk free, she'd know where she was now and which direction would take her home. She gasped. She'd lost track of time and needed to get home before Pa did. Jack Rushton had a temper and she didn't want to witness it tonight.

"Are you an angel?"

She turned to face the woman and grinned. "No, Ma'am. I am not an angel, although I like to think God gave me this gift."

The woman pulled her skirt down, recovered from her shock and said in a rough voice, "Well if you ain't no angel, than what in hell are ya?"

Taken aback at the woman's gruffness, she knelt down beside her. *Here we go, either she understands or she runs away delusional and screaming.* "I… I am a healer." She waited.

The woman said nothing instead she narrowed her eyes and stared. "A witch?"

Nora winced.

"No, not a witch. I need you to promise you won't tell anyone what happened here today." Her stomach in knots, she waited for the old woman's reply.

"You think I'm some kind of fool?" She stood and stretched her leg. She stared at the healed limb before she hopped on it a few times. "People already think I'm crazy. Why would I add more crap to their already heaping pile of shit?"

Oh my. The woman's vocabulary was nothing short of colorful, and she liked it.

She smiled and stuck out her hand. "I'm Nora Rushton. It's nice to meet you."

The woman stared at her for a few seconds before her thin mouth turned up and she smiled. "Jess Chandler." She gripped Nora's hand with such force she had to refrain from yelling out in pain. "Thanks for your help, girly."

"I don't think we've ever met. Do you live in Willow Creek?"

"I own a farm west of here."

"How come I've never seen you?" *I never see anyone, Pa's rules.*

The wind picked up whipping Jess's hat through the air. "Max," she called over her shoulder, "fetch my hat."

The horse's ears spiked and he trotted off toward the hat. She watched in awe as the animal retrieved the Stetson with his mouth and brought it back to his master.

"I've never seen such a thing," Nora giggled and patted Max's rump.

Jess took the hat and slapped it on top of her head.

"Yup, ol'Max here, he's pretty damn smart."

"I'd say he is." She remembered the companionship she'd enjoyed with the baby hawk she'd rescued a few weeks ago. She'd miss the little guy. His feedings had kept her busy during the long boring days at home. "Miss Jess, I'm sorry to be short, but I have to head on home."

"Hell, girly, I can take you." She climbed up onto Max and wound the reins around her gloved hands. "Hop on. He's strong enough for two."

"Are you sure?"

"It's the least I can do."

She clasped Jess's hand and pulled herself up behind her. "Thank you, Jess, for keeping my secret." Placing her arms around the woman's waist, she gave her a light squeeze.

"Darlin," Jess patted Nora's hand, "you can rest assured I will take this secret to my grave." She whistled, and Max started toward town.

Otakatay sat tall on his horse as he gazed at the lush green valley below. The town of Willow Creek was nestled at the edge of the green hills. He'd been gone four round moons, traveling to Wyoming and back. The rough terrain of the Rocky Mountains had almost killed him and his horse. The steep cliffs and forests were untouched by man.

On the first day in the Rockies, he'd come up against a mountain lion, a grizzly and bush thick enough to strangle him. He used his knife to carve into the dense brush, and his shotgun to defend himself. When he could, he stuck to the deer trails, and in the evening built large fires to keep the animals at bay.

He glanced behind him at the brown sack tied to his saddle. Inside, there were three. This time he'd ask for more money. His bronzed jaw flexed. He would demand it.

The sky was bright blue with smudges of gray smoke wafting upward from the homes and businesses. The weather would warm as the day progressed and the sun rose higher into the sky. His eyes wandered past the hills to the mountains behind them, and his insides burned.

He clicked his tongue, and his mustang sauntered down the hill. Wakina was agile and strong. Otakatay knew he could count on him always. Over the years Wakina had kept pace with his schedule and relentless hunting. The emerald stocks swayed and danced before him as he rode through. The grass brushed the bottoms of his moccasins, and he dunked his hand into the velvety green weed. He'd make camp in the forest outside of the mining town.

Wakina shook his head and whinnied. Otakatay brushed his hand along the length of his silver mane.

"Soon my friend, soon," he whispered.

The animal wanted to run down into the valley, but resigned himself to the lethargic pace his master ordered. Wakina tossed his head. Otakatay slapped Wakina's sides with the loose ends of the reins, and the horse took off down the hill clearing a path through the grass.

The rolling blanket of emerald parted as Wakina's long legs cantered toward the forest. Otakatay's shoulder-length black hair whipped his face and tickled his neck as his heart pounded lively inside his chest. It was rare that he felt so alive. His days consisted of planning and plotting until he knew every detail by heart. The eagle feather tied to his hair lifted in the wind and soared high above his head. For a moment he allowed himself to close his eyes and enjoy the smells of wildflowers and wood smoke. The sun kissed his cheeks and he tried to hold onto the moment, savoring the last bit of calm before rotten flesh and wet fur filled his nostrils.

His eyes sprung open. He pulled on the reins, and rubbed his nose to rid the smell, to push out the visions that saturated his mind. The scent clung to him burrowing deep into his soul and he mentally fought to purge it from his consciousness. He shook his head and concentrated on the fields, trying to push the memories away. He didn't want to do this, not now. He didn't want to see, feel, smell, or taste the memory again.

The rhythmic clanking echoed inside his head, and he squeezed his eyes closed. Sweat trickled down his temples. He clenched every muscle in his body. His hands skimmed the jagged walls of the damp tunnel. He stumbled and fell onto the rough walls, burning his torn flesh. He moaned. Every bit of him ached with such pain, he was sure he'd die. His thin body shook with fever. He reeked of blood, sweat and fear.

With each step he took, he struggled to stay upright and almost collapsed onto the ground. The agony of his wounds blinded him, and he didn't know if it was a combination of the sweat dripping into his eyes, or if he was crying from the intense pain. His back burned and pulsed with powerful beats, the skin became tight around his ribs as the flesh swelled.

He tripped on a large rock and fell to the ground. The skin on his knees tore open, but he didn't care. Nothing could ease the screaming in his back. Nothing could take away the hell he lived every day. He laid his head against the dirt covered floor. Dust stuck to his cheeks and lips while he prayed for Wakan Tanka to end his life.

CHAPTER TWO

The full moon brightened Otakatay's path into town. He'd been to Willow Creek before and knew the streets well. He stretched and accidently kicked the brown sack hanging from his saddle. He never looked inside the bag. Even when he'd shoved the contents inside, he closed his eyes.

He pulled his duster back around him. Although half Sioux, he chose to wear the white man's clothing. It allowed him to move about towns and be discreet. But he never took the eagle feather from his hair and he always wore it down, acting as a mask of sorts it shadowed his features from any prying eyes.

He tugged on the left rein and rode past the jailhouse. Inside the barred windows, a musty office displayed wanted posters for murderers, men who killed for greed and lust. Men like Gabe Fowler, wanted for the slaughter of three children and their parents outside of Rapid City, and Leroy Black, a bank robber who killed anyone that stood in his way. Men he'd hunted and destroyed.

It didn't matter to him if they were wanted dead or alive. Most times he brought them in slung over Wakina's back. It was easier that way. He'd learned long ago never to turn his back on the men he sought. A dead outlaw was better than a wounded one. He helped capture the worst kind of men—men like him.

He was a slayer of men and women—ruthless and unforgiving. He was Otakatay, one who kills many. A bounty hunter that killed men that needed killing. He received good money for the lives he stole. He had a purpose, a reason for ending their lives and nothing would stand in his way. Killing was what he did, and it had never bothered him until two years ago when he took this job. Now he preyed on something else. Now he killed innocent women.

He went from being a bounty hunter to a murderer. No better than the criminals he'd dumped at the sheriff's feet. The bitter taste of his transgressions tainted his mouth, making it hard to swallow. He spat, remembered his promise and justified his actions. There was no time for pity. No time to remember the way he was. He would never be those things again. He was evil. He was a nightmare come to life. He was death.

His horse trotted down the street. All the stores were locked up for the evening. Houses black, their residents fast asleep. He glared at the homes of the white eyes. He despised them. A half breed, he wasn't given the same rights as the wasichu.

He was not wanted in the white or red race. His village long ago disowned his family casting them from their tribe. Two years ago, the government had ordered all natives onto reserved land. He didn't even know where his people were and he didn't care. They'd shunned them, cast them into the world of the white man to be ridiculed and treated no better than a dog.

He was alone. He depended on no one and he liked it that way.

He led Wakina into the forest to the clearing by the river. There he dismounted and waited for the wasichu to arrive. A half hour later he heard branches cracking. He leaned against his horse's side and waited for the white man to appear.

"You're early," the wasichu said. "Did anyone see you?"

"No one saw me."

The man lit a cigar, and the sweet aroma puffed in a cloud above his head. "Well, did you bring them?"

He grabbed the bag and flung it at the wasichu.

"There are only three in here. You've been gone almost four months and you only found three?"

"I have other jobs."

"I don't care if you have fifty jobs, you do mine first." He held up the bag. "This comes before anything else."

"You got what you wanted."

"There should be more in here."

Otakatay shrugged.

"No more jobs until you've killed them all."

"I take orders from no one," he growled.

"You work for me, and I want my job done first. Do you hear me, breed?"

It was the name he'd been called since he was young. The name that separated him from any other race. He gnashed his teeth, and stepped forward, ready to kill the bastard with the tailored vest and pressed pants. Otakatay's hand pressed into the man's throat, squeezing he lifted him until his toes touched the ground.

"You will call me Otakatay," he snarled and squeezed some more. "Or you will call me nothing at all."

The wasichu's face turned red. His mouth opened and closed, trying to suck in air.

Otakatay released him and watched as he fell to the ground gasping. His knife, sheathed to his side, poked his hip. The wasichu would die, but not until he had all he needed from him.

"Where's my money?"

The man stood, while rubbing his neck. He reached inside the pocket of his dress shirt and pulled out a roll of bills.

Otakatay ripped the greenbacks from his hand and counted them. "You owe more."

"Are you absurd? I've already given you way more than you're worth."

"No, white man, you owe more."

"I've given what is owed."

The arrogant fool wasn't backing down. But that would change. Otakatay would get what was owed to him.

"The price went up."

The wasichu swung the sack against his pant leg. The rhythmic sound brought back memories of his Ina as she'd sit around their cooking fire, tanning and raking the hide of a deer. He shook his head.

"You charged more last time."

"I kill women." He stepped forward, towering over the man.

"You've always killed women." He held up the bag. "*They* are all women."

He hung his head. He battled with the guilt over what he'd done. He never looked into their eyes. Never heard their voices—never saw their faces. From behind he slit their throats and took their lives.

"More."

"No!"

Otakatay stepped forward glaring. "You will pay."

"And if I don't?"

"You will die."

The wasichu's brow furrowed and his lips formed a thin line.

He waited.

The wasichu pulled out a twenty dollar bill and slapped it against Otakatay's hard chest. "You better find me more than three next time. They must be repopulating. What about children?"

He tore the money from the man's hand and gave him a shove.

"I do not kill children." He would kill this man and enjoy doing it. "The numbers have dwindled. There are few left."

"I don't give a damn if there's one left. You will find her and you will kill her."

He placed the money in the waistband of his denims. He'd been doing business with this jack ass for two years, and he was getting tired of the white eyes. Tired of the nightmares his duties caused. But he needed the money, and he'd made a promise.

"When will you return?"

"I will stay around here for a while."

He strode up to Otakatay. "No. You will leave. I can't chance someone seeing you."

He smiled. A toxic smirk with no sincerity attached to it. "I do what I want."

"No. You do what I damned well tell you."

He pulled the knife so fast the wasichu didn't know what was happening until it pinched his throat. "I'm beginning to think you have no brains, white man. No one tells me what to do."

He gulped and nodded.

I should kill this ass right now. As much as he longed to drive his knife into the wasichu's heart, he needed him for a little while longer. He put his knife back in its sheath.

The man walked to the river and dumped the bag's contents. "Contact me when there are more."

Otakatay watched him leave. By the next round moon, he would slide his knife across the wasichu's throat.

CHAPTER THREE

Nora waited an hour after lunch before slipping out her bedroom window. Father hadn't come home for the now dried and unappealing sandwiches she'd made. She knew she had time to sneak into the forest. She followed the path behind the stores so no one would see her. The day was hot for the beginning of May. Flies buzzed in front of her and she sidestepped so she didn't run smack into them.

The back door to the Mercantile was open, and she heard the owners, Willimena and Fred Sutherland, bickering. She didn't know them well, but from the few times she'd been allowed to go inside the clean, organized store, that's all they seemed to do.

Willimena, everyone called her Willy, was a large woman with a boisterous voice. Fred was short and slight with a bald spot on top of his head. It was clear to Nora from the first day she went into the store that Willy made all the rules. There was no credit allowed, except for the doctor of course. However, Fred was known to give candy sticks to the children who came into the establishment.

She picked up her pace, longing for the cover of the forest. She felt safe there. She loved to listen to the birds and watch the deer while she sat and reflected on her life, which would be easier if she didn't heal anyone. She knew this, but she couldn't turn a blind eye to those in need. God had given her the gift to heal wounds and save lives. To waste such a gift was immoral.

On the other hand, Pa might trust her, and she'd be like everyone else. She frowned. But how was she supposed to walk away from someone who was injured? How could she stare into the eyes of a person in pain, knowing she could help? *I can't.*

Jess Chandler had been hurt. The old woman would've died had Nora not healed her. Yet, her father refused to understand this. He saw the danger her gift caused and kept her locked up in the house all day. She was like a bird in a cage, longing to spread her wings and fly. To be free.

Pa had become distant and spent most of his free time at the saloon. She feared he'd begun to resent her for the life they lived. She couldn't blame him. It wasn't easy moving all of the time, or the constant worry he felt when she'd used her power to heal someone. She closed her eyes.

Pa's tirades were justified. He'd stomp around and yell at her for putting her life in danger while throwing their meager belongings into bags. It was a scene she'd witnessed many times. Even though she wanted to argue, she always went along with him. She could never leave him, not after everything he'd done for her.

The long days on dirt roads, sometimes not even on a road, had worn on pa. She could see that now. Once a handsome man, his face now bore creases and sharp edges. His dark blue eyes seldom reflected the happiness she used to see in them as a child, instead they were bloodshot from the horrible habit he'd formed. When he looked at her, all she saw was anger and bitterness.

She sighed. She loved him. He'd always been there for her. Even though he was over bearing and demanded she live confined to his rules, her love for him would never change.

The elm trees rustled their leaves, welcoming her as she entered the thick woods. *I will make him see he can trust me.* She walked with a spring in her step, determined to work on this problem with Pa.

She made her way to the clearing by the river, her favorite spot. Water swished as it rushed by. Crickets chirped in the distance, and the birds whistled up above. She sat on a large rock and inhaled the air around her. Dirt, water, the musky scent of the spruce trees and the pungent smell of fish surrounded her.

She slipped off her boots and peeled off her stockings. She dipped a toe into the cold water, scrunched her face and dunked her whole foot in. Hands clenched at her sides, she waited for the shock to wear off and her muscles to relax before she put the other foot in. She giggled as the water rushed between her toes. Nora kicked her feet and splashed water onto her skirt. She could sit here all day.

A horse whinnied nearby, and she glanced across the river to try and catch a glimpse of the animal. She held her breath, when she saw a man standing amongst the trees. Branches rested on his wide shoulders. He was tall. A black duster hung to his shins. She squinted against the sun's rays to try and see his face. The Stetson he wore was pulled down low so she could only make out a square jaw and long black hair.

Nora slowly released the breath she'd been holding without taking her eyes from him. She pulled her feet from the water and sat up taller to get a better look. If she didn't know any better, she'd say he was glaring at her from across the river. She shivered. He didn't seem friendly that was sure. In fact he looked like an outlaw. Determined to stay where she was and not scare off, Nora held her position.

Her bottom slipped down the back of the rock, and she reached out to stop herself from falling onto the ground. Minutes passed while she righted herself, when she looked up, he was gone.

She searched the outline of the trees for the stranger and saw nothing. The hair on her neck stood, and she touched her feet to the mossy ground.

The sound of breaking branches startled her and she froze. *The stranger.* She stared straight ahead. Her hands balled into tight fists as she waited for whoever stood behind her to make themselves known.

"Afternoon, Miss Rushton."

The voice seemed pleasant and somehow familiar. She searched her mind for anyone with the clipped tone and southern drawl. One face came to mind, Doctor Spencer's. She listened to his long strides as he came closer and stood beside her.

She glanced up at him from her log. "Hello, Doctor."

"Miss Rushton." He tipped his round hat. "You shouldn't be in the forest alone. With the mine nearby, you never know who might be passing through Willow Creek."

She thought of the stranger. Doctor Spencer was right. She'd seen the men that sauntered in from the mountain. One man in particular disgusted her. Elwood Calhoun owned the mine and had taken an interest in Nora. He'd come to call several times, even though Pa or she had turned him down.

"Come on, I'll walk you home," Doctor Spencer said and offered her his hand.

On the few occasions she'd seen the doctor, the elderly man had always been kind to her. She sighed. She didn't want to leave the forest, she'd just gotten here, but rather than tell the doctor about her troubles, she put her stockings and boots back on and took his hand.

"Thank you, but I can find my way home, Sir."

He chuckled.

"Well, that may be, but I'm headed into town so we may as well keep each other company."

Even though she liked the doctor, she wanted to walk home alone. She was a strong individual but, fighting with Pa was a losing battle.

She scanned the countryside as they made their way out of the forest. Colors melted into one another as brown, green and orange smeared across a canvas of swaying stalks. She'd give anything to be able to run through them right now. She wanted to live without restraints. She wanted to stomp her foot and demand her father see her for the woman she was.

The doctor's long strides had her taking two steps to his one to keep up. He smiled as they walked into the street. Nora froze. She always went around back and crawled in her bedroom window.

He stopped also and gazed at her with kind brown eyes.

"Everything okay, dear?"

"Yes, yes. Everything is fine."

She smiled.

"I have to attend to some business at the Mcaffery home. Seems little Billy has broken his arm and I need to check on it. You'll be okay?"

"Of course. Thank you for accompanying me into town."

He nodded while taking out his pocket watch. "Very well." He glanced at the time. "Good day, Miss Rushton."

"Good day, Doctor."

She scooted toward home the back way, passing by Sheriff Reid.

She tipped her head and continued walking. She liked the Sheriff, but couldn't afford to stop and talk. Pa could venture out for a walk and see her. She glanced back into the forest. She'd never seen the stranger in the woods before, and her curiosity was champing at the bit to find out who he was. Why was he in Willow Creek, and why had he stared at her for so long?

"Miss Rushton." Sheriff Reid tipped his hat. "How are you this fine day?"

Damn it. "I am well, Sheriff." She took a step but he blocked her path.

She craned her neck to stare up at him. He had a square chin with a dimple in its center and was clean shaven. The sheriff was Pa's age, but that didn't stop her from thinking he was handsome. She'd bet in his younger years he'd broken a few hearts.

She inhaled and could smell the hint of cigar on him. She felt sorry for the lawman. His wife had died a year ago of pneumonia. They'd had no children, and she wondered if he regretted it now that he was all alone. She liked him, even if the town gossips thought he drank too much. She never took to gossip, and in her judgment he was a good man.

She fidgeted with her hands.

"Are you all right, Miss Rushton?"

He missed nothing. "Yes, yes I'm fine. Anxious to get home is all." Her insides tightened, and she pivoted on her heel. "Good day, Sheriff."

He didn't move.

She tapped her foot and peered around him toward the blacksmiths.

"I know you moved here last year, and Willow Creek is pretty quiet but you shouldn't wander into the forest by yourself."

Odd, first the doctor and now the sheriff was warning her to be careful? Did this have something to do with the man she'd seen earlier? Maybe he was an outlaw. His attire did fit the bill if the dime novels she'd been reading held any truth to them.

"I'd been thinking on talking to Jack about it, too."

Nora's breath caught in her throat. She pulled her gaze from the blacksmiths to stare up at the sheriff. She didn't know what to say without giving away that she wasn't allowed anywhere past the yard. If he told Pa she'd be in hot water.

"I'll do right to remember that. Thank you, Sheriff." She smiled and willed him to step aside so she could get home.

"If it's just the same, I'll walk you home and speak with Jack." He headed in the direction of the blacksmiths.

He was relentless. *Damn it. What in hell am I going to do now?*

Father wasn't going to be happy. She frowned. She didn't want to move again and that was always the outcome when Pa felt like things were beyond his control. Her shoulders slumped. She had to figure a way out of this. She had to stop the sheriff.

"Um, Sheriff Reid." She paused, unsure what to say next. "Thank you for your concern, however I am an adult and my father has no say over where I go during the day." *Seem convincing. This is my one shot.*

"Is that so?" he said and gave her a long look.

She tipped her chin up and nodded.

Their pleasant conversation had shifted to an uncomfortable silence, and she knew it was now or never.

"Thank you again, Sheriff, but I think I will walk the rest of the way on my own."

He stopped and glanced down at her. His eyes held a hint of sadness while they gazed into Nora's. "Good day to you," he said. His gun belt sat low on his hips and hugged his backside as he walked away.

He missed his wife. She'd seen the loneliness in his eyes. Understanding settled like a rock in her stomach. She knew what it was like to be alone and wish for someone to talk to—someone to confide in. She turned toward home and came within inches of being trampled by two horses pulling a fancy black wagon.

Would this day ever end?

She jumped out of the way, lost her balance and landed face first in a puddle. Mud caked the front of her dress and hung from the skirt. She pulled herself up and smacked her hands on the ruined dress. She licked her lips and regretted it the instant she tasted the mud. Nora ran her arm along her mouth. *I just want to go home.* She lifted her head to apologize to the driver for getting in his way. When she recognized him and cringed.

The wagon stopped.

"Miss Rushton." Clean white teeth smiled down at her. "You should be more careful. I'd hate to hit a pretty little thing like yourself."

She didn't want to talk to Elwood Calhoun. She didn't want to be anywhere near him. The black wolf dog tied to the wagon growled, and she stepped back. The mud-soaked dress clung to her legs making it difficult for her to move.

"Sorry," she called and turned from the mangy dog and his owner. *Keep walking.*

"Miss Nora, Miss Nora." The voice stopped her. *Joe.*

Elwood came into town once a month. Always clean shaven and dressed in the latest fashion, he boasted of the coal he got from the mountain. He was very well-to-do and flaunted his money in the saloon while gambling. His son Joe was what folks called simple. Born a cripple, he got around with thick wooden sticks that he leaned into and used as legs. Nora had seen him a few months back waiting outside the bank for his father. She was drawn to the kind boy and every time he was in town she'd made an effort to talk with him.

"Hi Joe," she said.

"I brought my cards. I brought my cards." He held up a stack of blue playing cards. "We can play old man, old man."

She smiled up at him.

"It's Old Maid, Joe," Elwood corrected and leered at Nora.

On his last visit to town she'd told him about the card game. "I'd like that, Joe, but right now I have to get home. I'm all wet."

Disappointment clouded his blue eyes, and he fidgeted with his sticks. Nora's heart ached. She couldn't let him think she didn't like his company, when in fact it was his father's she despised. Elwood had come to call each time he'd been in town. He wanted to court her and thank goodness Pa said no, shutting the door on the fancy dressed miner. He was getting irritated with the constant no's, and she wondered if or when he'd give up.

"How about tomorrow?" she asked. "I'll come by after lunch."

His face lit with joy and he tossed his head from side to side. "Okay, okay," he shouted.

She couldn't keep the smile from her face when he clapped his hands.

"Well, that's right kind of you," Elwood interrupted. "I'll make sure I'm there and we can all dine together. My treat."

Nora's smile disappeared. That was the last thing she wanted. He had a tendency to touch her, a hand on the shoulder or the back and she didn't like it one bit. She didn't want to owe him anything either and dinner with him was sure to have its obligations. "That won't be necessary," she said.

The sun reflected off of his gold tooth as he smiled down at her.

She stood stiff trying not to show her disgust.

"Dinner will be at five. We'll see you tomorrow," he said.

Unsure of what to say, she waved at Joe and spun around to head home. Her arms spiked with goose bumps and she shivered. The last time Elwood was in town he'd caught her behind the livery and tried to kiss her. The thought of his hands on her caused her stomach to revolt. She shook her head. Thank goodness for Seth the stable boy. He'd come around the corner while Elwood had her pinned up against the barn wall. If Seth hadn't shown up, she hated to think what would've happened.

Elwood had made it no secret that he wanted to marry her, and he seemed insulted that she wanted nothing to do with him. Other women gushed over his good looks, fancy clothes and wealth. But it was the cold look in his eyes, and the sense of entitlement to anything and anyone that had her running in the other direction.

Look what I've gotten myself into now. Mud ran down her ankles and into her boots as she walked. She couldn't let Joe down. The boy had a soft wit about him, and she wished she could heal his legs without any repercussions from his father. But she knew without a doubt, Elwood would use her for his own benefit. He did the same with his own son.

She listened to him brag to the townspeople about what a loving father he was to his simple son. He brought Joe to town for the sympathy and free wares the business owners would give him. She despised the shifty miner for using his own flesh and blood as a pawn.

Joe's wide smile stayed in her mind as she stepped over manure and continued on her way. He was a wonderful boy, and she couldn't figure out how someone so pure and kind came from something so arrogant and scary. It must be from the boy's mother, whoever she was.

How on earth was she going to avoid Elwood tomorrow? The man repulsed her. Every time she saw him, she could feel his eyes undressing her. *I will be in the dining room, he won't try anything there.*

She sighed.

She rounded the corner, relieved to be home. The acrid smell from the blacksmiths filled the air around her. She recognized the aroma from the town often aiding in telling her what time of day it was and when to get home. The morning's air tossed hints of baked bread, afternoon's sweet peas, honeysuckle and grain, and in the evening's wood smoke permeated the air with its spicy scent.

She hesitated at the gate. Pa wasn't home yet. She eyed the livery and then her muddy dress. She scrunched her toes and they squished against soft mud. She really should go home. *A few minutes won't hurt.* The door to the livery let out a sorrowful moan as she pushed it open and went inside. She came here almost every day to see the horses, and after her encounter with Elwood she needed something to calm her nerves.

The strong majestic animals fascinated her. The doctor owned the livery, but Seth Holmes ran it. The boy was no older than sixteen and Nora liked him. He let her come into the barn anytime to feed and groom the horses. Best of all, he sensed that it was to be a secret and never mentioned it to Pa.

She unlatched the palomino's stall. He was the most beautiful animal she'd ever seen. The white mane and tail stood out against his honeyed hair. It was the animal's regal posture that drew her to him. She didn't know who he belonged to, but he was always here when she came.

She glanced behind her at Seth cleaning an empty stall. She wanted to ask him who owned the animal and why they didn't ride him, but she decided not to bother him with her nosey questions. It didn't matter to her who he belonged to, as long as he was here when she came to visit. She'd give anything to climb on his back and let him run through the valley. *I'd probably break my neck.* A risk worth taking to feel the wind in her hair. To feel fear. Exhilaration. A pulse inside her chest.

Her life wasn't filled with much excitement. The one thing that got her heart racing was sneaking around town. But now, after doing it for so long, she almost wanted Pa to catch her so she could yell and scream and fight with him. So she'd feel something other than the dull, repetitive, ho-hum emotions blended into the tasteless broth that was her life.

She grabbed the brush from the bucket and she nuzzled her face to his.

"Hello, Ghost."

CHAPTER FOUR

Elwood drove the wagon toward the white-washed hotel at the edge of town. He couldn't get the image of Nora Rushton out of his head. She was beautiful, and he'd love nothing more than to have her for his wife. When would she come to her senses and marry him? He was tired of waiting. She was a prize. A delicate little morsel he could nibble on whenever he needed.

Her long black hair and striking blue eyes held a hint of what lay beneath her dress. He was as sure as the money in the bank, under the frills and lace there was more to take his breath away. Hell, everywhere he'd go people would be jealous with her on his arm. He could show her off when he wanted to and keep her locked up until their children were born.

He snickered.

Joe hummed beside him. It was annoying and he glared at him.

"Stop that hummin' boy, or you'll be sorry."

"How come, Pa? How come?"

The invalid often repeated himself, and it drove Elwood crazy. Joe's brain didn't work like everyone else's. He was a burden, but he had value. People felt sorry for him, Nora in particular, and Elwood used that to his advantage by bringing Joe to town.

June waited outside the hotel for them, and he was glad the hotel maid had finished her errands in time to take Joe off his hands. He tipped his hat to two ladies walking past. Most of the people in town liked him, but it was his money and his business they liked more.

He didn't give a damn about the good people of Willow Creek, or any others for that matter. All he cared about was how much coal came out of his mountain and how fat his wallet was.

Five years ago he'd sold a few hundred acres of land near the mine at two dollars an acre above the price it was worth. He'd loaned the farmers money when the banks wouldn't. His plan had worked great. He charged high interest rates and collected regularly. And if he wasn't paid on time, he'd take the land and whatever was on it.

He'd raked in some good cash and was one of the wealthiest men in the area. Women threw themselves at his feet begging for a taste of his attention, and he'd obliged of course, using them for what he wanted and then discarding them. But Nora had never glanced his way. She never batted her lashes or pushed her breasts up at him.

He hunched over to set the brake. There were a few things that money couldn't buy and he'd made his living on taking whatever he wanted. He wanted Nora and damn it he'd get her.

"C'mon, Joe. We're here." Elwood jumped down from the seat and got their bags. The boy shimmied his way to the edge, and Elwood helped him down. At sixteen, Joe acted more like he was five. His head bobbed from side to side, and he started humming again.

"Joe," Elwood growled.

"Is June-bug here? Is she? Is she?" Joe propped one thick stick under each arm and hunched into them. Over the last two years, his back had curved and he'd grown a bump behind his neck. The Doc said it couldn't be corrected and Elwood didn't care. The more pitiful Joe appeared the more sympathy his loving father got. He took hold of Joe's arm and helped him along the walk. The bags were heavy and the boy was slow. He squeezed Joe's arm.

"Hurry up, Son," he whispered through a fake smile.

"Yes, Pa. Yes. Yes."

Joe's legs shook and Elwood held him upright. Once inside the doors of the hotel, Elwood handed Joe over to June.

"Mr. Calhoun," June greeted him. The older woman had worked at the hotel for years, and Elwood paid her a handsome amount to watch over Joe while he was in town. Lucky for him, she'd taken to Joe right away.

"Afternoon, June." Elwood moved around her to drop his bags onto the polished floor of the hotel lobby.

"Mr. Calhoun, glad to see you back in town, sir," Milton Smith, the owner, said. He picked up Elwood's bags. "Your room is ready. This way, sir."

He followed Milton to a room on the second floor, and headed straight for the bottle of whiskey he always demanded be there when he came to town. He poured himself a drink from the heavy glass decanter while June helped Joe up the stairs.

Elwood shrugged and took another swig.

The kid was more of a pain in the ass than anything. He poured himself another drink. But Joe's friendship with Nora served a purpose.

"I'm hungry. I'm hungry," Joe said as he hobbled into the room. His crutches scraped on the wooden floor and made Elwood wince.

"Pick those damn things up." He pointed at the boy's sticks.

Joe did as he was told and lost his balance. He would've fallen over if June hadn't caught him.

"Joe, darling you go ahead and scrape those sticks all you want to. It doesn't bother me none." June glared at Elwood.

Joe's blue eyes began to tear and his bottom lip trembled. He shook his head from side to side.

"Elwood, you tell this boy he can use his sticks the way he did before."

June was angry, and Elwood knew if he didn't say something to Joe, the whole damn town would know what he'd done. June sat on all the town committees. His horrible manner toward the boy would spread like wildfire and he'd be shunned.

"Go on." He waved his hand. "Walk with 'em the way ya were." He emptied the glass in one gulp leaving a trail of fire down his throat.

"Come now, dear, I made cookies today in hopes you'd stop by. They're in the kitchen."

"Mmmm. Cookies. I love cookies. I love cookies."

The maid giggled. "I know, dear. I baked them for you, and once you're settled we'll go down and get a few."

"Thank you, thank you, June-bug." His eyelids fluttered like butterfly wings.

Elwood rolled his eyes at the way people fawned all over the crippled kid. If June knew how he treated the boy back home, she'd shoot him for sure. Hell, he couldn't be expected to care for a simple minded kid. He didn't even like him. But he was his ticket to getting what he wanted.

He filled his glass again and swirled the gold liquid around before bringing it to his lips. The heady scent filled his nostrils and he inhaled. Yes, he'd have what he wanted. All of it. And no one would stand in his way.

CHAPTER FIVE

He saw the shadow on the stone wall. The long black snake snapped and buckled in the air behind him. The crisp crack echoed throughout the damp chamber. His hands were bound to a thick wooden pole, the same one he and two other boys had pounded into the ground a month ago—for this purpose. For pain. For torture. For fear.

He braced himself, closed his eyes and took a deep breath holding it within his lungs until they ached with the need for air. He pictured his Ina. Crack. The pain was instant. His flesh burned, and he could feel his skin as it hung in ripped pieces from his body. Crack. Again the long snake wielded its coiled end and bit into his back. Blood splattered onto the dirt floor. He tried to focus on the tiny dots that melted into the ground and disappeared at his feet, but his vision blurred.

Crack. He couldn't take anymore. He gasped as his body screamed in agony while his flesh was forever branded. The pain sliced through his ribs and into his very soul, filling him with hatred for the wasichu. His stomach rolled. Yellow bile spewed from his mouth and ran down his chest. Crack. The weight of the whip buckled his knees and he hung from the leather band tied around his wrists. The wounds on his back oozed and throbbed. His head lulled to the side, and he closed his eyes.

Otakatay woke from the dream panting. His heart thundered in his chest, and his body was moist with sweat. The moon was still high in the sky. He lay motionless on his sleeping mat and listened to the crickets sing, as the light breeze clapped the leaves together. The nightmare still vivid in his mind, he tried to abandon the awful memories and think of something else—something peaceful.

Had he been anyone else, peace might've come easy. But for him, a slayer of women and men, there was no such thing. He hunted with purpose, for a promise made. And he'd do whatever was necessary to fulfill it.

He thought of the man who hired him to kill the *witkowin*, the crazy woman and his lips thinned. The wasichu was evil, like his father. They both had the empty stare but one still walked this earth.

He sat up and struggled for a breath that wasn't paired with a sharp pain in his ribs. As he stretched his strong arms above his head, his back seized and spasms shook his whole body. The muscles didn't recuperate after the last time. The wounds had healed, but the flesh was a mangled, deformed mess. Rigid and raised the scars drew a grotesque pattern on his back and sides.

He traced a long, bevelled scar down his forearm. He would never forget the pain he'd endured. It intoxicated him and afterward he felt delusional. Full of angst and fear wondering if he was ever going to escape the dreadful memories of the life he'd been thrust into. He grabbed his shirt. Within the vacant eyes of the forest he went without one. When living among the wasichu, he never took it off.

He ran his fingers through his shoulder-length hair to untangle it. A fingertip caressed the eagle feather tied on the side, and his chest seized. *I promise.*

Wakina neighed and stomped a hoof, and Otakatay came alert. He grabbed his knife, rolled to the side and in two quick, soundless strides was behind a tree, waiting. He heard a branch snap, and then another and another. He raised his blade.

A deer pranced through the campsite and stopped at the bushes on the other side. The large buck stared straight at him.

He lowered his knife.

The deer bolted, disappearing into the trees.

"You should've known it was a helpless deer," he said to Wakina.

The horse turned his head, ignoring him.

He smiled and dug into his saddle bag for an apple. He sliced the shiny red globe in half, gave one piece to Wakina and took a bite out of the other.

The horse didn't even chew it, but swallowed the fruit whole.

"You, my friend, are a glutton."

Wakina bowed his gray head and nudged Otakatay's hand for more of the apple.

"I don't think so." He held up the fruit. "This is mine."

After he finished his half of the apple, he picked up a few dry branches and brought them to the pile of ash near his bed roll. Once he had the wood smoking he blew on it to fuel the fire. Satisfied with the height of the flames, he gutted and cooked the fish he'd caught yesterday.

Leaning against his saddle, he picked at the trout on his plate. The moon made its descent. The sky changed to orange and yellow as the first rays of dawn shone down.

Nora woke early and prepared some coffee. She added two more tablespoons of the grounds to make it extra strong. Pa had been out late the night before and lay slumped over the sofa. One arm dangled to the floor, while the other was tucked under his chest. She checked the tin in the cupboard above the stove. The money was gone. There had been thirty dollars in there. He'd taken it to gamble and drink, again.

Her face heated as anger raced through her veins. They were never going to have their own place if he continued on like this. Now with all their money gone, how would they survive until the end of the month?

She checked the cupboards, cornmeal, yeast, baking soda, one jar of fruit, one jar of meat and nothing more. She was thankful for her garden, but that wouldn't feed them for long. The garden was planted for the purpose of supplementing their meals. With no meat and no money the garden would feed them for another week.

Oh Pa, why? Why did you do this? She poured coffee into two cups.

"Pa, it's time to get up," she sang. "You don't want to be late for work."

She sat at the table and watched through half-closed eyes as her father dislodged his arm from under his chest. He groaned. The front of his shirt was stained brown, and an overwhelming odor invaded her nostrils. She covered her mouth and nose. He'd thrown up all over himself and the sofa.

Pa's face lost all color, and she knew he smelled the vomit, too.

She stood. "Here, Pa, let me help you."

He waved his arm at her. "No."

"But, Pa."

He swayed and almost fell from the sofa.

"Leave me be."

Tears formed in her eyes. What was happening to him? He was no longer the man she knew. She went to him and placed her hand on his shoulder.

He pushed her hand away, and ripped the soiled shirt off tossing it onto the floor. "I don't need your damn help."

She stepped back toward the table.

His pale face contrasted with swollen red eyes that glared up at her. "You left the yard. Jed said he saw you walking toward the forest yesterday."

Oh dear.

"I didn't go far, just enough to set the hawk free, that's all."

He swayed. "You know the rules. You've disobeyed me."

She held her tongue. Pa was provoking her. She'd seen this many times before when he'd had too much to drink and wanted to put the blame on her. If she took the bait, he'd be packing up their things and they'd be gone within the hour.

"I'm sorry, Pa. It won't happen again."

He tried to stand, and swayed to the side falling onto the sofa and into the mess there.

She grabbed the wet cloth on the counter and brought it to him.

"Here, let me help you."

"Get away from me." He swung at the cloth in her hand missing it by a foot.

She dropped the cloth onto the table and fled to her room closing the door behind her. She could hear him trying to get up off the sofa. The table shifted and something banged against the far wall. She cringed.

Pa went to work feeling the effects of his drinking almost every day, but this morning was different. He was still drunk.

She gnawed on her bottom lip while she waited for him to wash his face, dress and leave for work. Wanting to escape, she glanced at the window. She'd just promised Pa she'd stay in the cabin but a walk in the forest would do her some good. He wasn't going to check on her or say goodbye. She'd clean the mess when she got back. She braided her hair and crawled out the window. The morning air smelled much better than the awful stench inside the cabin.

Pa's drinking had always been a problem. When she was younger she'd find him in an alley curled up in his own vomit and urine sobbing about how he couldn't save her mother. Not strong enough to carry him home she'd sit and console him. He drank to forget and Nora was the reminder of what he'd lost. When he found out she could heal, he drank even more, distancing himself from his only child. He spent every night at the saloon gambling and drinking. She hadn't seen a glimpse of happiness in him in years.

She shook her head. Was their life that bad? Sure, she'd complained and argued with him for freedom; she'd do anything for him to loosen the rope tied around her neck. But was this life terrible enough to become inebriated every night? She pursed her lips.

She passed the Mercantile, and her shoulders slumped. They had no money. He'd gambled everything. How was she supposed to fix this? She couldn't get a job.

"Oh, damn it."

She shoved her hands inside her apron pockets. The hotel stood at the north end of Main Street and backed onto the forest. She had no problem walking past it except when Elwood was in town. She shivered and pulled her hands from the apron to rub along her arms.

When the mine owner was in Willow Creek she stayed close to home, but this time she'd have to see him. She promised Joe a game of cards this afternoon, and she couldn't let the boy down because his father was no good.

She was determined to visit with him over a card game and not let Elwood intimidate her.

Lush moss blanketed the forest floor. She untied her boots and slipped them off. A squirrel ran along a branch above her, hesitated and then jumped to another. She giggled. Animals always had a way of calming her. Life never seemed awful in the thick of the forest.

Roots burst from the ground mangled and barbaric, and she stepped over them. She inhaled and her mind filled with the fresh, balsamic scent of pinecones. She skimmed the prickly pine leaf. She always loved the spruce trees. They never lost their glorious greenery in the winter like the others. Tall and magnificent, they stood like proud soldiers within the dense forest. They looked beautiful at Christmas time decorated with ribbons and candles, too.

A branch broke to her left, and a hand clamped over her mouth. She tried to scream, but nothing came out. Her heart hammered inside her chest. She struggled for air. She squirmed, trying to wiggle loose, but her arms were held tight to her sides. Cold steel pushed into her throat, and she froze.

"Quiet wasicun winyan—white woman," a low voice said from behind her.

She could see from the corner of her eyes, a dark hand across her mouth. *Indian!* She was going to be taken captive. She would be a slave for the rest of her life. Visions of wild Indians tearing at her clothes invaded her mind. Their filthy hands pawed at her virginal skin, taking from her what she fought to keep. She tried again to move, but his hand tightened around her mouth and he pushed the blade closer.

The forest floor swayed before her as the truth of what her future would be slammed into her chest. She pushed forward vomiting into his hand and all over her cheeks and chin.

A loud growl erupted from behind her, and she was thrown to the ground.

"Ahh, shit." His back was to her as he knelt down and washed his hand in the river.

She saw the glint of the knife in the shallow water. She needed to run, to scream, to get the hell out of there. She tried to move her legs, but the limbs proved useless.

"Clean your face." He stood over her now.

Afraid to make eye contact, she examined his moccasins. She'd never seen a pair this beautiful and wondered if his wife had made them. She'd heard of Indians taking more than one wife, and she drew back. *Oh, God. Please don't let that be his plan.*

"Go!"

She crawled to the river, cupped her hand in the cold water and splashed her face. She swished water in her mouth and spat it onto the ground.

"Get up."

She struggled to her feet, and her stomach rolled. She tucked a loose strand of hair behind her ear.

Nora's eyes met his. Her breath caught, and she took an unconscious step back. It was him. The stranger she'd seen the other day. Long, black hair framed his face. Dark stubble covered a strong jaw and high cheekbones. He wore black pants and a shirt opened halfway down his chest. She could see the muscles bunched there.

A scar peeked out of his collar and ran up his neck disappearing behind his hair. He stood at least a foot and half taller than her. Almond shaped charcoal eyes bore down upon her. If he meant to intimidate her, he had succeeded. He resembled evil, hatred and death all rolled into one. She shivered. The urge to run consumed her.

She tried to speak, but a lump had lodged inside her throat and nothing came out.

He stepped toward her.

She squeezed her eyes shut and waited.

He grabbed her braid and pulled her head back, exposing her throat. This was it, she was going to die. A tear slid down her cheek. Her heart hammered inside her chest. She had to calm down. She felt the Indians chest rub against her shoulder as he exhaled beside her. Leaves scrunched under his moccasins. The frigid blade bit into her flesh.

He pushed her away and growled, "Go home, little girl."

She almost tripped and fell, but grabbed onto a tree to catch herself. She stared at him. Had he told her to go home? He wasn't going to kill her?

He slid the knife into the leather sheath strapped to his pant leg, and she saw more scars around his wrists. Nora's hands heated and before she knew what was happening, she took a step toward him.

His head shot up and he glared at her.

"I'm Nora." What the hell was she thinking? The man almost killed her. *But he didn't and he'd been hurt badly one time in his life.*

He continued to glare at her. "Go home."

His voice reminded her of sand paper run along a block of wood and the low baritone key on the church organ.

"Are…are you passing through Willow Creek?" *Do as he says. Go home. What am I thinking?*

"Are you deaf? I said leave." He pointed behind her. "Go home."

He spoke English well. She assessed his face, his clothes, his skin tone. He wasn't only native, he was white, too.

He hadn't moved his arm from the stiff position.

She glanced in the direction he'd pointed with no intentions of leaving. Something about him fascinated her. At first she was scared to death and now she wanted to know something—anything—about him.

"I'm quite capable of finding my way home, mister."

He spoke in his language, and she knew by the way his face twisted with fury he was angry. He pulled the wide blade from its sheath, and sinister eyes glared into hers. His full lips lifted up at the corners, but not in a kind way and he ran the tip of the knife along his cheek.

She retreated. He advanced until they stood so close she could smell campfire on his skin.

He grabbed her braid and weaved the knife through it. "What a nice trophy this would make."

He is going to scalp me! She closed her eyes and enlisted any courage she had left deep inside her. She wasn't going down without a fight. She stood taller and lifted her chin. Inside she was panicking, but she'd rather die than allow him to take her beautiful hair.

He laughed, but there was nothing merry about it. He pulled a clump of hair from her braid and sliced it from her head.

She gasped and felt her head where he'd cut the hair.

He pointed the blade, the tip pricking her throat. "Go. Before I change my mind and take it all."

Without so much as a second thought, she rushed through the forest she loved, leaving behind the birds and the eerie stranger who scared and excited her at the same time.

CHAPTER SIX

Nora ran as fast as she could over the uneven ground. Branches slapped her face and pulled at her hair as she went by. She didn't look back until she stepped onto the path behind the hotel. Her heart thumped, and she wheezed low moans from her throat. She slumped against a tall spruce, put her hand on her chest and shivered as she glanced behind her into the dense forest. The dark trees were no longer welcoming. But she was more concerned with the stranger that lurked among them.

She turned and almost collided with Elwood's dog, Savage. The black half-wolf was wild and mean. Savage's fur was matted and dirty. An ugly looking scar that pulled the skin sat above his left eye and deformed the face. The hair on top of his head stood up, and his ears lay back and pointed. He hunched low as a deep threatening growl rumbled toward her. She glanced up at the street beyond the buildings. Where had he come from?

"Savage," she said in a commanding voice.

The dog's lip curled, large fangs dripped with saliva. The dog had chewed through the rope that tied him to the fancy wagon, and she doubted Elwood even knew he was missing.

Savage growled.

If she weren't in danger of losing a limb, she would've thought his growl sounded more like a giant cat's purr, a roll of the tongue making the sound rippled. Her toes scrunched, and she realized while running for her life in the forest, she had forgotten her boots. *Great.*

Savage crouched lower. The hair on his neck stood and his tongue dashed out to lick his fangs.

Oh, this isn't going to be good. All animals could smell fear and she stunk of it. Sweat trickled down her neck. She didn't dare move her hands from her sides, for fear the deranged animal would see her shaking and lunge for her throat.

She spotted the mercantile and the blacksmiths next door. She was so close to home. If she screamed would there be enough time for someone to come running and stop the animal from ripping her to shreds? *I doubt it. Besides, Elwood may be the one running and he's the last person I want to see.*

Another growl and this time a large paw stepped toward her.

Oh dear. She loved all animals, but this one was different. He was mean and wouldn't think twice about ripping her arm off. She thought of the stranger in the woods. He was similar to the wolf-dog. He, too, was a mixed breed, who would hurt, or even kill if the opportunity arose. After all, he was going to scalp her. *But he didn't. Yes, yes, he didn't but his dark eyes said he would.* And she knew without a doubt he was capable of anything.

His presence exuded arrogance—it reeked of danger, need and hunger. By taking his knife to her hair he'd accomplish scaring her to death, and making her run away terrified. She glanced at the dog, now two feet from her. She inched back into the tree, trying to melt into the trunk.

Savage growled.

"Savage, you go home." Her voice trembled. "You heard me. Now get going, right now."

The filthy animal barked and showed his teeth.

I'm dead.

"Nora, Nora," Joe yelled from between two buildings. He leaned into his walking sticks and waved.

She didn't dare move. The dog was so close now she could feel his breath on her hand. Joe's feet shuffled in the grass. She wanted to yell at him to go home, but didn't move for fear Savage would strike. She watched as Joe struggled to get to her. How she'd love to heal his mangled legs. Her hands grew hot and tingled. *I can't help him. If Elwood found out, he'd never stop pursuing me.*

Joe came up beside her. "Why ya way out here? Out here?"

She watched as his beautiful blue eyes rolled; something she'd seen him do many times.

Savage growled again.

"Oh, puppy, stop it. Stop it." Joe reached for the dog.

Savage twisted his head and dug his teeth into Joe's hand.

Joe screamed and clutched his bleeding hand to his chest. He shook his head from side to side and opened and closed his eyes repeatedly.

Nora kicked the dog's snout with her bare foot and felt the jab of sharp teeth against her toes. She kicked him again, this time in the side. The horrible beast lunged at her and she kicked him harder. She knew the dog wouldn't stop now that he'd tasted blood.

She picked up the crutch Joe had dropped and swung at the dog catching him in the neck. He rolled backward and shook his head before he came at her again. This time she was ready. She'd never played baseball, but she watched a few games out on the church lawn. She positioned the crutch like a bat. Joe screamed in the background as Savage leapt toward her. She squeezed her eyes and swung. The wooden stick vibrated in her hands. The dog yelped and began to whimper.

She opened her eyes. Joe was crying and Savage lay on the grass, whining. *What have I done?* She dropped the crutch and knelt in front of him, but he got up and limped away. She stood and watched Savage until he disappeared into the trees behind them. Joe's crying became louder. She went to him and took his hand. The boy was beyond sobbing now, he gasped as fat tears messed his face. There was blood everywhere, and Nora's stomach rolled.

"I will fix it, Joe. I promise."

The boy's body rocked back and forth, and he almost lost his balance.

"Joe, you need to sit down."

He shook his head again, and she didn't know if he was answering her or if this was one of his odd behaviours. She slid the stick out from under Joe's arm and leaned him against her. She lowered them both to the ground. With Joe positioned against the tree, she took his hand once more.

Oh my. The tip of Joe's thumb hung by a few pieces of flesh. She couldn't see the rest of his hand, there was too much blood. Nora's hands shook with the need to heal him. Red blotches covered her palms, and the tips of her fingers were the color of Joe's bloodstained ones. She wondered if he would tell anyone, or what his reaction may be once she made this right. There was no time to debate the outcome. She needed to heal him.

Joe continued to cry, rocking back and forth.

"Here we go." She placed her hands on his to bring the thumb into place with the torn bone and flesh. The heat in her palms intensified and she squeezed.

Joe tried to pull away, but she held him to her. The boy's pain shot down her arms to nestle back into her own thumb. She swayed. The earth spun around her. She dug her knees into the grass and closed her eyes. She absorbed the wound until she felt the thumb was no longer dislodged.

The boy was silent when she released his hand.

She walked a few feet away into the forest where she threw up all over the bushes. She waited and vomited a second time. Still light-headed, she wiped her mouth with her apron and faced Joe.

The boy held his hand in front of his face. The thumb no longer bloody and looking horrid.

"How's your hand, Joe?" She knelt in front of him.

"It's all better. Look, Nora. Look." He shoved his hand into her face.

She giggled. "I see that. Are you okay now?"

The boy smiled and his eyes lit up. "You made me better. You. You. You," he shouted.

She smiled.

"Yes, Joe, I did. But you mustn't tell anyone."

"I know. I know. Like a secret."

"Like a secret,' she confirmed and squeezed his hand.

He tilted his head and scrutinized her for a long time before asking, "Are you a witch?"

The word sobered her. All of Pa's fears echoed in her mind. "No, Joe, I am not a witch."

"They're real you know. Pa says. Pa says."

"I'm sure they are, but I am not one of them." She eyed him. Did he believe her? She didn't need him telling folks she was a witch. People didn't like someone different, and if word of her gift got out they'd lynch her for sure.

"What are you? What are you?"

Nora sat a moment. She'd done this enough times to know the right answers. But she'd never healed someone like Joe, someone with a simple mind.

"Well, I'm—"

"I know. You're a good witch." He smiled.

Oh dear. "No. No I'm not a bad, or a good witch, Joe. I'm just a girl with a gift."

"Like a present? A present?"

"Yes, like a present." She could work with this. "You know on Christmas morning how all the gifts are wrapped and under the tree?"

He shook his head and glanced at the ground.

She wondered why he didn't know. Elwood must buy his son gifts at Christmas. She put her hand on his shoulder.

"Well, they are wrapped up so you don't see what's inside. Like me. I'm wrapped up so no one sees my gift."

"Oh, you're a special present."

"That's right." She smiled and ruffled his hair.

"Nora, Nora I won't tell anyone you're a present," he whispered.

"Thank you, Joe. You're a good friend." She hugged him. "Now, let's get you cleaned up."

She took his hand and wiped the blood as best she could onto her apron. She looked like she'd slaughtered a chicken, but there were no signs of trauma on Joe.

"I'm going to head home and get cleaned up. Then I'll come back to the hotel and play a game of cards with you in the dining room."

She stood, helped him up and handed him his crutches.

"Okay. Okay!"

They walked to the street and before she left him, Nora brought her index finger to her lips. "Shhh."

Joe smiled and limped toward the hotel door.

Nora's feet were sore and her big toe was cut from Savage's teeth when she'd kicked him. She needed her boots. They were the only pair she had. She'd go home first and change then head into the forest to find them, before going to see Joe.

As she got closer to home, the morning altercation with her father came rushing back. Was he home? She doubted it. He'd go to work, because he didn't want to see her. Nora's eyes misted. She'd never felt so alone. Pa didn't want anything to do with her, other than to tell her where she could go and what she could do. There were no conversations about her day, no card games, no moments filled with laughter. They didn't talk to each other anymore. She was isolated in the tiny shack, forbidden friends, enemies and love.

She hiked up her skirt and climbed through the window. The smell of vomit filled her nostrils. Pa hadn't cleaned up the mess. She glanced at her bloodied, muddy apron and decided not to remove it until everything was tidied. She placed her ear to the door to listen, in case he was still home. Silence.

In the kitchen, she stood back and assessed the situation. Pa had left his clothes, dirty and smelling to high heaven, in a pile on the floor. The cushions on the sofa were still wet from his vomit. *Oh pa. What am I going to do with you?* She tossed the clothes out onto the porch to be washed. She filled two buckets, threw pa's clothes into one and carried the other one back inside.

From her knees she scrubbed the fabric on the sofa as best she could and sprinkled baking soda on top to rid it of the awful smell. Next she opened all the windows to air out the house and washed the floors. Nora's hair hung from her braid in damp wisps that stuck to her cheeks. The hammering and clanking from the shop echoed into the kitchen, and she wondered if she should go and see how her father was faring. The gesture would anger him. She'd be better off fetching her boots.

She peeked at the clock on the mantel. It was ten minutes past noon, and Pa wasn't coming home for lunch. He wouldn't be able to keep anything down anyway. Knowing it was safe to escape for a while, she went out the window.

Otakatay packed up his bedroll and tied it behind his saddle. He didn't like being this close to town. He inspected the place he'd slept for three nights. All evidence that he'd slept there had disappeared under the thick blanket of branches and leaves.

He mounted Wakina and guided the animal through the trees. Noise from town pushed through the swaying leaves to swirl around him. Horses pulled wagons, boots heels clicked on the wooden walk and children's laughter eased into his mind. He set his jaw against the reminders of a life he hadn't been allowed to enter. The streets he'd never walked along without being stared at or judged. The homes he'd never been invited into.

His eyes narrowed and his rugged features hardened. He grabbed the reins once more. He hated the wasichu. He hated their towns and their homes and the very ground they walked on. He hated that he had to mingle within their communities and buy goods from their establishments.

He tightened his hold on the reins until his knuckles paled. The white man took what he wanted without thinking of the consequences. They held themselves higher than any other creation while they pranced around like kings in this rough, uncivilized land.

His father was white, the first wasichu he learned to hate. Buck Morgan had been a useless piece of shit, mean to the very core and Otakatay despised him. He wished that instead of killing the snake so quickly he'd have prolonged his suffering. The son of a bitch hadn't deserved to live as long as he did. Otakatay ground his teeth until his jaw ached.

He could see the mountains through the tree tops. He'd return soon and claim what was stolen from him years ago. He patted his thigh where he'd sewn an extra piece into the pant leg for his money. He needed more. One more kill. The man will pay triple next time. One more victim and he'd have the amount he'd need to fulfill his promise. He caressed the feather in his hair.

He no longer wanted to kill the witch women. The softness of their skin, the smell of their hair—he'd never forget. He open and closed his hands. He could still feel their blood run down his arm after he sliced their throats. He could hear the quiet moan that seeped from supple lips as life wafted from their lungs. Sweat bubbled on his forehead and his stomach roiled. He bowed his head and inhaled until he collected himself. He scowled and hid behind the evil mask he'd perfected.

He sat up tall in the saddle. *I am Otakatay, one who kills many.*

He was vile and grim. He sat for a long moment listening to the squirrels rustle in the trees. Branches cracked as a fox bolted into his den. The muggy air filled his lungs leaving the familiar taste of pinecones, horse and earth on his tongue. Here, within the depth of the forest he felt welcome.

He clicked his tongue, urging Wakina on.

The river was quiet, and the chickadees chirping in the trees indicated it was safe to stop for a drink. He dismounted and released Wakina and watched as he made his way toward the rushing water. The horse trotted toward him with a black boot protruding from his mouth.

He pulled it from Wakina's strong teeth. The boot was old, the leather creased and soft from wear. He flipped it upside down. Two holes the size of his baby finger dripped water. The heel was worn down, smooth and shiny.

He thought of the crazy girl with the braid. This must be her boot. He scanned the area for the other one and spotted it by a rock. Both boots were wet and in need of repair. He often wondered why the wasichu didn't wear moccasins. The soft leather moulded the feet and kept them warm. He hung the boots on a branch to dry out. The girl would come back for them.

She was feisty, that one. He didn't understand why she wasn't afraid of him. Why hadn't she run the first time he'd told her to go? Most people never hung around long enough to be told to leave, but she did. And she even wanted to know his name.

His features softened for a moment before he tightened his mouth and narrowed his eyes. He pushed any warm thoughts from his mind. The notion of even one kind thought toward a wasichu was enough to make him sick. He swatted at the boots hanging from the tree, until they tumbled to the ground.

Wakina snorted.

"I will not help a wasichu," he said to him.

Wakina snorted louder and bared his teeth.

He glared at his horse. There was no pity left within him. No remorse for the things he'd done. He couldn't be the soft, timid boy who would sit on his Ina's lap and listen to stories. That person was no more. He was gone and would never return.

Wakina walked over, picked up one of the boots and placed it gently on a rock sitting in the sun.

"Do not touch the other boot, Wakina."

The horse snuffed at him, picked up the other boot and placed it next to its partner.

Otakatay strode toward the rock.

Wakina blocked his path.

He grabbed the reins, and looked straight into his eyes. "You, Wakina, I will eat one day if you keep this up."

He left the boots where they were and went back into the forest in search of a new camp.

CHAPTER SEVEN

Elwood paced the length of the dining room. He pulled out his pocket watch. Two o'clock.

"Damn it, Nora should've been here an hour ago to play cards with Joe."

She'd said after lunch. He clicked the watch closed and shoved it into his pocket. He glanced out the window, but there was still no sign of the dark-haired girl.

He eyed the liquor cabinet in the corner. Wine, whiskey and bourbon called to him. He hadn't had a drink since this morning and he'd been hankering for one the last hour. His stomach lurched. He'd been up half the night drinking and thinking about Nora and what it would be like to have her as his wife.

He'd grown restless at the mine, and he was bored with the women at the saloon. He wanted a wife and Nora was the one. She'd add immeasurably to the wealth he'd already obtained. The best part about his plan was he'd be able to take her whenever the need arose, and she wouldn't be able to do a damn thing about it.

He pulled on the collar of his shirt and undid the top button. Red and Levi were due back from the saloon any minute. The two men went everywhere with him. They were an extra pair of guns when he needed them and they helped keep order at the mine. He needed to collect on a few homesteads, and he'd be taking them with him.

Jess Chandler owed him more than the rest of the farmers he'd sold to. The crazy crow was a good shot and damn near put a bullet in him last time he'd been out to her place. He'd set her straight today. He'd bring old Savage and the boys. The mutt would attack anyone Elwood commanded him to, and Red could clip a whiskey bottle a hundred yards away. Elwood would love to see that devil woman thrashing on the ground with a chunk of her throat missing or a bullet in her chest.

He peered out the window once more and groaned. There was still no sign of Nora.

"Joe," he hollered. "Joe, come on in here."

The boy had been sitting in the lobby, waiting for Nora.

The shuffle of Joe's feet grew louder as he got closer.

"Yes, Pa. Yes, Pa."

Joe stood in the doorway wearing a blue shirt buttoned wrong and tucked into his denims. His rounded back was more prominent today, and the sadly buttoned shirt did nothing to hide it. His dirty-blonde hair stuck out in all directions, while crumbs from the cookie he'd been eating gathered at the sides of his mouth.

"Look at you." He motioned with his chin. "You're a mess."

He walked toward him.

"Damn it, boy, why can't you clean yourself up?" He raised his hand and the boy flinched.

He chuckled. The kid was afraid him. A rush of excitement bolted through his veins, and he brought his arm back down to his side. Some days he had to show the kid who was in charge. He'd done enough damage that it didn't much matter what he did to him anymore. Joe usually followed the rules, but when he didn't, Elwood had a way of reminding him.

He loved seeing the fear in Joe's blue eyes and the way he'd withdraw whenever Elwood was mad. The kid was useless around the mine, and most days he was locked in his room.

"Do you remember when Miss Rushton said she was stopping by?"

"I like Nora. I like Nora." He swayed his head.

"Yeah, I get that." Elwood went back to glance out the window. Why wasn't she here? He wanted to make sure they had dinner together. "Damn woman."

"Nora's not a damn woman. Damn woman. She isn't a witch, a witch either." Joe stopped, a loud moan came from his wet lips and his eyes rolled back.

Elwood turned from the window. "Ah, hell."

He grabbed Joe's arm, brought him to a chair and shoved him into the rose-colored fabric. He was getting mighty tired of these episodes and considered leaving the kid in the middle of nowhere. Be rid of the invalid for good. Spit dripped from Joe's mouth, and his whole body twitched. Elwood took his time removing his expensive suit coat which he placed neatly on a chair.

"I need a drink." He rummaged through the liquor cabinet.

Joe's arms were rigid, and his fingernails dug into his palms. The front of his shirt was wet, and a high pitched sound hummed from his lips. His boots tapped on the floor and grated on Elwood's nerves so that he knocked over a bottle of Champagne.

"Where's the damn whiskey?" He pulled out a dusty bottle of scotch and decided that would do.

Joe was still in the full effects of his fit.

Not bothered by it at all, Elwood uncorked the scotch, smelled the bottle and poured himself a drink.

The boys crippled legs bounced up and down in perfect cadence. Damn, this was taking forever. When this happened at the mine, he'd make sure he was nowhere near the kid. He downed the alcohol, poured himself another glass and walked toward Joe. He glared at him and gave his leg a little kick. The boy continued to shake, his body stiff.

He'd had enough. Elwood brought his leg back to kick him again, a little harder this time when he heard voices coming into the dining room.

He swallowed the remaining scotch and knelt in front of Joe when a man and woman entered the room.

"Son, come out of it. Daddy's here," Elwood crooned.

"Oh, dear." The woman rushed toward them. "Is your boy okay?"

"He suffers from fits." Elwood frowned and made his eyes water. "I hope he comes out of it soon."

"Oh, you poor thing."

June came into the room, a bag in each hand. She dropped them when she saw Joe. "How long has he been like this?"

"He just started. I've been trying to make him comfortable." Elwood feigned concern.

"Did you call for Doctor Spencer?" June asked.

Elwood hadn't even thought to call for the doctor. He masked his irritation. "No, I didn't have time. I didn't want to leave my boy."

June glared at him before she focused on Joe. "Dear, can you hear me?" She rubbed his shaking arms and started singing Mary had a Little Lamb, with compassion showing in her old eyes.

Elwood wanted to leave. He had better things to do than sit with the damn kid, especially after that episode. He wanted nothing to do with cleaning Joe up either. He eyed the scotch on the mantel. He could use another drink.

When he thought it couldn't get any worse, a crowd gathered. He had to keep from pressing his fingers into Joe's arm. The kid did this stuff all the time back at the mine. Hell, he was a constant nuisance and most times Elwood left him alone to deal with the aftermath by himself.

A bystander brought a chair for June to sit on.

"Try to make him comfortable," another person said and a woman wearing a black skirt covered with an apron brought in a blanket and laid it across Joe's restless legs.

Elwood eyed the liquor cabinet.

Joe's legs stopped twitching and his body gradually relaxed. He opened his eyes, glassy and dazed.

"Joe, can you hear me?" June rubbed his hand. "Are you all right?"

The boys eyes filled with tears, and it took all the strength Elwood had in him not to slap the kid across the face.

"Could someone get the boy a glass of lemonade, please?" June asked.

"My head hurts, my head hurts," Joe slurred.

"Would you like me to go for the doctor?" A young man asked.

"He'll be right as rain in a few minutes. Happens all the time," Elwood said as he ignored June's glare and grabbed the Scotch. He downed two glasses before the woman came back with Joe's lemonade.

The crowd disbursed after wishing Joe well. Elwood couldn't stand to be near the kid any longer.

"Seein' as how the boy's come out of it, I've got business to attend to." He left June and Joe in the dining room.

He walked around the back of the hotel to check on Savage. He picked up the chewed piece of rope. Savage was gone.

"Damn mutt. I should've shot him years ago." He whistled for Savage to come. "But the bastard does come in handy now and then."

He wanted to take him along while he collected payment from certain farmers, especially that crotchety Jess Chandler. She had a way of ruffling his feathers. Her and that damn shotgun. She won't mess with Savage, that's for sure. The vicious dog was feared by most men. He whistled again.

"Savage, where in hell are you?"

He scanned the edge of the forest and the street out front. There was no sign of him and he didn't have time to wait. His palm itched for some cash and his throat needed some whiskey. He'd take care of the dog when he got back. He'd make sure the son of a bitch never ran off again.

He glanced back one more time before he headed to the saloon to round up his men. The bloody dog would feel his whip when he found him. He laughed and weaved his way through the people on the boardwalk.

CHAPTER EIGHT

Nora's boots were placed on a rock beside the river. The one she'd sat on while dipping her feet into the cool water earlier. Hands on her hips, she scrutinized the area. She'd tossed her boots to the side, close to the water's edge, but not onto the rock.

Wondering how her boots got there, she pivoted on her heel and searched the area around her. She spotted a large footprint in the mud. *The Indian!* She ran her fingertips along the edge of the print and thought about the stranger she'd met this morning.

He had scared her half to death, coming up behind her the way he did. Goodness, he even made her vomit. Her cheeks glowed, embarrassed by how easily she'd spooked, but it wasn't until she looked at him that she was truly shaken. He was huge. A beast of a man—wide, jagged, rough and mean. Someone she didn't want to remember that was for sure, or run into twice.

She quickly searched the trees around her. Shades of green and brown blurred as she scanned the outlining area of the forest. Thinking of the Indian made her nervous. She swore she could feel his dark eyes upon her even now, and the hair on her arms rose. In his presence, she sensed danger and, worse yet, death. But there was something else. She could feel it, deep within her soul. Curiosity pushed her to find out more.

I'm crazy. He's dangerous. People didn't behave horrible for no reason. She thought of Savage, Elwood's dog. The signs were all over the animal that someone had mistreated him and she'd bet it was the rich miner. The black fur was matted, bald in places and his snout was deformed. She figured he'd been kicked or beaten with a stick and that was why he was so mean. The dog was born an innocent pup, as the stranger was once an innocent baby, but through circumstances beyond their control both of their paths had turned in the wrong direction.

What in the stranger's life had caused him to become so hateful? What pushed him to be cruel enough to threaten an innocent woman?

Determined to find out, she made a vow to look for the man tomorrow. If he was still around she'd do her best to befriend him, if he didn't kill her first.

She picked up her boots, still damp and sat down on the rock. While tying them, she listened to the rushing water and wondered where the river was going in such a hurry. If she had a boat she'd ride out the currents to see where they'd take her. She'd never been on a boat, but she imagined the wind in her hair. Not a care would enter her mind. There would be no running, no hiding and no disappointing her father.

If I had a friend, we'd go together. A tear formed in the corner of her eye and she blinked it away. Friends weren't going to be popping up anytime soon. Willow Creek's women had long ago given up on befriending the blacksmith's daughter, thanks to Pa. Because of his selfishness, most of the women would rather talk behind her back than to her face. She cringed. During the first few months after moving here, the women came to call bringing pies and scones, but sadly she'd turned them all away. Even though she'd done so with a smile and a polite thank you, they never returned.

She shrugged.

"Yes, well it's not meant to be, and I can't sit around feeling sorry for myself, now can I?"

There was no answer, but she didn't expect one. She stood and straightened her skirt. Her shoulders slumped as the bereft feeling she'd known so well eased within her soul to nestle there, familiar and warm.

Nora walked down the boardwalk from the hotel. Poor Joe. The boy was resting after a bad fit this afternoon. Her chest constricted. She couldn't ease the seizures, or the mind, but she wished she could heal his legs. She battled with herself each time she saw his deformed limbs, wanting to help him. The boy didn't deserve to have so many problems.

When she asked, Elwood told her Joe had been born that way, but Nora wasn't too sure. Joe's legs were knurled and his calves pointed outward when he stood. But it was the hunch on his back that made her second-guess his father. If Joe had been born crippled, his hump would be much larger than it was now.

She shook her head. She shouldn't be thinking such horrible thoughts, but Joe had planted himself inside her heart, and she wanted to protect him. She considered him a friend. *Friend.* The word stuck in her mind and a smile spread across her face.

Joe was the one person who hadn't judged her. He allowed her to be who she really was, not someone she was told to be. Not a girl locked in a cabin with hopes and dreams, and a gift. She accepted him for his differences as he accepted Nora for hers.

She'd mended his thumb earlier and he never questioned her. He may have thought she was a witch, she grimaced, but when she explained things to him, he understood and promised to keep her secret. Even though Joe had a simple mind, she knew without a doubt the boy wouldn't tell a soul about the episode behind the hotel.

She glanced back at the building. If she'd come earlier, Joe might not have had the fit and they'd be sitting on the porch playing Old Maid. Nora felt terrible for making him wait. She would come back tomorrow and hope he'd be well enough to see her.

She took the path behind the stores home. The aroma of coal stoves heating up dinners wafted toward her. Smoke filtered up from the chimneys and dissolved into the gray sky. Her pace quickened. Pa would be home soon.

What was she going to make for dinner? There wasn't much in the tiny cupboards to cook and Pa had drunk away all their money. She sighed. He needed help, and she had to make him see that he was destroying his life as well as hers.

She climbed through the window and closed it quietly behind her. In the kitchen, she skimmed through their meager supplies, not bothering to take down the box that held her mother's jewelry. No, she wouldn't sell the few things she had left of her.

There was one jar of peaches and one jar of pork left, and she placed them on the counter. The bag of cornmeal was the last thing left on the shelf. She'd use that in the morning for their breakfast. They would make do.

She looked out the window at her garden. A handful of carrots and two hills of potatoes remained. They could get by for most of the week, if she were careful. She could make potato soup. The meal would last them a few days. She opened the icebox. Her shoulders sagged and her bottom lip trembled. No milk. She glanced back to the counter. A teaspoon of flour was left in the jar, and she'd used all the baking soda on the sofa earlier.

Inside the cupboard, two empty shelves stared back at her. She squeezed her eyes shut to stop the tears from flowing and pressed her forehead to the wood.

What will we do? Oh Pa, what will we do?

The door swung open and her father came in, harried, filthy and stinking of stale alcohol. How did Jed work with him all day and not be sick?

She planted a smile on her face. "Good evening, Pa. How was work?"

Pa's eyes narrowed. "It was work." He pulled a chair out and slumped down into it.

She fidgeted with her hands, twisting her fingers until they hurt. She opened the jars and put the meat in the frying pan. She needed to talk with him, but she didn't know how. Every time she confronted him about going out or having friends, he'd fly off the handle and spend the rest of the night drinking at the saloon. But she had to say something now. She had to. There was no food left.

He hunched over in his chair half asleep. He was drinking himself to death.

She cleared her throat. "Um, Pa?"

The meat in the pan sizzled and she flipped it with a fork.

He angled his head toward her, but didn't say anything.

She chewed on her bottom lip while wiping her hands up and down on her apron. *Quit being a ninny.*

"Pa?" she started again. "We need to talk about...about your drinking." She braced herself for what was to come. From head to toe her muscles tensed.

He was silent.

She took two plates of peaches and fried pork to the table. She watched, as he moved the rubbery meat from one end of the plate to the other, never bringing the fork to his mouth. She couldn't blame him because it didn't look appealing.

She stared at him. Was he going to say anything? Taking his silence as a sign that he was willing to listen, she put her fork down and said quickly, "Pa, you have to stop going to the saloon. You have to stop gambling."

He stared at his plate for what seemed an eternity.

She inhaled and waited for him to speak.

He placed his elbows on the table and folded his hands. His blue eyes penetrated right through her. "No daughter of mine will tell me what to do," he growled, deep and low.

"But, Pa, you've spent all our money again. You gambled and drank it all away."

He slammed his fist onto the table. Plates rattled against their forks.

She jumped.

"The money you talk of is mine. I work for it. I hammer every day for hours to put food on the table, and this is the thanks I get?"

"No, no I appreciate all of those things, I do." She knelt in front of him. "But, Pa, you're drinking more and more every time."

"Sheriff Reid mentioned that he spoke with you yesterday."

The damn lawman was a boot-licker.

"I... I went for a walk. I wandered a little too far. It was nothing." She fidgeted with her skirt.

"You broke the rules, Nora, and at the end of the month we will be moving."

"No, Pa. I thought it best to get some fresh air, that's all." She stood and walked to the counter.

"What do you know about what's best? You're still a child."

"That is not true, Pa. I am almost nineteen. Most women my age are married with children to care for." When he rolled his eyes and threw his fork onto his plate she knew this conversation wasn't going to go well. *I'm in it now, no sense turning back.*

"Marriage will never be in your future, Nora. I've told you that time and time again. You are different, and you need to accept that."

"I know I'm different. But I can still have a normal life—I can still be a normal girl."

"No, Nora, you can't."

"Mama could heal, and she married you." Bringing her mother into the conversation was a sure fire way to anger her father. Prepared for battle, she waited for him to say something.

"Your mother didn't tell me until it was too late, until I found her hanging from a tree with a rope around her neck." He pushed his plate away.

Tears filled her eyes, as she leaned against the counter. She knew how her mother died. Accused of being a witch, the townspeople broke into their home while her father was away and hung Hannah Rushton on the tree in their yard. Nora was a baby. Her father found her hours later nestled in the trunk in their bedroom. Afraid the angry posse would come for Nora, Pa took her and they fled in the middle of the night.

"I am not Mother. No one here knows about my gift."

"Gift?" he sneered. "You call what you have a *gift*? It's a damn curse."

"I can't change who I am."

"No, you can't. That's why you must obey the rules I have set for you." He tapped his fingertips on the table, a sign he was frustrated and needed a drink.

"But I—

"I know, Nora. You want to be normal. But you're not," his voice grew louder. "You are different, not by choice, but different just the same."

Desperation pulled at her sanity. She needed him to understand. "I have no friends. I want to get married some day. How can I do any of those things if you keep me locked up in the house?"

He stood and raised his voice, "Are you not hearing me, daughter? You will never have those things. There will never be anyone who can be trusted enough to know. They will kill you." He ran his hand along his red face. "Do you understand? They will kill you." He slumped into his chair and murmured, "I could not bear finding you hanged from a tree, too."

She went to him. "Please, Pa, I've been good. I promise. Let me have a little freedom."

"No."

Nora's cheeks flushed and she frowned. "I've met your end of the bargain. I stayed in the house," she yelled. "But you haven't kept yours. We have no money. You've gambled and drank it away."

His face twisted and he glared at her.

Nora stood her ground. She would not back down.

"I'm the head of this house. I say where the money is spent." He grabbed her arms and leaned in so close she thought he would fall on top of her. "Do you hear me?" He shook her. "I am tired of you accusing me of not giving a damn. If I didn't, I'd let you roam the hills using your *curse* on who ever needed it."

She looked into bloodshot eyes. There was no way to make him see. He was sick, and there was nothing she could do to help him. "I understand," she whispered.

"I don't think you do." He wrenched her closer. "You want to have friends, and go out, and get a job. But you're too stupid to understand what will happen when they find out you're cursed."

"I am not cursed," she shouted.

"Yes, you are." He tossed her to the ground as he stood. "You're the very reason I've had to move all over this damn country. You're the reason we've been chased down by people you've healed." He pointed a finger at her and his voice rose. "You are why there is nothing left of what we once had."

The words sliced through her and piece by piece he tore her down. Her soul begged for a kind word from him. Nothing but blame came from his lips. Blame, blame and more blame.

He hated her.

I will not cry. She blinked back the tears, and stood tall while he hurled insults at her.

"I'm sorry."

"Sorry?" He knelt down beside her and lifted her chin. "I love you, Nora." His eyes watered. "But some days I wish you were never born." With those words he left, shutting the door behind him.

Nora's heart broke. The one person she'd ever relied on, ever cared for, ripped the heart from her chest. The pain was almost too much to take. She brought her knees up and hugged them to her. How could he be so cruel? How could he say he loved her but then say those words? She wiped at a tear. Over the years, Pa's disposition had faded from joyful and light to ugly and dark. He resented her for the life they had to lead. He accused her for the alcohol he consumed.

She brought her forehead to her knees. *When did he begin to hate me so much?* She held out her hands. They had caused this—her gift. Maybe he was right.

Maybe her hands were cursed after all. But how was she to stop helping those in need?

She shook her head. *If someone is hurt I need to help them.* She thought of Joe. If she hadn't healed him, he'd have no thumb. If she hadn't helped Jess Chandler, she might've died. And what of the animals that she found shot, in traps or wounded? She couldn't walk away from them either.

She couldn't do what Pa asked of her. She squeezed her hands together. She'd sacrificed her relationship with her father to save lives. Why couldn't he see the good she'd done? Instead, all he saw was a curse that had taken everything away from him.

She blew out a ragged breath.

If she received nothing else from her ability to help those in need but to see their joy, then it was worth it to her. She couldn't change who she was, even though Pa would love nothing more. If she didn't use her gift at all and walked away from those in need, would he love her again? Would he take back the awful words he said? Acceptance weighed heavy upon her soul. Without saying the words, she knew the answer.

Nora gathered the dishes and pushed the untouched food onto one plate to be saved in the icebox for tomorrow. Her stomach lurched. The thought of eating the tasteless meat tomorrow night was enough to make her sick.

After she cleaned the kitchen, she heated water in the pot. A cup of tea would ease the tension in her neck and the headache she felt coming on. She took yesterday's leaves and dumped them into her cup.

She went to the window. The kerosene lamps lit the street. There was no sign of father. She knew where he'd gone. The water boiled and she poured some into her cup. She stirred the leaves and took a sip. The hot minty taste wasn't as strong as when she first used the leaves a couple of days ago, but it did the trick. And she didn't have a choice, there was no more left.

CHAPTER NINE

He lay awake listening to the sounds of a night he knew would end badly. He leaned over and placed his hand on his younger brother's chest. Little Eagle's soft breaths feathered his skin. Good, he was still asleep. A crash echoed through the tiny cabin.

He removed the thin blanket covering him and his brother. The straw-filled bed crunched under his weight as he shifted to roll off and touch his bare feet to the dirt floor. The fireplace on the far wall gave little light to the one room home, but he could still make out the table flipped on its side, two wooden chairs and a makeshift counter—a plank on top of three tree stumps.

Another bang followed by a pleading moan. Ina! He crawled around the bed to try and see what was going on, even though he already knew.

The warm glow from the fire cast the room in welcoming shadows, but the beast standing over his mother turned it into a nightmare. A meaty fist raised high in the air and rushed toward her as she lay on her side, bleeding from the temple. The thud of flesh meeting flesh sent his stomach rolling. He squeezed his eyes shut, tucked his head into his chest and prayed it would stop.

The dull sound continued. He covered his ears, tried to shut it out. If he were taller, stronger he'd be able to help her. Guilt consumed him, and a tear slipped past his black lashes.

A low whimper came from his Ina, and he wanted nothing more than to go to her. He needed to hold her in his skinny arms and tell her he loved her.

Tears wet his face, but he didn't bother to wipe them. More punches came. When would it end? How much more could she take? His chest heavy, the air seized within his lungs, as he muffled a sob into the straw-filled bed. His fingers gathered the blanket, gripping it tightly.

He needed to help her. He rubbed his cheek against the mattress, the straw poked through, cutting his skin. He searched the room for something—anything that he could use as a weapon. There was nothing. No gun, no knife, no magical spell to cast like in the stories he'd been told.

Silence. The room held an eerie stillness, and he strained to hear any sign his Ina was alive. He opened his eyes. The swine still stood above her, a bottle of brown liquid in his hand. He took a long drink and spat it all over her. She didn't move. The brute nudged her with his boot. Still nothing.

Rage bubbled hot and feral inside of him. Ina lay beaten and bloodied on the dirt floor while the monster, the beast—his father kicked her! He dug his hands into the dirt floor and squeezed, feeling the black residue filter through his clenched fingers.

A warrior's cry burst from his mouth as he bolted toward his father. Arms flailing, he punched and kicked trying to kill the wasichu. A large hand clipped his chin, dazing him, but he wouldn't give up, he couldn't. He had to save her.

He scratched and bit puncturing the skin, on his father's arms. Another backhand across the head sent him sprawling into the counter, breaking dishes and toppling it over. His arm was cut, and the side of his head pulsed with pain. A knife bounced to the floor and he grabbed it.

Arm held high he charged at his father. With one swing the knife was knocked from his hand, and thick fingers dug into his throat. He struggled for air as his feet left the ground. He kicked at the space around them, his vision blurred.

When he came to, it was still dark outside and his father was gone. His throat sore and swollen, he winced as he swallowed. He crawled toward Ina. Each move he took sent spasms throughout his scrawny body. By morning he'd be covered in bruises.

He would never forget these moments. The punches, smacks, kicks permeated his mind and stole to the very depths of his soul. His brother was awake. Three winters old, Little Eagle clutched the tattered blanket close to his mouth and stood over Ina. Little Eagle's round face was damp with tears.

He struggled to get closer. His tongue fatter in his mouth, he tasted blood when he licked his lips. He knelt beside them and held his little brother's hand.

"Misu, iyunke—Brother, lay," he said and guided him down to lie beside their mother.

"Ina, Ina?" Little Eagle whimpered.

His breaths came in quick puffs as his heart pounded in his throat. He placed their mother's head onto his lap. How was he going to fix her? Old bruises mingled with new ones coloring her face. A nasty scrape bled from the side of her head and into her blue-black hair. He ran his hand along the soft tresses, something he'd done since he was little. The motion had calmed him and helped him sleep.

He slowly got up, dunked a dirty cloth into the bucket and tenderly cleaned her wounds. Her deerskin dress was ripped at the neck and arms, traces of too many times their father had abused her. He ran the cloth along the cut on her head, trying to pull the dry blood from her hair. He'd cared for her several times in his twelve winters, and each time she grew weaker and weaker. He'd watched his Ina change from a strong, lively woman to a shell, a whisper of who she once was.

He turned a hate-filled glare toward the door where the man who called himself a husband, a father had left. He had no feelings but those of disgust, at the vile wasichu who stole from them a life filled of happiness and love.

He kissed her cheek and rested his face against hers.

"Ina, Ina, please wake up."

He lay like that for half hour, until he realized he could feel no breath touch his cheek. He sat up and watched her chest. He shook her.

"Ina, you've got to wake up."

His mother didn't move, and he gasped unable to accept what might be. He glanced at Little Eagle, nestled close to their mother on the floor.

"Wanbli Cikala—Little Eagle. Ina needs to stay warm. Go fetch some firewood."

The boy shook his head. "No, no," he cried clutching Ina's hand.

"Go. You must be big. You must help."

Little Eagle nodded and laid his blanket over Ina.

"Two logs," he said and his brother ran outside.

Hands shaking, he placed his finger into his mouth and held it in front of her nose. There was nothing. No air flowed from her lungs! He scanned the room searching for something or someone to help him. He shook her, once, twice a third time. No air. No air!

"Ina? Ina?"

He watched as her dark head lolled to the side, and he knew there was no life within her.

"Ku, ku, ku—come back, come back, come back."

Tears spewed from his eyes onto her face as he sobbed, clutching her body to his. He inhaled the wood smoke, the pine, the fresh scent that was her alone. He didn't want to forget. He didn't want to let go. He couldn't. He couldn't. He couldn't!

Wrenching sobs wracked his body in uncontrolled shakes. The pain inside his soul pricked and pierced at his sanity. He rocked her back and forth, clutching—grasping at what he once had. He pulled her closer and wept for the mother he'd lost, for the stories he'd not hear, for the love he'd never see in her eyes again. He wept for the brother he'd have to tell, and the life they'd live without her.

He stumbled to his feet and searched for something to ease his pain. Something to take away the fire from his insides, the weight of hopelessness, anguish and fear bore down upon him and buckled his knees.

Ina, Ina, Ina. His mother was gone.

His hands shook as he gripped the knife he'd tried to kill his father with. He sliced his chest four times. The misery, the torment poured out from inside of him. He howled, and as the blood ran from his chest, so did the tears from his eyes.

He rubbed his bleeding flesh, smearing two lines along his cheeks. He fell to his knees before his mother and gathered her into his arms. A low humming floated from his lips in between moments where his body broke down and trembled. He took Ina's hand and sliced her palm, before slicing his own and bringing them together.

"You will be with me forever, my Ina."

Otakatay tossed back the bed roll and sat up, panting. His lungs burned with the intensity of the dream and the vivid memory of his last moments with his Ina. His bronzed flesh glistened. Four scars stood out among the others.

He closed his eyes. The ache in his heart radiated, encompassing his whole back. *Ina.* Oh, how he missed her. How he wished for that day back. He let her down. He didn't protect her. He didn't save her.

I couldn't. Years passed before he'd avenged that day and all the others that led up to it. But no matter what he did, no matter who he killed, the hurt stayed with him, a constant sickness that crippled him.

He remembered the suffering Ina went through, the anguish that followed afterward, the life they were thrown into. He touched the feather in his hair, a constant reminder of a promise he would fulfill at all costs.

There was no way to make it right. No way to change what had happened. He wiped at the tears that wanted to fall. He would not cry. He showed no weakness.

But he was so sorry he'd let Ina down. He'd let them all down. He studied the scar on his palm. *I will never forget.* He was no longer the happy boy who loved stories and whittling wood, or who had taught his brother to shoot an arrow. He was a killer, a violent, deadly man who with the skilled swipe of his blade had ended many lives.

I am Otakatay, one who kills many.

A chill swept over him and he pulled the deerskin shirt from his saddle bag. The leather was smooth and warm against his damp flesh. He rubbed the faded yellow skin between his fore finger and thumb taking comfort in the texture of the shirt and the rhythm of his fingers. A night owl hooted. The day was going to be long.

He placed the shirt back into the bag and threw his arms into the black cotton one he wore every day. He was restless, sleep eluded him. He gathered wood to stoke the fire.

Now warm and comfortable, he felt the feather tied in his hair. It was becoming dense and falling from the quill. He would need to get a new one.

He didn't think he'd find any witkowan in town, but it didn't hurt to have a look around. He needed one more kill. One more scalp to bring to the wasichu who hired him. Then he could take back what was his. He didn't have to kill anymore.

In a few hours he would put his black duster on and head into town. A nervous tension settled inside of him. No welcoming party would greet him. Instead, people would stare, point and run. Doors would be locked, windows closed and shutters brought down. Children herded indoors by fearful women and men with rifles.

He shook his head. His presence among the wasichu had disaster written all over it. He learned long ago to read the white eyes. He knew their actions before they surfaced in their own minds. Which gun they'd use to draw on him and where his bullet would strike, killing them instantly. He could spot the cowards that would attack from behind and the sensible men that didn't want any trouble at all.

He pulled the knife from his pant leg and sharpened the blade on his whetstone. If he had to venture among the wasichu, he'd go prepared. He was never without two knives and a rifle. Sparks flew from the blade as it scraped along the smooth stone. The owl's voice blending with the swipe of the blade played an earthy song that he embraced, allowing the melody to become a part of him.

Chapter Ten

Elwood pushed himself back into the wooden chair. A thick fog of cigarette and cigar smoke along with the scent of lustful women filled the saloon. He squinted through the haze and scrutinized the players around the table.

Ted Blair, the banker, sat stiffly in the chair across from him, his pointy nose buried in his cards. Levi and Red passed a bottle of whiskey between them and laid their cards on the table face down. They were here to fix the odds. Jack Rushton flopped close on his right and swayed back the other way again.

He glanced at his hand, a pair of kings and three ten's, a full house. Red had slipped him the winning card, and because of the ruse he'd won almost every hand. Dollar bills, coins and even a ladies watch piled high in the middle of the round table.

"You sure on that, Jack?" asked Ed Morgan, the dealer.

The gold watch was dainty, a pretty piece with clean lines and a round face. Elwood knew it was worth more than money.

"I'm fine with it. Nows let's play cards." Jack was well into the bottle before he sat down at the table and started tossing jewelry into the pot. He'd lost the gold wedding ring he wore in the last hand and threw in the watch so he could continue playing. The blacksmith was a tall man with a slight build and Elwood figured not worth a damn. He'd heard the man spent more time in the saloon drinking and gambling than at home with his pretty daughter.

He eyed Jack. Gambling with precious jewelry was a sign of bad things to come.

"I can give you a loan if that's what you need, Jack." Elwood pointed to the table and the loot awaiting his pocket.

Jack slumped toward him, and the smell of sour mash liquor followed.

He inched back.

Jack was so intoxicated he didn't even know what he'd said. Elwood didn't give a damn if he understood him or not. Hell, he didn't need anything from him other than control. He wanted what Jack had the pleasure of seeing every night.

He dug into his pocket and pulled out a handful of bills. "How much do you need?"

Jack swatted at his hand. "I ain't needin' yer money."

He balled his hands into tight fists until the urge to strangle the blacksmith left. He picked up the watch and cradled it in his manicured hands.

"Don't sell the pretty watch. You've already lost your ring. What will Nora think?"

Jack's bottom lip quivered and he blinked. Elwood knew he'd struck a chord.

"You don't talk about Nora. Sh...she is never going to marry you." He pointed at Elwood while swaying and almost falling from the chair.

"I've come to accept that."

"Leave her be. I won't condone it," he slurred.

Elwood had to refrain from kicking the chair out from under the drunken ass. He didn't give a damn if the old man condoned his marrying Nora or not, it was going to happen one way or the other.

"I can lend you the money." He held the watch in front of Jack.

"Leave it there," he stammered and tried to grab it from Elwood's hand.

Elwood persuaded people with his money in order to get what he wanted. He'd done the same thing with his land, and the best part was he could kick the farmers off if they were a dime short. The power he held over them made him giddy. He ran the mine the same way. He lorded over those brats for years, and he loved that they feared him. He paid them nothing and got labor in return.

Pretending to be kind was something he was good at, and Jack Rushton would fall for it like all the rest. Jack had the one thing Elwood wanted. Nora.

"How about I loan you the money for the watch?" He dangled the yellow band on his finger. "I will give it back once you've paid me." A lie of course, he'd use the watch to entice Nora.

"Hurry it up, Jack. We have a game to play," Ed growled.

Jack looked from the watch Elwood held, to the money on the table and back again. He peered out the window for a long while. "You'll leave Nora alone?"

He nodded a dark smile upon his lips.

"All right, you have a deal."

Elwood had to conceal his excitement. Soon Nora would be his. He dropped the watch in his pocket, counted out twenty dollars and handed the green backs to Jack. He'd given more than the watch was worth, but that would all come back to him tenfold when he had Nora in his arms and in his bed.

The game continued and within a half hour Jack had lost the twenty dollars, his pride and according to Elwood, his daughter. He watched as the man stumbled out of the saloon, falling over his feet a few times on the way. He stretched across the table and scooped up his winnings.

"Good dealing tonight, Ed," he said and slipped the dealer five dollars before following Jack outside.

CHAPTER ELEVEN

Nora stood at the window and watched Pa walk across the lawn to go to work. She didn't come out of her room until she heard the front door close. After last night's argument a conversation wasn't what either of them wanted. She ran the brush through her long hair, listening as it crackled.

She loved pa, but she didn't want to be a burden any longer. She had no control over why she'd received such a gift. Why her mother and grandmother bore the mark, or why they died.

She didn't know much about her mother, only what Pa wanted to tell her. Hannah Rushton was a healer, a woman with a curse, according to father. Whenever she'd ask about her mother, he usually held his lips firmly together and never said a word. On the rare occasion he mentioned her, she sucked in his words and buried them deep within her heart.

No matter what she did, or where she went, she knew she'd never change. People wouldn't expect Doctor Spencer to walk away from a sick child without giving him some medicine. If it came down to saving someone's life, she'd risk losing hers to save another's.

She braided her hair and tied the end with the same piece of leather she'd used since she was a girl. She held the tail of the braid close and examined the tanned leather strip. She often fantasized that her mother had worn it.

She opened the cupboard, stood on tiptoes, and grabbed the box. Her shoulders sagged at what she was about to do. *I have no choice.*

Faded blue flowers graced the sides of the box, and she skimmed her finger along the edge. Pa had given it to her for her tenth birthday. The only gift she'd ever received. She didn't want to take the treasures inside. They were the last things she had left of her mother. The hinges creaked in dismay as she lifted the lid. She blinked. *It can't be.* She placed her hand over her chest to ease the dull ache. The watch was gone. The beautiful gold watch that had rested on her mother's wrist wasn't there. Her eyes filled with tears. She pushed aside the silver brooch and gold ring with a ruby. The watch was gone. Pa had done this.

All for another drink and a game of cards.

She picked up the ring and placed it on her finger, turning the band. Pa had stayed out late last night. Now she knew where he'd gotten the money to do it.

She lowered her head. The watch was gone. He'd sold it for a bottle of whiskey, a damn bottle of whiskey. She slammed her hand onto the counter. Anger packed around her heart and fueled her irritation. She placed the brooch in her pocket, and went out the door, heading straight for the blacksmiths.

Inside, her nose burned with the heavy scent of ash, sweat and smoldering wood. She straightened and walked around a barrel full of water. Tools she'd never seen before leaned inside the tub, cooling off. The clanking and tapping reminded her of when she was little, sitting on a stump watching Pa work. Happier days assaulted her mind, forcing her anger out.

When she spotted him, her resolve faltered. She watched as he hunched over a large fire, heating a long piece of metal. Sweat dripped down his forehead, and his eyes squinted. He was tired—worn. She saw the wrinkles on his face, and the thought of tearing a strip off of him didn't seem to have the same effect anymore.

He glanced up.

Sadness reflected in his blue eyes and spread across his face. She stood still, waiting for him to say something. But when she saw a tear drop from his eye, all her anger left and she went to him.

"Oh, Pa." She placed her arms around his neck and hugged him.

Strong arms wrapped around her waist. "I'm sorry, Daughter."

The embrace didn't last long, but it was enough for her. He smelled of stale liquor, but she didn't care. For this moment he was her pa, the one who raised her. The father she missed very much.

"We will get through this," she whispered.

He nodded.

She wished she could take him home and feed him a warm meal. He needed to rest. His skin held a yellow tint, and the black circles under his eyes belied the late nights filled with drinking. He wasn't well.

"Pa, let me take you home. You should rest."

"No, I must work." His eyes shifted toward the ground, "I need to make up for the mistakes I've made."

"We'll make do. We always have."

He tensed, and she knew she'd touched a nerve.

"I don't need you telling me what to do, Nora." There was an edge to his voice, a warning.

"Yes, sir."

She kissed his forehead, and without glancing back, she went out the double doors and into the street. She was challenging him, and she waited for the shout, the hand on the arm to stop her but nothing happened. No fight. No argument. No admonition to go home and stay there.

She should've been relieved to have some freedom, to no longer be hidden from the world. Instead she felt horrible, incomplete, a puzzle in which Pa was the missing piece. He didn't care. He didn't love her. She stepped out onto the street.

She could come and go as she pleased, and yet it didn't please her one bit. The sun shone brightly in the clear blue sky, and she closed her eyes feeling the warmth on her face. The freedom should be exhilarating. She should be jumping for joy, but all she could think about was the distance he had placed between them, and she didn't know how to fix it.

She stopped before the boardwalk and swallowed thickly. She fingered the broach in her apron pocket. The bell over the door jingled a warm welcome as she entered the Mercantile. Doctor Spencer was leaving, so she held the door for him.

"Thank you, Miss Rushton," he said supplies in his hands.

"You're most welcome, Doctor." She couldn't hide the sadness in her voice and prayed the doctor didn't notice.

A quick look around told her no one else was in the store.

"Good morning, Miss Rushton," Fred said, with a bright smile.

"Good morning, Mr. Sutherland." She pulled the brooch from her pocket and laid it on the counter. "How much will I be able to buy with this?"

The shop owner glanced at her over his wire rimmed glasses, before he picked up the brooch to examine it. She saw a glimpse of pity in his wrinkle-framed eyes, but ignored it and waited patiently for his answer.

"I can give you three dollars for it." He placed the broach on the counter.

Three dollars wasn't much. She'd only be able to get a few things and they needed more. She caressed the ring on her right hand, slipped it off and laid it next to the broach. Her cheeks heated and she swallowed past the lump in her throat.

The shop owner picked up the ring. "This is nice. This is nice indeed."

She dipped her head to hide the tears threatening to fall. Hands folded in front of her, and she concentrated on squeezing them together.

"I will give you seven dollars for this one," Fred beamed.

Unable to find her voice, she nodded and waited while he counted out the money from his register. With a shaky hand, she scooped up the green bills, not knowing if he'd given her the correct amount or not.

She walked aimlessly around the store, the tins, boxes and fabrics all became a blur. She pulled the handkerchief from her pocket, tipped her head and blotted her eyes. She no longer cared about buying food. All thoughts of surviving left her, replaced with a mourning she'd never felt before. Her chest tightened as sharp pains spread to her back. She wrapped her arms around her to keep from crumpling on the floor and bawling like a baby. The brooch, the ring, the watch—they were all gone.

Mr. Sutherland held her mother's ring up to the light shining through the window. A bright smile creased his face. She needed to get out of the store before she ran over and took the ring back.

Head down, she pulled the door open, heard the faint jingle and stepped outside. A strong force sent her flying onto her butt. Before she realized what had happened, two large hands cupped under her arms and yanked her up.

Flustered, she flipped the hair that had fallen in her eyes to the side and stared up at—him. It was the Indian, the one who threatened to kill her. He was right here in front of her. She couldn't see his eyes because of the black Stetson low on his forehead, but there was no mistaking the square jaw and the feather peeking out from behind his ear. Nor was there any mistaking the smell of danger that seemed to surround him.

"Thank you," she said and smiled.

A low grunt was all she heard and then she was staring at his backside as he walked away. Children and their mothers hurried out of his way, panic and fear on their faces. She could see why they were scared. He was a frightful person. The black attire he wore didn't help, but she guessed it had more to do with his Indian blood than anything.

He walked with lethal prowess, a hunter seeking his prey. He held his shoulders straight and flexed his hands at his sides, ready to pull the knife he'd used on her the other day. There was no mistaking his aura; he was not someone you tangled with. She'd bet ten to one he'd come out the winner every time.

As people shuffled to the other side of the street and hastily went into shops, she knew he wasn't here to harm any of them. If he wanted to, he'd have done so by now. He was simply walking down the boardwalk, scaring the hell out of them instead.

Not bothering to right her skirt or apron, she trailed after him, curious about who he was and why he was here. He was heading out of town in the direction of the forest, and she was determined to follow.

She waited until he disappeared into the thick of the trees before going in after him. The smell of pine and moss tickled her nose as she took soft steps. Sun light burst through the trees and lit up the forest floor. She continued on, before she figured out he was no longer a few yards in front of her. She picked up her pace and scanned the trees around her, but there was still no sign of him. He'd vanished.

Where did he go?

She stopped, did a full circle looking into the dense bushes around her, but he was gone.

She glanced back toward town. She didn't want to go home. She had hoped to find the stranger and talk with him. She continued on her way deciding to sit by the river and collect her thoughts. After selling the last of her mother's jewelry, she didn't have it in her to go back to the mercantile.

They needed food and she'd buy it, but not right now. Not when her insides ached with such despair and guilt. She wondered if Mr. Sutherland would consider holding the items for her until she could get enough money to buy them back. The brooch maybe, but she doubted he'd give up the ring. For all she knew it could be on Wilimena's chubby finger by now.

She walked along the water's edge and watched while it receded in and out, leaving a trail of twigs and leaves. She rounded a bend and spotted a horse standing next to a tall oak. The lean creature stood still. The color of his coat was beautiful and resembled a storm filled sky. She inched forward and held out her hand. The horse didn't move.

"You're beautiful." She stepped closer.

A saddle was cinched around the animal's middle and a bedroll tied to his back.

The horse stepped toward her and placed his snout into her palm.

She smiled.

"You're a friendly one, aren't you?" She ran her hand between his eyes and down the length of his nose.

"You should not touch other people's belongings."

She spun around as the Indian made his way through the trees toward her. Where had he come from?

"I... I was walking and saw him."

"You were following me." He came closer, and instinct told her to run.

"My name is—

"I don't care who you are."

He took the horse's reins and pulled the animal away from Nora. The horse yanked his head back toward her.

"Wakina," he growled and tugged the reins again.

"What a beautiful name. What does it mean?" She examined him, trying to make out if he was frowning or if his lips were always pursed together.

Reins in hand, he turned and walked away.

She fell into step beside him. "What does your horse's name mean?" She wanted to know something—anything about the man. He was a mystery to her, and she could see he needed a friend or maybe it was her in need. She shrugged, it didn't really matter, and she was too darn curious to let this go. She saw the scars on his right forearm and her fingers pulsed.

"Sir, what does Wakina mean?"

"Go away."

He stared straight ahead, hat still on his head, he worked his jaw. She was annoying him, but he intrigued her so much she didn't care. "Sir."

He spun around almost knocking her to the ground a second time and leaned into her face. "Leave."

He's going to kill me. And judging by the gleam in his eyes, he was envisioning the way to do it. She shuddered. Something quick and effortless was probably the way he'd go. The knife across her throat or right into her heart. She wouldn't feel a thing. She pushed all thoughts of the consequences aside, tipped her chin up and stepped forward so her breasts brushed his chest.

"No. I think I'd like to stay."

"You do not get a choice," he uttered through clenched teeth.

He smelled of leather, smoke and a spice she couldn't quite put her finger on. She refrained from touching the feather in his hair, and instead stared into his troubled eyes. Sadness, anger and purpose melded together in the dark depths.

She smiled.

She never heard the sound of the blade until the tip pricked her throat. Black eyes, lethal and wicked, bore into hers. Tanned features tightened to conceal any hint of kindness and were replaced with evil and disgust. It was fascinating how he changed. How he masked any emotion other than hate and punched it forward onto his enemy, onto her.

She gasped. The enormity of his revulsion smashed into her, heavy and compressed. She felt dirty. Had her people done this to him? Had they mistreated him, pulling the hate from him, so anger was the sole emotion he displayed? Oh, if this was so, she needed to fix it. She needed him to see that not all white people were the same.

She closed her eyes. She had no idea where the courage came from to place her hand lightly over his. She felt the cool metal blade on the tip of her thumb but did not move her hand away. *If he is going to kill me, let it be quick.* She opened her eyes and watched as curiosity, anger and hate flickered across his face.

"Go," he rasped.

"No."

"I will kill you."

She gulped.

"Then do your best, because I'm not leaving."

He flexed his jaw, pushed the knife into her throat. The skin broke and she could feel the blood trickle down her neck. *Here we go. Please let Pa know how much I loved him.*

She held her breath and met his eyes.

Time stretched. His broad chest rose and fell as he exhaled onto her face. She refused to look away.

He growled, flung her to the side and threw his knife. The wood split as the blade struck the tree. She checked to make sure he hadn't sliced her throat before he threw the knife. Blood smeared her fingers, and she pulled a handkerchief from her apron.

CHAPTER TWELVE

Otakatay pulled the knife from the tree. What in hell had the wasicun winyan been thinking? He glanced back at her. She sat on a tree stump blotting a white cloth to her neck. He'd cut her. Not enough to kill her, a nick from the tip of his blade to scare her. But it hadn't worked. Instead she'd challenged him with her blue eyes, pushed him to harm her.

He threw his knife again. Every muscle vibrated, wanting to release the energy alive and coursing rampantly through his veins. He should've smacked her. She'd be running away in fear then.

He shook his head. He didn't hit women. *No, I only kill them.* His stomach pitched. He looked at her again. He murdered women like her, women with kind smiles and bright eyes—women who haunted his dreams. He massaged his chest. He didn't want to think of them.

He grabbed his knife and slid it into the leather sheath strapped under the coat on his back.

"What do you want?" he barked.

She stopped dabbing her neck. "To be your friend."

He had no friends and didn't want any either. "I don't need a friend."

Without missing a beat she piped up, "Everyone needs a friend."

He saw sadness flicker across her face, and he stiffened. She was the one in need. He didn't give a shit what she needed. He wasn't it. There were plenty of wasichu in town she could mingle with. He went to Wakina, wrapped the leather reins around his hand and walked away. He heard her steps beside him. *Why won't she go away?* She was like a fly, a nuisance that hung around until you swatted it away or killed it.

He grunted. He'd tried that, and it didn't work.

He glanced at her through his lashes. He couldn't kill her. He didn't kill without reason, and as irritating as she was, it wasn't a good enough excuse to end her life.

"Sir, where are you from?" She skipped beside him.

He walked faster. A hand touched his arm and he pushed it away.

"Wakina means *Thunder* in Lakota," he said, still feeling the heat from her hand on his arm.

"Well, that makes perfect sense," she puffed.

He didn't know why he'd told her Wakina's Lakota name, or why he hadn't jumped on the horse's back leaving her far behind him. He scowled at her and an innocence he'd witnessed before surrounded her. *Ina.*

There had been nothing soft, nothing warm in his life for years and he didn't know what to do with it—with her. She had an aura that illuminated a goodness he'd thought forgotten within the wasichu.

She was different.

"He is the color of thunder clouds, dark gray. I see why you named him that." She ran her hand along Wakina's mane.

He ignored her.

"Where are you from?"

He avoided the question the first time. He didn't know, didn't want to remember. "I've lived all over."

She nodded, satisfied with his answer. "Do you belong to a tribe?"

"No." *I belong to no one.*

"Oh." She was silent for a long time, and he thought she was done asking questions until her full lips opened again. "Are you white, too?"

Not by choice. "Yes."

She stopped. He didn't, and soon he heard the rustling of the leaves as she caught up.

"You're a—

"Half breed." He didn't know what she was going to say and he didn't give a damn. Half breeds were outcasts. He'd been reminded every day of his life what he was.

"I wasn't about to say that," she whispered.

"It is what I am."

"It is cruel."

He tripped on a root but continued walking. "Why would you think it is cruel when your people continue to use it?"

"My people may use it, but it doesn't mean I do."

He'd brought her to his camp. *Damn it.* What the hell had he been thinking? He'd let his guard down for five minutes and this is what happens. *Why won't she go away?* Hell, even men feared him, yet this little minx walked beside him as if he were a preacher giving the Sunday Sermon.

He frowned.

She lifted her skirt, and he spied the white of her calves. His pulse quickened.

She plopped down onto the ground and crossed her legs. "You enjoy sleeping under the stars?"

He'd enjoy it if she'd leave.

"What is your name?"

"Otakatay."

He smiled, knowing what would come next.

"What does it mean?"

"One who kills many."

He watched amused as her mouth opened and closed a few times. White delicate hands fidgeted on her lap. "Why would your mother name you that?"

Ina. He made a fist, constricting the muscles within his arms. He could not change the past. He couldn't make things right. He touched the feather in his hair.

"Have you killed many?"

Her words seemed far away. "Yes." There was nothing more to say. He'd killed more than he could remember, more than he should have. More than he wanted.

"Are you a bounty hunter?"

Why was she asking so many damn questions and why in hell was he answering them? He left Wakina to wander and sat down across from her. He threw her a menacing glare, but the little nit didn't even flinch. He pulled the knife from his back and with brisk movements, sharpened it.

"Is that what you do?"

"I kill for money."

She chewed on the inside of her cheek.

She was troubled, he could tell. He hoped she'd get up and leave, now that she knew what he was.

"Have you ever killed someone who was innocent?"

He held the blade of his knife up to his cheek. "I kill those who are deadly and those who I'm paid to kill."

"Even if they are innocent?"

"It doesn't matter to me what they are as long as I get paid."

"Even...even women and children?" She folded her hands together, twisting them until the knuckles were white.

His face hardened. "No children."

"But, but you've killed women."

He remained silent.

"Oh my."

He'd had enough of the questions and decided it was time for her to leave. It was time for her to see what she was sitting across from.

"I am a killer." He dragged his blade slowly across the whetstone. "I've gutted, sliced and pitted bodies for greenbacks. I'm a shadow lurking in the corner, waiting to." He threw the knife, missing the side of her face by less than an inch, into the tree behind her.

She lifted a shaky hand up to her head and patted her hair. When her eyes met his there was no malice or hate within them. No trace of fear. He blinked. Why wasn't she scared? Why didn't she curse at him, yelling savage, lowlife, breed? *Why is she still here?*

She was not like any other wasichu he'd come across in his twenty-six winters. She was familiar in a peculiar way. He stomped down any gesture that might lead her to believe he was a good person. He wasn't.

He stood, and so did she. Dainty hands ran along the front of her skirt. The fabric should be burned, the edges frayed, the brown color faded and worn. He analysed her features. She was pretty, in a different sort of way. Pale skin, blue eyes and black hair were an odd combination, but one that seemed to compliment her. She was fine-boned, with dainty hands and short legs. Underneath the rags and braided hair, she was strong, a fighter. His previous attempts to scare her told him that. There was also kindness within her, and he'd seen it with his horse.

He shifted from one foot to the other, curled his fingers into fists. He wanted nothing to do with the wasicun winyan.

"I have to go," she said.

He watched as her eyes darted from him to Wakina. She went to the horse, placed her cheek against his and whispered something he couldn't hear.

"Goodbye, Otakatay."

He remained silent and watched her walk into the forest. When he couldn't see her anymore he let his shoulders fall, and kicked dirt over the ashes left from his fire last night. He broke branches throwing them onto the ground. He was moving camp. He didn't want her coming back with more questions. Shit, he'd rather face a den of rattlesnakes.

A terrifying scream carried over the trees and slammed into him. He pushed his feet into the ground, planting himself so he wouldn't move. She was fine, probably saw a snake.

Another scream echoed throughout the camp.

Wakina tossed his head and bared his teeth.

"No."

Two hoofs sprung into the air and landed with a puff of dirt onto the ground.

"Wakina."

The horse raised one leg, bared his teeth again and took off into the forest.

"Son of a bitch."

Otakatay pulled his knife from the tree and sprinted after Wakina. His moccasins allowed him to run with silent steps. A gift he'd acquired after much practice. He swatted at the branches, as he followed the sound of Wakina's hooves. He spotted the girl through the trees. She sat on a rotted stump by the river, holding something in her hands. Wakina stood next to her, his snout resting on her shoulder. *I will eat the animal yet.*

He set his jaw and pushed through the last tree in front of him. He saw the black fur on her lap. "Why are you holding a dead animal?"

Nora's tear-streaked face looked up at him, and he realized it wasn't an animal. It was a scalp. He ground his teeth together.

"It's a...a...a"

He yanked the wet hair from her lap and threw it into the river, making sure it was within the rapids.

Her hands shook. He didn't know what to do. He didn't want to help her, he couldn't.

"I will walk you to the end of the forest."

She didn't move, instead continued to shake worse than before.

"It was a scalp, Otakatay. It was a woman's scalp." More tears burst from her eyes, making the blue within them shine.

He didn't answer. He knew what it was. Remorse, grave and intense, weighed on his shoulders. He swallowed. He had nothing to offer her. He placed his hand upon her shoulder for a mere second, before snapping it back to his side. He was a killer. A low-life half-breed that belonged nowhere. There was nothing gentle within him.

He left her and went to stand by a tree. The distance helped to bring back his senses and the overwhelming urge to help the girl. Wakina stayed by her side and he glared at the horse.

She wiped her eyes with the back of her hand and gave Wakina a shaky smile. He scanned the river for more floating scalps and exhaled when he saw none.

She wrapped her arms around the horse's neck.

He'd never seen a wasichu show affection for an animal. He waited until she twisted toward him before ushering her out of the forest.

"Why, Otakatay, would someone scalp a woman?"

He clamped his lips together so he didn't confess.

She caught her foot and stumbled.

He grabbed her before she fell onto her face. He turned her in his arms and gazed into her eyes. They reminded him of a stormy sky, sapphire with a dark ring around the outside. A jolt of lightning shot through him, and he couldn't look away. He couldn't see anything but her.

He leaned forward, hovering above her pink lips. She smelled of roses, dirt and horse, and before he could control himself, before he could talk some sense into his thick skull, he grazed his lips over hers.

Softly, he melded them together, branding this moment into his mind forever. The sun's rays filtered through the trees and onto her hair, transforming the dull color to a shimmering shade of dark blue. She brought her arms up, wrapped them around his neck and tilted her head to deepen the kiss. He stilled, and his arms fell listlessly at his sides.

She dropped onto the ground with a thud and gaped up at him confused.

I have to be sure. He yanked her up and cushioned her back against his chest. He kissed her neck and pushed the hair to the side. Delicately, so he didn't startle her, he moved his lips up to her ear.

Amidst her braided hair, nestled so it wasn't easily seen sat his destiny. He hugged her to him as a wave of nausea bloated his stomach. Beads of sweat formed on his forehead. *One more. I need one more.* The demon inside him whispered, *slit her throat.* He squeezed his eyes shut. *Do it. Kill her.*

He fought with the hunter he'd become, and the promise he'd set out to fulfill. *One more. One more. One more.* He shoved her from him and watched as she hit the ground.

He took a step back.

"What?"

"Go." He pointed in the direction they'd been walking.

"But…"

"Get the hell away from me, witkowan," he growled. *She'd be the last one.* He stretched behind him, his fingers tightened on the handle of the blade.

She got up and wiped the mud smeared on the front of her dress. Confusion and hurt swarmed in her eyes. She walked away.

He pushed his heels into the ground as the words screamed in his head, *she has the mark.*

CHAPTER THIRTEEN

Nora walked through the last of the trees and onto the street. She'd refused to go back, or even turn around after he'd cast her out. She swiped at the hair falling into her eyes. The air was muggy and she fanned her face with her hand. *I kissed a bounty hunter.* She groaned and wiped her forehead.

Why had Otakatay told her to go? What had she done wrong? She thought he wanted to kiss her. *For heaven's sake, he started it.* She'd been so caught up in the moment she didn't know what to do.

It all happened so suddenly, first he was kissing her and then she was on the ground. She'd seen his face change from serene to disturbed within seconds, but there was no reason why. Not one she could see. She made a face. She never should've allowed him to kiss her at all.

"Damn it."

He was a killer, a bounty hunter. Her stomach turned. But she was drawn to him, determined to be his friend, even though it was clear he didn't want to be hers. In his eyes she saw sorrow, a yearning for acceptance, for peace. She'd never seen such misery, so instead of running from him, she'd taken a giant leap toward him.

She knew it was unsafe to be around him. *He threatened to kill me twice.* But no matter what he'd shown her or how badly he scared her, she was compelled to prove that not all white people were as cruel as he thought them to be.

She brushed her fingers across her lips. She could still feel his kiss—still taste him on her tongue. *Was it the kiss?* Was that the reason he wanted nothing to do with her? She paused. He'd changed after their embrace. His brown eyes hardened, and his features grew jagged and firm. *It had to be.* She must've done something wrong. She'd never been kissed like that before.

I've never been kissed at all.

She was inexperienced and was shocked when his lips met hers. She followed his lead, and look where that got her. She glanced back into the forest.

Not forty-eight hours before, he'd threatened to kill her and then he was kissing her. When his lips touched hers, excitement stirred within her and she instinctively kissed him back. She didn't think of the consequences, or why he'd kissed her at all. Nora's desire pushed all thoughts from her mind.

She was sure he found her amusing, a white girl easily seduced. He played a game, one she didn't want to be a part of. She wanted to be his friend, but he used and humiliated her. Nora kicked at the rocks on the road.

She'd never seen Otakatay before. Why was he here, in Willow Creek? *A bounty.* She froze. *But who?* She searched the street, wondering who Otakatay's next victim would be. Outlaws hid all over the territory and they could hide in Willow Creek without difficulty. Fear crawled up her spine, making the hairs on her neck spike. She'd pay more attention to who roamed the streets and to her flippant emotions when it came to the bounty hunter. She didn't want to be caught off guard if things went awry with either of them.

She shoved her hands into the pockets on her apron and felt the money. They needed food. She glanced at the mercantile. She needed to gather a few staples. She chewed on the inside of her cheek. After her encounter with Otakatay she didn't feel like eating lunch at all, and after Pa's night of drinking she doubted he would either. But there was always breakfast in the morning and a possible dinner tonight. She glanced down at the dried mud on her dress. She was a mess and she couldn't go into the store looking like a ragamuffin. But they needed food.

"Oh, hell." She hiked up her skirts and headed toward the store.

The bell jingled when she opened the door, and after the day she'd had, she found the bell to be more irritating than welcoming.

"Afternoon, Miss Rushton," Fred said merrily.

She nodded a polite hello and continued to the back of the store. She stacked flour, sugar, cornmeal, yeast and Willimena's raspberry jam in her arms. She placed them all on the counter. She'd worry about meat and eggs later. Right now she needed enough to make a few loaves of bread and the jam to spread it on.

"Will this be all?" Fred asked.

"A half pound of coffee, please."

The door to the back room swung open and a robust Willimena Sutherland sauntered through. A pale blue dress pulled tight over her plump hips and even larger breasts. "Miss Rushton," she said and her chubby hand swept across her forehead.

Nora saw it right away. There was no missing the ring on Willimena's pinky finger. She was sure the woman had shown it to her on purpose. She probably had no clue it was Nora's, and one look at Fred's uneasy stance told her he hadn't said a word about who the ring belonged to before he gave it to his wife. The ruby seemed quite a bit smaller than she remembered on Willimena's fat finger. Eyes downcast, she forced air into her lungs.

The ring didn't belong on anyone's finger except hers. Nora's cheeks flushed, and she bit her tongue to keep from shouting at them both. She balled the fabric on either side of her skirt into her hands and squeezed. She loved that ring. She loved the brooch and the watch wherever it was, whatever Pa had done with it, she loved that, too.

She focused on the counter. Nine brown and black smudges marked the wooden plank. She couldn't contain the hurt any longer. She handed Fred his money, scooped up the packages, and ran out of the store. She moaned, a strangled sound, and one by one the tears ran from her eyes. *I will not cry.*

The watch was gone, she'd sold all her mother's jewelry and she'd let Otakatay kiss her. She'd never been anything to anyone, and for a mere moment she'd allowed herself to get caught up in the affection of having someone other than her father care about her. What a fool she'd been. She sniffled, wiped her face on her sleeve, tilted her chin and carried on.

She unlatched the wooden gate on the short fence, glad to be home. Voices came from around back, and she went to investigate.

Elwood and two men she didn't recognize stood with her father in the yard in a heated discussion.

"I will pay you back. We settled that last night," Pa said in an even baritone. He used the no-nonsense voice whenever she was in trouble, and she knew something wasn't right.

"I am aware of what the agreement was, and I've come to collect," Elwood said.

He wore navy pants and a white shirt open at the collar. Had he not been so shady, or tried to accost her every time he was in town, she'd of thought he was handsome. But his attitude and forceful nature made him one of the ugliest men she'd ever seen.

His eyes roamed the length of her, and he smiled.

Goosebumps covered her arms and she shivered. The man repulsed her. Why would Pa have anything to do with him? He knew as well as she did that Elwood was a devious business man, ruthless to the core. He'd strike an old woman down to get what he wanted. A head taller than her father, Elwood was wide and powerful, which didn't bode well for people who could be intimidated. Plus he had two men with him, the odds didn't favor them.

"Pa, is everything okay?" She eyed Elwood while she put the packages down.

Pa faced her. The lines on his forehead more prominent then the day before matched the deep frown on his face. "Nora, go into the house."

She didn't want to leave. She wanted to stay right here and see what this was all about. Back rigid, she walked past Elwood when he grabbed her hand and brought it to his lips.

"I'd be obliged if you'd accompany me to dinner tonight, Nora."

"Elwood," Pa warned his face beet red.

She swallowed and forced herself not to shiver in disgust. "I'm sorry but I am not allowed to take suitors."

Elwood's beady brown eyes squinted, and he squeezed her hand. "I say you are, and so does the money your father owes me." He tossed his head back and laughed.

Nora stared at her father. "What is he talking about?"

"Never mind," Pa said.

"I loaned your father money to gamble and now he owes it back," Elwood said. "However, I'm kind enough to waive the loan for a night out with you."

"No." Pa grabbed Nora's other arm and pulled her toward him.

She didn't move. Elwood had a firm grip on her wrist. Pa wasn't going to answer her, so she decided to take matters into her own hands.

"I'm sorry, Mr. Calhoun, but your money issues are with my father, not me. So kindly let go of my arm."

She glared at him, and when she felt his grip loosen, she yanked her arm away and stepped behind her father. She watched the two men on either side of Elwood and wondered if they'd killed anyone like Otakatay had. Their clothes were dirty and by the look of them they hadn't been washed in weeks. But it wasn't their attire that had her heart in her throat; it was the soulless eyes that glared back at her. She concentrated on Pa's back, praying they'd all leave soon.

Elwood took the watch from his pocket and held it up. "You will not even think about it, Nora dear?"

He smiled when he heard her gasp.

No.

Of all the people Pa could've sold the watch to, it was Elwood, the filthy bastard. She clenched her jaw.

"One night with me and you can have the watch back."

Nora couldn't take it anymore. She went to step around Pa, when he pulled her back behind him. She glanced at the watch in Elwood's hand. She could do it, one night with him, for the watch. She had nothing left of her mother, and the watch was so special to her.

"Pa—

"No, Nora."

She watched from behind Pa's shoulder as Elwood shook his head and dropped the watch onto the ground. She took another step, but Pa's hand held her still. She wanted nothing more than to grab it and clutch it to her chest.

"Dinner with your daughter?" he asked Jack one more time.

There was a long pause, and Nora wondered if Pa had changed his mind, but he shook his head.

"No."

Elwood motioned to the tall red-headed man on his left. She watched horrified as he raised his large black boot and smashed the watch into bits.

The sound of the gold being crushed turned her stomach and bile rushed up her throat. She swallowed the bitter taste, and pushed the scream that wanted to burst from her lips back down. She tried to focus on anything but the watch. She refused to make a scene, when all she wanted to do was fall at his feet and cling to the bits and pieces lying on the ground.

Elwood would not see how this affected her. She blinked back the tears hovering within her lashes. She glanced at her father and saw his chin quiver.

"You'll pay your debt one way or another, Jack," Elwood said and winked at Nora. "And it will be *my* way. It always is."

They both sighed when he left the yard.

"It's okay, Pa." She placed her hand on his shoulder.

Pa stared straight ahead, lost within his own thoughts, and she wished she knew how to reach him. He shrugged her hand away and left without saying a word. She stepped back, stunned as he walked in the direction of the saloon. Thick tears fell from her eyes and soaked her face. Her arms hung frozen at her sides, she didn't have the energy to wipe them.

She knew he felt horrible for selling the watch, and as much as she didn't want to resent him for it, she didn't understand why it had to be to Elwood. She picked up the pieces. Holding them in the palm of her hand, she examined the broken heirloom—the shattered glass face, the deformed gold links. It would never look the same again.

She closed her hand and brought it to her chest. There were no memories of her mother to pull from her mind whenever she needed to. No lullabies, no stories, no kisses when she was sick. All she had were the fantasies built in her mind, and the pieces of jewelry Pa had given to her. She squeezed her hand until the knuckles went white. Now all that was left were broken bits, like her heart.

A low whine caught her attention, and she glanced out onto the street. Two more long moans floated toward her. She stood, dropped the pieces of the watch into her apron pocket and walked down the path behind the buildings.

The whine grew louder, and she peered into the woods. A brown burlap sack was tossed over something moving underneath. Curious, she pulled the rough fabric slowly away. She covered her mouth to conceal the loud gasp. Savage, Elwood's dog, lay beaten and bloody on the ground.

"Oh, no."

She eased past the branches and crawled toward him. A low growl met her as she came closer.

"Shush. It's okay, boy."

She inched her hand toward him. Savage bared his teeth and his head snapped to the side, almost taking her hand off.

How was she going to help him if he was going to bite her? She observed the street through the trees, glad no one could see them. Elwood could come back anytime, and she didn't want to be caught in the forest alone, with no one to protect her. She took a deep breath, held it and stepped closer again. Savage growled, but she laid her hand on the dog's side. In a flash he lunged and nipped her finger.

"Damn it." She clutched her finger close. Nora's hand throbbed as blood ran from her finger down her arm. He'd bit her good. The wound stung and by the way the skin was torn, she was sure a few stitches would be needed.

She shook her head and focused on the task at hand. She forced her hand back to Savage's fur, moving it soothingly over his coat. A growl rumbled from his chest, but he didn't move, and she exhaled.

"Okay, boy, I'm going to wrap the sack around you and lift."

Savage gave a high pitched whine, and Nora's heart broke. He was in pain and until she got him into the cabin to examine his wounds there was nothing she could do to help him. She wiggled the fingers on her uninjured hand. The need was there, both hands pulsed and heated.

The process of lifting the dog so she could slide the sack underneath him took forever, and she was sweating by the time she was finished. Blood flowed from wounds she couldn't see because of his fur. She didn't know where to place her hands so she wouldn't hurt him. Her finger hurt like hell and she needed to stop the bleeding. She ripped a piece of the fabric from the hem of her apron and bound the finger, using her teeth to tie it tight. She winced as the last knot was made and her finger was bandaged.

She peeked at the dog. "Here we go."

She shoved her hands underneath his belly before lifting him from the ground. She hadn't realized how heavy he was, and she took two quick breaths before hastily walking toward the cabin.

She laid Savage on her bedroom floor. The animal whimpered. She struck a match and lit the lamp on the table. When she lifted the sack from him, she couldn't believe what she saw. He'd been beaten with a stick or a leather rope. Pieces of his fur were missing from where he'd been cut. Slash marks sprawled across his back and under to his belly. She swallowed. The poor thing, he'd never had a chance.

Damn you, Elwood. She'd always known the man was cruel, but this was far too disgusting for any human to do. Savage had always been mean and it was as she'd suspected, someone made him that way.

The shaking began in her hands, relentless and unstoppable. She didn't know where to start, there were so many cuts. The white cotton wrapped around her finger stuck out as she laid her hand over Savage's black fur.

"Okay, boy, let's start slow."

One hot hand crept with ease over the longest cut. She closed her eyes, allowing his pain to encompass her body as the aching in her ribs and right side intensified. She drew in a quivering breath as she dragged her hand along the rest of the wound.

Savage moaned.

She was able to heal two more gashes before her stomach rolled and she puked in the bucket beside her. She wiped her mouth with her forearm and swept the braid back over her shoulder. The poor pup. While healing his wounds, she'd felt his pain. She rubbed her right side and inspected him. There were still so many.

A lock of hair fell in her face and she tucked it behind her ear. She'd heal the deep cuts first and then make a poultice for the others. She thought of Otakatay. The scars she'd seen on his neck and arms appeared similar to the ones Savage bore. *He'd been beaten.*

"Oh, dear God."

What had he been through? Who would do such a thing? Elwood's face shot across her mind and she scowled. He'd beaten his dog. She always knew he was a louse and this confirmed it. After a few long minutes of inspecting Savage's wounds, she knew which ones needed healing fast and which ones could be bandaged. She laid her hands over the cut feeling the skin close underneath. A burning sensation sliced across her back and around to her stomach. She arched and sucked in a hissing breath.

She healed four more wounds, but before she was done the last one, her stomach heaved and she threw up all over herself. It seemed like an eternity before she was able to bring her head up from the bucket. Spasms sliced through her middle, and damp hair clung to her temples. Her finger throbbed. She was so weak that instead of emptying the bucket or gathering bandages, she laid her head on the floor and closed her eyes. Savage placed his nose beside hers and they fell asleep.

CHAPTER FOURTEEN

Otakatay heard the branches break, and listened to the uneven melody hum throughout the forest. He patted the knife tied to his leg and flexed his back, feeling the leather casing shift slightly. The wasichu didn't care about their heavy feet. They didn't care about anyone other than themselves. Their arrogance and ignorance was what he hated most about them. He ground his teeth together and leaned against a tall pine to wait.

The wasichu stepped through the trees and came toward him. He didn't bother to conceal his disgust for the man who had hired him. They both had a purpose for using the other and once he was done, he'd kill the white eyes.

One more kill. He shook his head. The reminder called to him, taunting and sinful, while evil fingers pressed along his consciousness squeezing out the last of his reason. Would the nightmares cease after he killed the last one? Would he forget the softness of their skin while he clutched them close, or the sound of his blade cutting their throats? He tensed. Visions of thick scarlet covered his hand, hot and sticky. No cry. No whimper. Silence—a quiet he will always hear—a stillness that will haunt him for the rest of his life.

The killer inside of him mocked him for letting the girl go. He heard the sneer, the laughter, the growl for blood. And he'd saved her, even if for one day. He pushed her from him. The need to finish what he'd started to fulfill his promise crawled over him, biting at his reason. When he closed his eyes, he saw the mark and the face that went with it.

"Have you found any more?" The wasichu's voice brought him back to the conversation and the task at hand.

Tall and lean, the wasichu stood a few feet from Otakatay and he wondered why the white man hired him to kill these women. He never believed they were witches, as he'd been told. But for some reason unbeknownst to him, the man was obsessed. The women consumed him, and each time they met he pressed Otakatay for more.

"There are none." He thought of the girl, Nora, and decided to keep the information to himself.

The wasichu eyed him and murmured, "I have someone I want you to follow."

"I do not follow anyone."

"She may have the mark. I need you to be sure." He smiled. "And then I need you to kill her."

There was someone else? Why he felt relief that it wasn't the girl, that it wasn't Nora, he didn't know, and he brushed the reprieve aside.

"Where is this one?"

"She lives behind the blacksmith's shop in a cabin with her drunk of a father."

He froze. *Ina.* He struggled to stay with their conversation as a rush of emotions crashed down upon him. He couldn't draw air into his lungs. His chest ached. Ina—mangled and bloody, his brother, broken and frail and he could do nothing. He dropped his head, and inhaled slow and steady before he said in a low growl, "Fifty dollars is the price for this scalp." He was done. No more killing. He would fulfill his promise.

"Damn it. That's too much." The wasichu took out a handkerchief and wiped his face. "I will pay the regular fee."

"No." Otakatay pulled his knife from his back and took a step toward him. "You pay what I want. Nothing less."

"Are you going to kill me, Savage? Out here in broad daylight?"

Otakatay sprung forward, pushing the wasichu up against a tree. With his forearm against the man's throat, he dragged the blade of the knife along the whiskers on his cheek.

"Today I am feeling generous." He smiled. "How do you prefer to die? A slice across the neck so you bleed out slowly, or punctured in the stomach and gutted?" He pressed the blade into the wasichu's flesh, cutting him.

Blood dripped down his cheek and the wasichu's Adam's apple worked up and down. "Fine, fine. I will pay the fifty."

He reached into the man's front pocket and pulled out two bills. "I will take half now." He shoved the weasel from him and walked toward Wakina.

"You will kill her, if she has the mark, right?" he asked, while rubbing his neck.

"It will be done."

CHAPTER FIFTEEN

A knock at the door woke Nora. She'd fallen asleep on the floor, and the uneven boards did nothing for her aching muscles. She rolled over, feeling the ridges of the wood dig into her skin. Every joint screamed in agony.

She wanted to crawl into bed and sink into the covers for the rest of the day. Savage was still where she'd left him last night, resting on the blood-stained burlap sack. She could tell by the even rise and fall of his chest, he was out. Slowly, and with great care for her sore back, she stood and stretched before going to see who was at the door.

She'd look at Savage's wounds this afternoon. They needed to stay clean, lest infection set in. The sun peeked through the window, bright and welcome. She didn't hear father come home last night and wondered if he'd gone to work this morning. The rumpled cushions on the sofa and the pale blue blanket piled in the corner told her he'd been here, but there was no sign of him now.

Even after they reconciled yesterday, he still wanted nothing to do with her. A razor sharp spasm slashed across her middle. She bent over and tried to draw in air that wasn't paired with pain. She was helpless to the way her body dealt with pa's rejection. Another knock. She tucked her mangled insides away and opened the door.

"Mornin'," Jess said, "Damn, girl, you look like hell." A worn Stetson sat lopsided on her head, and a broad smile spread across her face.

Nora hadn't realized how terrible she looked until Jess had mentioned it. She glanced down, shocked to see the blood from last night still smeared across her apron and along her arms and hands. She'd fallen asleep and forgot to change. She lifted a hand to try and fix the stray hairs that had fallen from her braid, but she gave up and stepped aside.

"Please, come in."

Jess smiled and sauntered past to plop down in one of the two chairs at the table. "Shit. Were you butchering a pig? Why in hell are ya covered in blood?"

The older woman's crassness was something she wasn't used to, but for all the spit and fire she was, Jess Chandler was indeed a kind hearted soul.

Nora sat across from her. "I rescued Elwood's dog, Savage. The bastard beat the animal just short of killing him."

Savage still had a long way to go until he recovered, but Nora had healed the worst of his wounds, the ones that would've killed him. She stretched her hands out on top of the table. The sleep had helped her to recuperate after healing the deep cuts, but it made her violently ill and very weak. Even now she still didn't feel up to grade.

Jess's eyes narrowed. "You be careful around that damn mutt. He's vicious and will kill if provoked."

She shook her head. "He's been mistreated."

Jess pointed to Nora's bandaged finger. "Where did ya get that?"

"He was scared and hurt. The animal was protecting himself. He's fine now."

The woman raised her thick eyebrows.

"Honest, he won't hurt me."

Jess took off her hat and placed it on the table. Her silver blonde hair was in a neat bun, and Nora noticed for the first time how pretty she was.

"Well, you better let me have a look." She held out her hand, and Nora laid her finger on the table. "That no good scalawag Elwood Calhoun is pure evil." She pointed her finger at Nora. "Probably could use a few stitches."

She winced.

"Pour a little whiskey on it and bandage it good. You don't want an infection."

She nodded.

"Listen here, girl. You'd be wise to stay away from Elwood."

"Oh, I can assure you that I plan to stay far away." She glanced at the doorway where Savage lay. "But he insists on courting me, even though I've refused several times."

"Well, to hell with him." Jess swatted the air and pulled a gun from the holster around her waist. "You point this in his direction, and I'll damn well guarantee that louse will be a runnin'." She slid the Colt .45 across the table and winked.

Nora didn't like guns. They scared her something fierce. But she saw her friend's point. If Elwood came by, she needed to protect herself and there was no better way than with a loaded gun. She ran her hand along the cool barrel and wrapped her fingers around the ivory handle. The gun was heavier than she expected, and she laid it back down on the table with a loud thud.

"Is it loaded?"

"Sure as hell is. Doesn't hold much use if'n it ain't." Jess paused. "You ever shoot one before?"

She shook her head.

Within the confines of the cabin, she learned how to load, cock and fire the gun. Nora placed the loaded weapon up in the cupboard.

"Time's a wastin' with that finger of yours. Get on over here so I can clean it up."

Nora sat across from her and watched Jess pull a silver flask from her pocket.

"What's that?"

"Whiskey."

Without another word, Jess poured the potent stuff all over Nora's finger.

"Hell and tarnation." She placed her head on the table and groaned.

"Ah shit, girl, you're tougher than that. I'm afraid you're in need of some sewin'." She doused the needle and thread with whiskey before taking Nora's hand and poking the skin.

Nora bit her lower lip and hummed. The sharp needle pricked her skin again, and she tensed.

"Almost done."

She hissed as the last stitch went through.

"Good as gold." Jess patted her hand.

Relieved the finger was bandaged and she'd never have to feel the fire from the whiskey on it again, she excused herself to change into a clean dress and apron.

"How long have you lived here, Jess?" she asked while pouring two cups of coffee.

"My husband Marcus and I bought our land ten years ago."

She saw the far off look in Jess's eyes and knew the woman was thinking of the past. Unsure if she should pry, she waited patiently for her friend to continue.

"Marcus wanted to be a farmer. And he was good at it, too. We had a few hundred acres back in Wyoming but lost everything from years of drought. We packed up and traveled around the country for a while. We buried two babies on those trails."

Nora placed her hand over Jess's. "I am so sorry."

"Ahh hell, it's in the past. Ain't nothin' nobody can do. After the disappointment and heartbreak, we decided not to try for any more children." She smiled sadly.

"We found Willow Creek and liked it here. I wanted to stay in town and work until we had enough of our own money to buy land, but Marcus was dead set on finding land first. And once Elwood had sunk his rotten teeth in, offering land and the money to loan us, Marcus signed the papers without even asking me." She took a long drink of coffee before she continued. "Four years later, my husband is shot out in the field and no one knows who did it."

"Why would someone kill, Marcus?"

"Money brings people to do things, horrible things."

Nora couldn't imagine losing a husband. The pain, the anguish Jess must have felt tore at her heart.

"Marcus found oil, and within two days of hearing it, Elwood was there willing to forget the money we owed him if we gave back the land. Marcus refused, and the next day he was found shot up in the east quarter of our spread. A week after I buried him, Elwood brought in his men to drain the oil. They didn't leave a drop. He's determined there's more on the land, but I won't let him near it. Between myself and the few cowhands I have left we protect what Marcus fought hard to keep."

"Oh, Jess, that's terrible."

"I get by. Marcus wouldn't want me to lie around and weep. I'm tougher than that. Hell, I'm made out of nails and I'll fight for what's mine."

"Your Marcus sounds like a fine fellow."

"He was, dear. He was."

She poured more coffee and enjoyed their conversation. The woman she'd come upon in the field weeks before had become her friend and she was thankful.

After Jess left, Nora went to check on Savage. The name irritated her, and every time it left her mouth she felt dirty. She thought of Otakatay and how he'd been mistreated. How he'd been called names and shunned by his people. It didn't matter to them that he was half white, when they stared at him all they saw was red. She was disgusted and ashamed to be a part of a race that was so cruel.

She ran her hand along Savage's black coat.

"Savage is for something wild or ferocious, and you, dear friend, are neither. I will call you Pal."

She smiled, satisfied with the name and the meaning it held. Nora inspected his wounds, a yellow crust had formed around the cuts. She needed to draw out the puss. She hurried into the garden and rummaged through the sparse rows. She scooped up the last cabbage, went into the house and boiled it.

On her knees, she placed the warm cabbage over Pal's cuts, breaking off bits to feed to him as well. There was no trace of meanness in him now. He put his head on her lap and nuzzled his nose into her hand. He was a good dog, part wolf, which made him intimidating, but she knew he'd never harm her again.

It was late afternoon when she'd gotten around to making bread, and she could now smell the mouth watering aroma throughout her kitchen. Pal had limped out of her bedroom to lay by the warm stove. She smiled and ruffled his fur when she heard Joe call her name from outside.

She opened the door and was greeted by a very happy Joe and the hotel's maid, June.

"Good afternoon, Miss Rushton," June spoke with clipped English in which every word was enunciated.

"Hello, Nora. Hello," Joe called from beside June.

"Hello, Joe." Nora laughed.

"Miss Rushton, I promised Joe I'd walk him over to visit with you. He's been wanting to see you for some time now."

"I'd love to visit with him. I can walk him to the hotel before supper." She moved to the side so Joe could shuffle in.

"That is most kind of you. His father sits down to dinner at six."

"Very well. He will be there by then."

June nodded and turned to leave. "Miss Rushton," she called, before Nora closed the door.

"Please, call me Nora."

"Nora, you can bring Joe to the back door by the kitchen. Mr. Calhoun never comes that way."

She eyed the maid. She'd never really talked to her, but June was aware of Elwood's infatuation with her and Nora was glad for the suggestion.

"Thank you."

She closed the door, turned and bumped right into Joe. His wide eyes gaped at the dog. Fear etched across his face, and his eyelids started to flutter.

"Joe." She touched his arm. "Joe, Savage is a good dog. He won't hurt you."

He shook his head from side to side and his bangs blew from his forehead.

"Let's sit you down." She walked him to a chair and eased him into it. "Savage was hurt real bad, and I brought him back here to help him get better."

"He's a bad dog. Bad dog."

"No, Joe, he's a scared dog. Someone mistreated him."

He peered into her eyes, and she saw something familiar within the blue depths. "Pa is mean to him. Mean to him."

"Yes, I know. I've fixed him up and he's on the mend."

Joe stood and went to the dog. He slid down the wooden sticks he used to walk, and sat beside the animal. "Poor puppy, poor puppy."

She knelt beside him. "Yes, he's been through a lot."

"Savage, Savage," he sang while playing with his fur.

"Joe, he's not a mean dog anymore, and therefore he needs a nice name, don't you think?"

"Yes, yes." He clapped his hands.

"I like the name, *Pal*."

She'd already named him, but she wanted Joe to take part.

Joe mouthed the words a few times before he said, "Pal, Pal. I like it!"

Nora laughed. The boy had nestled himself deep within her heart, and she cared for him like the little brother she never had.

CHAPTER SIXTEEN

Nora woke to the sound of a gunshot. The moon shone through her bedroom window allowing her to see without lighting the lamp. She grabbed her robe at the end of the bed and slipped it on. Pal got up slowly and moved to her side. Injured, the dog must've sensed her concern and she exhaled relieved to have him there. She hurried out into the kitchen to check on Pa.

He wasn't there. The blanket still folded nice and neat on the end of the sofa. A dreadful sensation stirred in her stomach and she shivered. She didn't know why, but she needed to find him. Without thinking, she went outside and headed in the direction of the saloon. Half way across the yard, she saw a crowd of people gathered around. She picked up her pace.

"Miss Rushton, you may want to wait until…" Fred said holding both her arms.

She didn't bother to stop, but instead yanked herself from him and pushed her way through the crowd.

"Pa!" she screamed and fell to her knees beside him.

He'd been shot. She frantically scanned his body as another muffled scream burst from her lips. The bullet went into his chest, and without thinking of the consequences she laid her shaking hands over the open wound, when her father grabbed them.

He didn't say anything. The look he gave her was enough. The white shirt he wore had absorbed the blood, and it clung to his skin. She searched the faces around her, the people who would hang her if they knew of her gift. Pa was right not here, not in front of them.

"I will get you home," she whispered, close to his ear as her tears fell onto his face.

Pale blue eyes stared up at her as he struggled to take a breath. Nora's head spun and she reached out, pressing her hands into the dirt road to steady herself. *This can't be happening. Pa can't be dying.*

He gasped, and she pulled at the rocks beneath her shaking hands.

"I need to get him home. I need to get him home," she said to the people huddled around her.

"Someone's gone for the Doc," Sheriff Reid said, and she smelled the liquor on his breath.

Nora glanced up at him, irritation melded with anger. *Damn it.* The need to fire away at the sheriff filled her, but she clamped her mouth shut instead. Starting a fight wouldn't get Pa home faster.

"Sheriff Reid, carry my father home."

He wobbled to the side and almost fell on top of her. She ground her teeth and glared at him. There was no time to wait for the intolerable sheriff to get it together. She searched the faces around her, but before she could ask anyone else, Seth came forward and without saying a word lifted Pa and carried him toward their cabin.

Nora followed on shaky legs. She needed to see how badly he was hurt. *I have to heal him.*

Seth laid Pa on her bed as the sheriff walked in. Pal growled from the mat in the corner, and Nora shushed him.

"What in hell?" Sheriff Reid said when he noticed Elwood's dog.

She didn't know he followed them into the cabin, and she didn't want him here once she started healing Pa.

"Thank you Sheriff, but I can take it from here." She ushered him outside with Seth and shut the door before he could utter another word. She ran to the bedroom. Hands hot and sweating, she ripped opened Pa's shirt. The bullet had gone into the center of the chest. How was he still alive? How did it not pierce his heart? It made no sense, but she was thankful he was still here. Her hands hovered over the wound, about to draw out the bullet, when he pulled them to the side.

"No, Nora, no," he rasped as blood formed at the corners of his lips and trickled down his cheek.

She wiped it away with her hand.

I have to help him. She had to make it right. She had to fix him. His skin had turned pasty and gray. Time was running out. Her heart raced and an overwhelming pressure filled her lungs. She couldn't breathe. Panic set in, eager to destroy the life she'd so easily taken for granted. She pressed her hands back over the wound.

"NO."

He was stronger than she thought, and he gripped her hands in his.

"Please, Nora. Let me go."

"No, Pa. No." What was he thinking? Why did he want to die? *God, please help me.* "I can't do that Pa, I can't." She tried again to pull her hands from his, but they didn't budge. Tears fell from her eyes and dripped from her chin.

"You can't fix this, Nora," he wheezed.

"Yes, I can." She tried again to pull free.

"I don't want you to."

She didn't want to hear it. She had no control and she stomped her feet. He was slipping away right before her and she couldn't do a damn thing. She struggled against his grip, trying to free her hands, but he held her still.

"Pa, let go," she sobbed. "Please, please let me help you."

She watched helpless as his eyes focused on her and a tear slid down his cheek. "I love you." He exhaled, and his hands fell to the side.

"No." She shook him. "No, no, no, Pa!"

She pressed her hands onto the hole in his chest and willed the skin to close—to somehow put the life back in him. Her hands no longer hot, she pressed harder, his blood covered them as she demanded the wound to heal.

"Please, please, please."

Nora screamed through clenched teeth and pounded her fists onto his chest.

"Please, Pa. Please come back."

She fell across him and wailed. The pain rolled over her, picking and pulling at the reality she didn't want to face. She shook him once more.

"Wake up, Pa. Wake up."

Blood soaked the front of her dress, and she shuddered. She ran her hands down his face and closed his eyes. Memories of their life together flashed across her mind, and she shook her head. Unable to hold on any longer, she ripped the hair from her braid and pulled at the strands.

She shrieked and fell over top of him. Every muscle tensed. Every bone ached, and her chest throbbed. She desperately wanted to wake from this nightmare. The anguish bore down upon her and compressed her lungs. She gasped. She clung to him, scratching the skin, wanting him to be here, with her.

"Please, God, bring him back." She grabbed his shoulders and shook. "Wake up, damn it. Wake up." She lay across him and buried her head into his neck, wheezing as bitter sobs burst from her lips.

"Nora? Nora, come now dear," Doctor Spencer pulled her from the bed.

"No." She wrestled with the doctor. She wouldn't leave Pa.

"He's gone."

She wrenched her arms from the doctor's hold and fell over top of her father. "He can't go. He can't. Pa, please, please." She clawed at the blood stained shirt, and wrapped her arms around his neck. "Wake up. You've got to wake up."

Strong arms guided her back from her father.

"I'm sorry, Nora."

She stared at her father, his chest still, his body covered in blood. Nora's knees buckled from the truth. Doctor Spencer caught her, and she wailed in his arms.

He helped her into the kitchen where Seth stood. The young boy had come back. He didn't say a word and she was glad. There was nothing to say. Someone had killed her father and now he was gone—gone from her forever.

She lifted a trembling hand to her eyes and wiped at the tears. She didn't care that they were covered in Pa's blood, or that her dress was ruined, stained beyond recognition. All she wanted was for someone to tell her this was a bad dream, for Pa to walk through the door alive and well. She sucked in a sob and bit the inside of her cheek.

The doctor came out of the bedroom and announced he'd prepared Pa for burial. Nora nodded, not knowing what to do next. She wanted to crawl into a dark hole and cry out all her sorrows. She wanted to scream at the top of her lungs and punch the wall. She wanted to die.

"Will you be okay, by yourself?" Doctor Spencer asked.

Dazed, she nodded. She wanted to be alone, and didn't hear the door close when they left. Pa's last words replayed in her mind, *I love you.* She'd never said it back. She never told him. She slid from the chair onto the floor, buried her head into Pal's fur.

"I'm sorry, Pa. I'm so sorry."

Otakatay heard the gunshot from the forest. It came from town. The wasichu didn't like to lose and he'd bet it was over a card game. There wasn't another shot fired and that told him it was intentional. The man didn't even know it was coming.

He slipped his knife into the leather casing tied around his shin. He had a job to do tonight. He sighed. The weight on his shoulders increased, and he was sure a mountain sat on top of them. He lifted his arms flexing the muscles. Tonight it would end. Tonight he'd have his last victim. The last throat he'd slice. The last scene he'd replay over and over. He touched the feather in his hair. *I do this for you.*

He tied Wakina's reins around a tree and walked toward town to find the cabin behind the blacksmiths. The piano from the saloon played a tinny, off key song that filled the otherwise silent street. He stayed in the shadows, watching as a few men left through the swinging doors and swayed down the street. There was no sign someone had been shot earlier. He shrugged. He didn't give a damn who had been killed or who had done it. All his senses focused on moving silently down the street to the cabin.

He eased up to the back window and peeked in. A man lay on the bed, and Otatakay immediately noticed the blood on the floor. This was the one who had been shot, the father. Was it a coincidence or pure fate that the father of the girl he was about to kill was dead? He examined the room. A brush and a few hair combs sat on the wooden dresser, and three dresses hung in the armoire.

With skilled movements he eased the window up, and silently climbed in. Light came from the other room, and he crept closer. He saw her sitting in a rocking chair in front of the fire. He stilled. It was her. It was the girl, Nora. A black dog lay at her feet, and he noticed the cuts and marks on his skin. The animal was injured and not a threat. He put him out of his mind.

He watched the girl. Blood smeared the front of her dress, and there was so much he wondered at first if she was injured. But after watching her, he realised that she was fine. Her pale skin was marked with red slashes of blood, and knotted black hair hung down her back. She rocked back and forth, and he saw the tears drip from her eyes onto her cheeks. Loud moans came from her lips as she brought her hands up to her face.

Why did it have to be her? He clenched his jaw. The lost look in her red-rimmed eyes told him she wasn't there at all. Killing her would be easy. She'd never see him coming. He pulled the knife from his back, gripping it within his hand.

Do it. Kill her. The heinous slayer inside of him screamed for retribution. He yelled, growled and whispered into the better part of his conscience. A veil of evil blanketed him and he was blind to what was right or wrong, the only thing he saw was death.

He shook his head, ignoring the executioner he'd become and focused on the girl. She was now on the floor, kneeling in front of the fire.

She hunched forward and he watched as her hands hovered above the fire. Her desolate sobs reached his ears, and a tiny part of him pitied her. Ina flashed across his mind, along with his promise, and he squeezed the knife. There was no time for pity, no time for caring. The assassin within him howled and he stepped toward her. The dog growled. He took another step when he saw her lean in toward the flames again.

What the hell was she doing? In two quiet steps he was behind her. The blade reflected the fire as he held it close. The dog growled again. She bent forward, and he knew she was going to burn them. He dropped his knife and sprung toward her. Grabbing her shoulders, he jerked her back as she placed her hands into the hot coals.

She screamed, and he didn't know if it was from the pain or the shock that he was there. He picked her up and set her in the rocker. He inhaled a couple times, before he took her hands and examined them. She'd burned them, not badly, but enough to need a salve to ease the pain and so infection didn't set in.

He made the mistake of gazing into her eyes. Sorrow filled their navy depths and for the first time in his life, he didn't know what to do.

A part of him wanted to help her, while the other wanted to leave and never return. He wavered on the edge of good and evil. He stood up to go, when she brought her hands up to her face and wept within them. The sound tugged at the boy inside of him, and he remembered holding his Ina when she died. He pulled the medicine pouch from around his neck and emptied some of the herbs into his palm. He spat into his hand and mixed the concoction with his finger until it was a green paste.

Otakatay took her hands gently in his, and with tender movements rubbed the medicine into the burns. She sniffed, and he glanced at her. Eyes closed she winced, and he moved slower, barely touching the skin. Blisters formed, and he knew she was in pain.

"Please, please do not help me," she whispered, her voice hoarse.

He frowned and continued rubbing the herbs into her palms.

She tried to pull away, but he held her to him.

"Otakatay, please leave them. They are no good to me anymore." She glared at her hands. "They are worthless." She started to cry all over again.

He stopped and waited while her body trembled. She squeezed her hands together and yelled out from the pain, but didn't release them. A low moan came from her throat as she hung her head and sobbed.

He didn't know what to do, and he wasn't sticking around to find out what would happen next. He pulled the medicine pouch from around his neck and laid it on her lap.

"Mix small amounts with water or saliva, and rub it into your hands once a day." He didn't know if she heard him. He watched as she shook her head and muttered apologies to her father. The urge to hold her in his arms stole over him. He took a step back and ran his hand down the length of his face. He grabbed his knife, and looked at her one last time before he walked away.

Nora stood at the graveside while two men lowered her father into the ground. He'd been gone two days, but to her it felt more like an hour. The pain still raw, she brought the white handkerchief to her face and blotted her eyes. Jed purchased the wooden casket and she was grateful for the help. She couldn't afford it and without Pa's income, there would be no money now.

She scanned the faces gathered around, a handful of people had come to see Jack Rushton buried. Aside from Doctor Spencer and the sheriff, she didn't know any of them. They resembled gamblers, unwashed clothes hung from their skeletal frames. She figured they knew her father from the saloon. Her stomach spun. She thought he'd drink himself to death, but she'd been wrong.

She hung her head. He'd died from a wound she couldn't heal. A horrifying moment she wished over and over to have back. She'd have done things differently, given him whiskey so he couldn't fight her, or tried harder to save him. A tear slipped down her face. *I should've tried harder.*

The sheriff stood off to the side, still embarrassed he'd been drinking the night Pa was killed. He assured her that he was searching for the killer and wouldn't give up until justice was served. Nora wondered if the killer was among them now.

It could be any one of the people mulling about the open grave site. She took a second look at them. They fidgeted, stepped from one foot to the other and their bloodshot eyes focused on the ground. They were itching to drink. She doubted any of them could aim a gun, much less pull the trigger and kill someone. All they cared about was where they'd get the next drink.

She blew a shaky breath and clutched the handkerchief. Her hands still tender, she loosened her grip on the cloth. Two men shovelled dirt over the coffin. The *scrape, scrape* of the shovels and the silence after they dropped it down the hole, she'd never forget.

Oh, how she wanted to be told it was all a misunderstanding. None of it happened. Pa hadn't died and she wasn't alone. She thought of Otakatay. She didn't know why he'd come the night Pa died, but she was glad, his presence offered comfort.

Had he heard the shot? Did he see her trying to save him? He'd been there afterward. A steady hand to help her when she'd burned herself. She remembered very little of that night, but she'd never forget the concern in his eyes as he smoothed the salve over her throbbing hands.

The shovels pounded on the hill packing the dirt over where her father was buried. He was gone. Her chest tightened. A mound of soil and a small wooden cross were all that was left of Jack Rushton. She blinked back tears and blew a kiss toward the ground. *Goodbye, Pa. I love you.*

CHAPTER SEVENTEEN

It had been six days since Pa's death, and Nora still couldn't make it through a day without crying. Her evenings were plagued with nightmares that carried over into the morning and followed her throughout the day. She was helpless to the visions that swirled in her mind of her father lying dead before her.

She shivered. She was captured within herself, and each day that went by, the burden she carried weighed so heavy she was sure she'd crumble. The pressure pushed her lower and lower, until defeat and exhaustion had her screaming at the walls.

She placed some wood inside the stove and threw in a lit match. She slid the tea pot over the burner. The wood crackled and she inhaled the sweet aroma.

She brushed her hands along her dress and looked at the array of food on top of the counter. There was more in the icebox, a mourner's gift from the townspeople. She hadn't touched any of it and found herself giving it away instead. Seth chopped wood all morning for her, and to show her appreciation she gave him one of the half dozen pies she had. Jess had stopped by yesterday, and she'd insisted the woman take a chicken pot pie home for dinner. She gave her back the gun too, not wanting to be a part of the violence it held.

She stacked the unwashed cups and plates beside the metal bowl on the counter. She'd wash them later. She thought of Jess. The kind woman had begged her to come and live out on the ranch. She made a good argument, too. Nora shouldn't be living alone. They'd give each other company.

The idea was tempting, and she wanted to say yes, but regret over the past lingered within her soul and she declined. She liked the older woman, and didn't want to offend her, but she couldn't afford to be a burden to anyone ever again. She'd been the anchor Pa tugged behind him for years, keeping him from living a normal life. And she'd never forgive herself for it.

She held her hands out. The burns had healed, and she still had feeling in them thanks no doubt to Otakatay's medicine. *I will never use them again. I will live like a normal girl.* No one would ever know she possessed such power. She tucked her hands into her armpits.

There wasn't a cloud in the sky, and a part of her wanted to get out of the cabin. The thick, dense woods called to her. A walk through the forest might be what she needed. Staying cramped inside the house wasn't good. But as she glanced in the direction of the tall trees, she couldn't find the strength to leave. She wrapped her arms around her stomach and leaned against the wall. She missed her father so bad some days she thought she'd die from the pain.

She pulled back the curtain. Wagons rolled by, and people walked in and out of shops. Their lives hadn't been interrupted like hers. A little piece of her resented them for their smiles and carefree attitude. Would the aching inside her heart ever go away?

A tall, dark shadow crossed the street, and she recognized Otakatay immediately. He hadn't come back for his medicine pouch, and she was beginning to wonder if he ever would. She'd used all the herbs inside on her hands and wanted to replenish the leather sack, but didn't know the plant that had been inside.

He glanced in her direction, but she couldn't tell whether he saw her or not. Her heart skipped and she brushed the warm feeling aside. He'd threatened to kill her, scared the devil out of her and kissed her all in a matter of days. Who was he and why did he stir such odd feelings inside of her? She must be crazy to even think someone like him would have the slightest interest in someone like her. He was the opposite of everything she believed in. He killed people. She saved them. *Or at least I used to.*

She sighed and her breath fogged up the glass. She wiped it with her sleeve. Her left hand was marked with red slashes that were raised like a welt. A sick feeling settled low into her abdomen, and she inhaled through her nose to ease the queasiness. She should've saved pa.

He was right. She was cursed. The reason they had run from town to town. The reason her mother died. She'd been selfish and refused to listen. Remorse choked her, and she fought the scream welling up in her throat. She'd never forgive herself for Pa's death.

The tea kettle whistled, and as she poured herself a cup someone knocked on the door.

Joe stood on the porch, leaning into his crutches as sweat glistened from his forehead.

"Hello, Joe. Please, come in." She looked around him for June. "Where's Miss June today?"

Joe shuffled into the cabin and sat down at the table. "She's busy, she's busy."

"Does she know you're here?"

He nodded and smiled.

"I can't believe you walked all the way over here on your own, Joe."

The poor boy was still trying to catch his breath, and her heart went out to him. How he must struggle. Everyday things she'd taken for granted didn't come easy for someone like him, and she felt horrible for the boy. She looked at his legs. *No, I will not even think of it.* She shoved the thought to the back of her mind.

"It was fun, fun." He tossed his head.

She smiled. "Would you like a cup of tea or some water?"

"I've never had tea, tea. Thank you, Nora."

He pulled a pack of cards from his front pocket and placed them on the table. Maybe a game was what she needed to take her mind off what she was going to do now. She took a dirty cup, dunked it in the cold water in the metal basin and dried it with a rag before she poured him a cup. She cradled the mug in her hand and sat down across from him. Joe's eyes watered and his lip trembled.

"Joe, are you okay?"

"I'm... I'm sorry about your Pa. I'm sorry about your Pa." He rocked back and forth.

Nora's vision blurred and she placed her hand over his. "Thank you, Joe."

He smiled, and it warmed her heart.

Curious, she asked, "Do you remember your mother?"

Joe didn't blink for a long while, and she grew nervous wondering if he was going into a fit.

He shook his head slowly.

"No. I don't remember her, I don't, I don't."

She could see the sadness reflected in his eyes. She had no intention of upsetting him. "I don't remember my mother either."

He squeezed her hand and blinked back tears. For all the things Joe lacked, the boy sure made up for them with compassion. He had a heart of gold, and she hoped Elwood would never steal that from him.

She grabbed the cards and shuffled them. "Let's play, shall we?"

Joe clapped his hands. "Yay, Yay!"

The sun was descending, casting gray shadows around them as she walked Joe back to the hotel. Pal trotted along beside them. The animal hadn't left her side since she'd healed him, and she was grateful. The long nights alone would be unbearable without him.

Joe gazed up at the sky, his blonde brows furrowed, and he moved his sticks faster.

"Joe, is something wrong?"

"It's getting dark, dark, dark." He tossed his head, and his eyelids fluttered.

She placed her hand on his shoulder. "We're almost to the hotel."

He didn't answer, and she moved her hand from his shoulder to his arm, offering support in case he fell. Joe's crutches made loud aggravated sounds as he ran them along the boardwalk. She scanned the street and noticed Fred Sutherland standing in the doorway of the mercantile.

"Good evening, Mr. Sutherland," she said as they passed.

"Good evening." He stepped in front of them. His brown eyes assessed her, and she stepped back. He was staring at her so intently she wondered if she had something on her face. She moved to go around him. He smiled, and pulled two candy sticks from his pocket.

"I know Joe has a sweet tooth, but I wasn't sure if you did."

Her hand shook as she grabbed the peppermint stick. "Thank you."

"Candy, candy." Joe almost jumped into Mr. Sutherlands arms.

The man laughed as he handed the candy over.

"Enjoy." The bell over the door jingled as he went inside.

The hair on Nora's neck prickled, and she pulled Joe along the boardwalk wanting to put some distance between them. Why she felt unsure around him all of a sudden, she didn't know. Goosebumps covered her arms and she pulled her sweater closed.

She glanced back. She could count on one hand the times she'd spoken to Mr. Sutherland. Maybe this was his usual demeanour. He'd been kind enough, and when she'd sold her mother's jewelry he was quite pleasant. She shrugged off the notion that the mercantile owner was anything but kind and continued walking.

Joe sucked on his candy with enthusiasm, and she smiled. The boy was a delight to be around, and she hadn't missed Pa as much while visiting with him today. She wondered why he was so afraid of the dark and decided to ask. "Joe, why don't you like the dark?"

He moved the stick to the other side of his mouth. "It's scary, scary."

"Yes, it can be."

"I go there when I'm bad, when I'm bad."

"When you're bad?"

He nodded.

She wanted to know what Elwood did to Joe when he was bad. Where did he take the boy that was dark and scary? She examined him with her eyes, searching for signs he'd been mistreated.

"Where do you go when you're bad?"

Joe pointed east to the mountain where the mine was. "There in the cave, cave."

"Elwood puts you in a cave?"

"Only when I'm bad, I'm bad."

He wouldn't. She stared up into the hills. He was a nasty man, but to harm a child, one with deficiencies like Joe, was heartless. She tried to process what Joe had told her. Had the doctor known? What about the townspeople, did they know? Were they all looking the other way while Elwood abused his own flesh and blood?

Nora's face heated as burning anger blazed through her. She wanted to confront the bastard. She wanted to stick up for Joe. Why hadn't she noticed before? Why hadn't she questioned Joe about Elwood? Guilt blanketed her, and she tried to push the feeling of suffocation away. *Poor Joe.*

She wanted to hug him, to tell him that not all people out there were as mean and vile as his own father. She thought of Pa, and her chest ached. He might've been a drunk, and he'd said unkind things, but he'd never struck her or left her behind.

She helped Joe to the back door of the hotel and was taken aback when he embraced her.

"Bye, Nora, Nora."

She hugged him back. If he could stand straight he'd be taller than her by at least a head. She blinked back the tear waiting to drip past her lashes.

"Goodbye, Joe. Please come by again."

He shook his head. "I go home tomorrow, tomorrow."

"Oh, I see. Well, next time you're in town, come and visit."

He nodded and went into the hotel.

She waited for the door to close behind him before she left. She followed the path behind the buildings back to the cabin, and was pulled into the shadows.

"Well hello, Nora."

Elwood's spicy cologne filled her nostrils, and she squirmed.

"Let me go." She tried to pull herself free of his grip.

He backed her into the side of the hotel and leaned in. The two men he'd had with him at the cabin stood blocking the entrance from the street. "Poor, Nora, you're all alone now, and need someone to take care of you." His fingers skimmed her cheek.

"Thank you for your concern, but I'll be fine." She tried to scoot around him, but he blocked her with his other arm.

"You'd have everything if you married me."

She searched the forest on her left and the street on her right for anyone she could call out to, but with Elwood's thugs blocking them from any prying eyes it was useless.

She tipped her chin and said hotly, "And why would I marry you?"

"Because bad things can happen to a woman living alone, I could protect you."

"I don't need protection."

"Don't you?" His finger skimmed her cheek.

"Please, let me go."

"I'm the wealthiest man within miles."

"What does money have to do with marriage?"

"Why everything, dear, and by marrying me you'll never be without it."

"If you think I'd marry you," She struggled to move away from him, "then you're dumber than I thought."

He laughed, a deep hollow sound, and she watched as his eyes hooded with desire. He brought her hands above her head and rammed his knee between her legs. She moved her head from side to side trying to get away from him. He gripped her chin in his hand and squeezed.

"You will have no choice," he sneered, nuzzling his lips into her neck.

She pressed into the wall behind her, the uneven wood pinched her back as she fought the urge to vomit all over him. The man repulsed her, and she rolled her hips trying to avoid his touch.

He caught her breast within his hand and squeezed.

She whimpered.

A low growl came from beside them.

"Savage, go on. Get outta here." He waved his hand behind him and continued to grind his groin up against her.

Nora pressed her nails into his hand trying to rip the flesh. She wiggled her head from his, avoiding his lips.

The dog barked and growled again, a low rumble that even had the hairs on her neck standing.

Elwood spun around. "What in hell?"

Pal was hunched low to the ground, his hind legs straight. Saliva dripped from his fangs as he showed his teeth.

"You son of a bitch." He kicked Pal catching him in the teeth.

The dog lunged for his foot, biting right through the boot. He shook his head, attacking the bastard's leg.

The two men ran toward them guns drawn.

"Don't shoot him. You may miss and hit me," Elwood screamed.

She eased away from him and faded into the shadows. Once she was a safe distance from them, she called Pal off.

"I'll kill that damn mutt yet, and then there will be no one to protect you." He wiped his mouth and spat. "I will marry you, Miss Rushton, if it's the last thing I do." He limped away smirking and his men helped him inside.

She wasn't waiting around for Elwood or his men to come back. She crumpled the hem of her skirt in her hand and ran all the way home, Pal beside her. She locked the door to the cabin and pressed her forehead against it. It wasn't until her heart resumed its normal rhythm that she knelt in front of her protector and hugged him.

CHAPTER EIGHTEEN

Otakatay packed up his bedroll and tied it to the saddle. He couldn't stay here any longer. He couldn't kill the girl. Unfamiliar emotions stirred inside him, and he didn't like it one bit. He was a killer, a breed. Not wanted anywhere but in hell.

He'd begun to care, to feel pity for Nora, and it pissed him off. He clenched his jaw. He didn't need some sniveling little girl getting inside of his head, making him feel things he had no right to feel. He had to get away and fast. He needed to find another victim, one whose face he hadn't seen.

He'd fought with himself for days about why he should kill her—why it was the right decision. She would be the last one. He'd have his money, have his freedom. He'd fulfill his promise. He flexed his hands.

He was going crazy. The killer in him shrieked of the good that would come from taking her life, he wanted her blood. Otakatay battled back and forth until all he saw when he closed his eyes was Nora's face. All he heard were her cries of agony, of hopelessness, and he understood. He remembered.

He pulled the blade from the deerskin case. It fit perfectly within his palm, and he stared hard at his reflection. The assassin he'd become cried out and he fought to control it. To calm the need for revenge—for the satisfaction of knowing she would be the last. *I've seen her face.* He'd heard her voice, kissed her lips. Sweat beaded on his forehead, and he tightened his grip.

He couldn't change the past, couldn't stop what he'd done, or what he'd become. He was Otakatay one who kills many, and he had. The last victims had been innocent—their only fault was a red mark upon their scalps. He killed for a purpose, and he'd paid the price. He'd never forget. Both the sleeping and waking nightmares would haunt the rest of his days.

Nora had the mark, the sign that could change his future forever. The answer to what he desired most. How could he walk away from everything he'd fought so hard for? The memories of the others plagued his mind, yet he'd had to do it to accomplish his goal.

He rocked back on his heels and threw the knife. The tree spat wood from the trunk as the blade struck it. Why couldn't he do it? Why couldn't he kill her? The act consumed him, kept him from sleep, from thinking of anything but her and the blue eyes set within a porcelain face. He made a promise, and this was all he needed to fulfill it. She'd be the last one.

"Shit."

There was no one to help him, to listen. There hadn't been since Ina died. He'd grown accustomed to living alone, to relying on no one. He closed his eyes. If he concentrated hard enough, he could see his mother's face. He could hear her, and on the days he felt most alone, he was sure he smelled her spicy, earthy scent.

He thought of his brother, Little Eagle and his heart ached. He hung his head and allowed the despair to fill him, drowning all thoughts of goodness from his mind. He wasn't good. Hell, he wasn't even close. Yet the one thing he strived for, the one purpose he had was what pushed him to do the things he'd done.

After seven years, he was so close to having enough money to fulfill his promise. Now, he was wrapped in a cloak that clouded his judgement and whispered words he did not want to hear. His mind was foggy, and the battle between the monster he'd become and the boy he once was raged inside of him.

He made a fist. He couldn't will them, or his mind to kill Nora. He yearned for a fight, for a way to get his emotions out, to calm the beast that screamed inside his head. He needed to smash something. He turned toward town. It'd be easy enough to find someone there to fight. The wasichu were always looking to put the lowlife breed in his place. He pulled the knife from the tree and placed it back inside the case. His body vibrating, he kicked leaves over top the ashes, when he heard someone approach.

"You haven't done your job," the wasichu said as he came through the trees. He stood face to face with Otakatay.

He growled, and did nothing to hide the angry expression on his face.

"The day is not over."

There was no need to tell the wasichu how he'd backed out the other night. How instead of killing her he'd helped her.

"You've had five days."

"It will get done."

"It damn well better. I've paid you half already, and I want her dead!"

The wasichu was no better than he was. In fact he was worse. He hid behind men like Otakatay to get the dirty work done, while sitting back and living as if he were the kindest of fellows. He was a deceiver, a manipulator, and Otakatay despised him.

The wasichu picked up a rock and tossed it in the air catching it in his palm. "If you do not kill her by tomorrow evening, I will find someone who will."

"Do you really believe she is a witch?"

He often wondered if any of the women held the magic the man spouted of, or if there was another reason, a personal reason for his wanting them killed. His people didn't believe in those types of things, and he found it hard to understand they even existed.

"Yes, of course I do. They're evil."

"Evil lurks on the earth in the killers I hunt, in rabid animals, and in men who pretend to be something they are not." He scowled at the wasichu, seeing right through him to the cold-hearted son of a bitch he was. "Evil is not in the face of a woman."

"What do you know? You're a bounty hunter. A damn breed." The man scrutinized him. "You haven't seen what they can do. I've been there. I've watched them kill by touching a person."

The urge to bust the wasichu's clean-shaven jaw vibrated over him. *In time, I will end his life.*

"It's in their hands. Their hands hold the power. They all have to die. They must," the wasichu went on half hysterical, and Otakatay watched as his eyes glazed and his face flushed crimson.

"Her father is dead."

"Yes, and soon she will be, too." He threw the rock onto the ground.

"Did you kill him?"

"Of course not," he scoffed. "Jack Rushton was at death's door anyway. If it wasn't a bullet that killed him, it would've been the alcohol."

Otakatay waited. He didn't care that the man was a drunk or that he'd been shot. All he wanted to know was if this wasichu had done it.

"You will do it. You will kill her."

He didn't know if it was the matter-of-fact way the man said the words, or because it was an order that caused him to bite down hard, and clench his fists. No one told him what to do. This was a job, nothing more. He chose to do it, and damn it, he'd choose when to end it.

"I want her scalp." He poked Otakatay's chest with his finger. "You will kill Nora Rushton, and you will do it by morning."

The fight he'd been looking for had presented itself. Otakatay smirked pulled back his arm and punched the man in the jaw. The wasichu stumbled backward, landing on his ass. A red welt brightened his chin and bled down the front of his shirt. He gaped up at Otakatay with dumb surprise.

"I work on my own terms." He glared. "Not yours." He grabbed the wasichu's throat and lifted him to his feet. "You touch me again white man, and you will die." He pressed his fingers into his neck.

The man nodded, his eyes bulging out of his head.

Otakatay released him with a shove.

The wasichu brushed the leaves and twigs from his pants. Fury and indignation shot from his eyes when he stared at Otakatay. He worked his hands at his sides, and Otakatay waited for him to charge. He wanted to smash the wasichu's face a few more times. He wanted to beat the life right out of the snake. But without saying another word, the white man pivoted on one heel and left.

Otakatay took a deep breath. The wasichu was the evil one, but he no longer held the money over his head. He'd find another way to get the remaining funds he needed. He'd stop by the sheriff's office and take a look at the wanted posters on the wall. It would be another month before his promise was fulfilled.

He rummaged through his saddle bags and pulled out the last of his pemmican. He bit into the dried meat and climbed onto Wakina. He thought of Nora. The wasichu would kill her.

He sat tall in the saddle, staring at the mountains ahead of him. He wouldn't allow the white man to take Nora's life. She was pure and innocent. A gem he'd not only had the pleasure to see but also to touch.

Thunder clapped in the sky, and he smelled rain. Dark clouds moved from the east toward town. This was going to be one hell of a storm. He took another bite of the meat and leaned forward to give Wakina the rest. They'd find shelter until dark, and then he'd warn the girl before he left town.

Nora placed a log on the fire and listened as the orange flames crackled, eating up the dry wood. The wind whistled through the cabin walls, and she sat back in the rocker while wrapping the quilt tighter around her legs. She hadn't been able to sleep in her room since Pa died, and tonight with the storm, she'd decided to sit by the fire with Pal.

A loud crack followed by an intimidating bang shook the cabin walls. Nora jumped. Pal whined beside her.

"It's okay. It's only rain," she said soothingly, unsure if it was for the dog's benefit or hers.

She glanced out the window and saw her reflection. It was darker than Pal's fur, and she couldn't help the slight shiver that shook her body. With her toes she pushed the chair back and forth, allowing the heat from the fire to warm her. Pa would've stayed in on a night like this and kept her company. Thunder clapped again, and Pal inched closer to her feet. She yawned and leaning her head back, she closed her eyes.

She needed to find a job. She had no money, and in time she'd have to restock the ice box. She'd stacked as much food as she could in there, but soon it would start to go bad and she'd have to throw it out. She'd find a job. She couldn't sit around here all day and do nothing. She couldn't stay in the cabin when all she thought of was Pa and how it was her fault he died.

She rocked the chair. Pal had nestled himself over her feet, keeping them warm, and she left them there not wanting to disturb him. She covered her mouth with her hand to stifle a yawn. The rain pelted the roof. The familiar and comforting *tap tap* lulled her to sleep.

Nora woke to Pal's growl. The room was black. She sat still. Someone was in the cabin. The hairs on her neck stood and her heart raced. The fire had burned down and the coals glowing orange offered little light in the room. She tucked her bottom lip between her teeth. Pal growled louder and the whites of his fangs glowed. She took a deep breath, held it and stood.

The blanket fell to her feet, and she turned around. A tall, wide shadow stood in front of her, and before she could scream the shadow lunged forward placing a hand over her mouth. She shrieked into the large palm cupped over her lips and went hysterical, thrashing her arms against a hard chest.

"It is me," a familiar voice whispered.

She inhaled through her nose as he pushed her closer to the fire so she could see his face. A loud sigh muffled against his hand when she recognized Otakatay standing before her. He stared into her eyes, waiting until she calmed down before he slowly removed his hand.

"You scared me half to death."

"There is no time. You must leave." He glanced around the cabin as if he were searching for something.

"Leave? But why?"

His eyes met hers, raw and obsessive.

Nora's stomach flipped. Terrified of what the feeling meant, she looked away.

"Someone is going to kill you."

Her head shot up. "What? Why would someone want to kill me?" *Did someone know? Had Jess or Joe told? It's what Pa feared all along.* She chewed her lip while trying to understand what he'd said.

"Because of something he thinks you have."

The room grew bright as lightning flashed outside followed by an ominous clap of thunder. The walls moved and she swayed to her right. He caught her arm. She blinked up at him and tried to focus on his face.

"But I have nothing."

"You must go." He pulled her toward the door. "Now! You must go tonight."

Things were happening too fast. She needed to know why and how he knew someone wanted her dead. She tugged her arm free and planted her feet into the wooden floor.

"But where would I go?"

He paused. "Where is your family?"

"I have no one."

Lightning illuminated the room, and she saw the hint of sadness cross his face. She touched his cheek. His skin was soft except for the whiskers, and she skimmed her thumb over his lips.

She couldn't explain why she'd touched him so intimately, other than she was drawn to him. Touching him felt right. She wasn't afraid of him, and she knew he wasn't the vile beast he proclaimed to be.

He moved closer, his hard chest pressed against hers. He bent and his black hair tickled her cheek. She felt his breath upon her lips and closed her eyes. He released her and stepped back, his shoulders rigid.

"You must go."

She stood motionless and watched as sadness, anger and confusion crossed his handsome face.

"I have nowhere to go."

"Then I will take you." He gripped the door handle as lightning cast the room in yellow shades. "I will be back." He opened the door and took off into the storm.

She glanced down at Pal beside her. The wind howled outside, and the rain banged against the cabin walls. Two gunshots drown out the storm. Without thinking, she opened the door and ran out into the pouring rain. Pal darted past her and around the corner of the cabin. She followed him while the rain pelted her, soaking her dress. She stopped and the blood rushed from her head to her feet. *Oh no. Not him. Please not him.*

Pal sniffed Otakatay's body as it lay in the mud. He'd been shot. She ran over and without examining him, she reached underneath his arms and pulled him toward the cabin. He was heavy, and she didn't know if she'd be able to get him inside.

Rain ran down her face and dripped off of her nose. Her hair was drenched, and she couldn't see it was so dark. She pushed her bare feet into the mud and pulled Otakatay another foot closer to the door. Pal whined and stared off into the blackness behind the cabin.

She huffed and tugged on him once more, moving him another two feet. If it wasn't for the mud, she didn't think she'd be able to move him at all. The wet dirt offered a slick path so it was easier to pull him. Pal came around, bit into Otakatay's shirt, and helped Nora drag him into the house.

She lit the lamp and carried it to the door. Pal stood outside on the porch and when she called him inside he took off, disappearing into the darkness. She yelled after him, but he didn't return and she needed to help Otakatay.

She knelt beside him and ripped open his shirt. Nora gasped when she saw the scars embedded on his chest, stomach and arms. *What happened to him?* The bevelled lines marked his skin in a criss-cross fashion, and her heart broke for him and what he must've been through. Her hands heated and her fingers pulsed. She clenched them and held them at her sides. *No. I will not do it. I will help him without using my gift.*

She put a pot of water on the cook stove to heat and gently washed his muddy chest. One of the bullets had gone clean through his shoulder. The other was still lodged in the center of his chest. She searched the house for a bottle of whiskey. She knew Pa stashed one around here somewhere. She removed the blanket from the basket beside the sofa and found the half-filled bottle nestled inside.

She dipped a clean cloth into the whiskey and blotted at the wound on his shoulder. Blood trickled down his arm, and she knew it would need stitches. She'd tend to that later, for now she needed to get the bullet out of his chest.

She felt Otakatay for one of his knives and pulled the large blade from his leg. She dipped it into the liquid. The water boiled, and she removed the pot and placed it beside her on the floor. His chest rose and fell in uneven breaths. She could taste the fear on her tongue. *I will save you.*

Nora's hands throbbed with urgency. She opened and closed them a few times before she pressed the tip of the knife into the hole in his chest. She stopped to see if he could feel anything, but he laid still, an ashen color already beginning to settle over his skin.

She dug the knife deeper and moved it around, trying to locate the bullet. Blood poured from the wound. Nora's hands shook wildly, and she dropped the knife. She squeezed her eyes shut, willed her hands to stop—to let her be normal, to save him without the power.

A lone tear slid down her cheek and fell onto her hand. She gaped at him. The ripped flesh was swollen and bloody. She didn't have a choice. She couldn't save Pa, he wouldn't let her. Otakatay was unconscious, there would be no fighting.

She couldn't remove the bullet with the knife, she didn't know how. She needed to save him and soon. She couldn't watch another person die without trying to help them first.

She blocked all reason from her mind and placed her hands over the wound. Strong blistering pain slammed into her and almost knocked her backward. The wound was deep, and she needed to work fast. She pressed both hands, one on top of the other over the hole again.

The nauseous feeling filled her belly as a fire exploded in her chest. She wheezed as the force sucked the air from her lungs. A piercing spasm radiated up and down her arms, zigzagged across her breasts and into her back. She bent forward and tried to ease the burning in her muscles.

When she inhaled, her lungs pinched as painful tremors rippled through her body. The enormity of it was too much. She didn't know how long she could hold on. Mouth dry, she tried to focus on his face as the room spun around her.

She pushed up onto her knees and forced her body to press into his. The heat in her hands intensified as she healed the deadly wound. Everything around her grew fuzzy, and she swayed to one side. She grew weaker and struggled to keep her hands on his chest. Her stomach lurched, and she held on until she felt the skin close underneath her palms. She removed them just in time to crawl to the basket she'd found the whiskey in, and vomited until she had nothing left inside of her.

Sweat ran from her forehead, and she trembled from the damp sensation. Her stomach convulsed a few more times. She laid her head on the blanket. The rain hitting the cabin was the last thing she remembered before she passed out.

CHAPTER NINETEEN

Nora woke with a start. Her chest ached, and her arms were numb. She flexed her hands to get some of the feeling back. She remembered Otakatay and crawled toward him. The room was still covered in shadows, but she knew it wouldn't be long before the sun rose.

The wound on his chest was no longer visible, and she laid her palm to his forehead. He was warm. She removed the cloth from his shoulder and shivered. Red and swollen, the wound was infected. There was no way she'd be able to heal him after closing the chest wound a few hours before. Her hands ached, and her arms were useless. She was drained and would have to wait until her body had recuperated.

"Otakatay." She nudged him. "Otakatay, please I need you to wake up."

He opened his eyes.

"I need your help to get you to the bed."

He nodded, and by the glossy look in his eyes, she wasn't sure he knew where he was.

She placed her arm under his and helped him to his feet. Her muscles cried out in agony as she ushered him toward the bedroom. He lost consciousness just as she sat him on the straw filled mattress. She eased him onto his back and propped a pillow under his head. She went to work removing his muddy pants and boots. As she unbuttoned his denims, she realized he was naked underneath.

Oh, no. Her hands hovered above his groin. She shook her head and frowned. She didn't have time for this nonsense. She threw the blanket over his middle and pulled the pants off. She was being ridiculous. This was a life and death matter. But she couldn't bring herself to steal a peek at his private area. She straightened the quilt the best she could. She picked up his dirty clothes and boots before she left the room.

She threw the pot of bloody water out into the yard and bolted the door, sighing when the wooden latch slid into place. She hadn't forgotten why Otakatay had come. Nora shivered and peeked through the curtain. *But who?*

There was still some water left in the bucket on the counter, and she dumped it into the pot to heat. She searched the cupboards for the lye soap and wrapped it in the wash cloth. The floor was a mess, with mud and blood smeared into the wood. She stared at it for a moment, deciding to come back and clean it later.

Nora dunked the cloth into the hot water and lathered the soap. She ran the cloth along his hard body, trying not to gape at the defined muscles on his stomach and chest. Nora's fingers skimmed the slashes on his shoulders and arms. There were so many she wondered how he lived through them all. She took the whiskey bottle, squeezed her eyes shut and poured it over the shoulder wound.

Otakatay bolted upright, knocking her backward, and yelled out in Lakota.

"I'm so sorry, but I have to clean the wound." She pressed him back down onto the pillow.

Amid red cheeks and clammy skin, glassy eyes gazed back at her. She laid her hand on his arm. He was sweating.

"One more time," she whispered.

He nodded and lay back down. She watched as his jaw clenched, and he closed his eyes. She leaned in and quickly tipped the bottle sloshing brown liquid onto the hole to run down his arm and chest.

A guttural moan came from his closed mouth, and his whole body tensed.

She took the whiskey soaked cloth and dabbed at the wound.

A strong hand gripped her wrist. "Burn it. Heat the knife and close it."

Was he insane? She couldn't do that. "I will stitch it instead."

"Do as I say," he growled.

"It is infected."

He squeezed her wrist, and she thought he was going to get off the bed and cauterize the wound himself when he passed out instead.

She sighed, doused the cloth in whiskey and placed it on the back of his shoulder, where the bullet had exited. She needed to stitch the torn flesh before he woke and demanded she melt it together with the blade of his knife.

Waves of nausea rocked her stomach causing her face to lose all color.

He was still too warm. She finished cleaning the area, pulled out her needle and thread, and dipped both into the whiskey.

Black eyes glared at her, and she jumped.

"Why do you not listen? Burn the damn hole."

"I... I don't think I can."

"It will get the infection out."

She held up the needle and thread. "But I cleaned these so I can stitch you."

He shook his head.

She wanted to brush the black strands that clung to his cheeks and neck.

"Where is the knife?"

"Please, Otakatay. Please don't make me do this."

He watched her for a long while before he said, "I will show you. Get my knife."

With no other choice, she grabbed the large blade sitting on the bedside table and handed it to him. He struggled to sit up and winced when he moved his arm. With his good hand he gripped the knife.

"You must build a fire and heat the end until the blade glows red."

She swallowed and nodded.

"Then you will place it over the hole until the skin is closed."

Nora's cheeks flushed. *How am I going to do this?* She glanced at Otakatay. *What if I throw up all over him or worse yet, pass out?*

He handed her the knife.

She willed her legs to walk into the kitchen. It wasn't more than a few minutes before the flames had grown, pushing heat into the room. She placed the blade into the fire and watched as it turned a bright orange-red. She wrapped her hand in the apron she was wearing, so she didn't burn it and pulled the knife from the heat. She hurried back into the room where Otakatay lay and stood over him.

"Do it. Quickly, do it now." He closed his eyes and clenched his jaw.

She focused on the bright tip of the knife as she moved closer to the swollen flesh. *I can't do this.* She chewed on her lip, and her hand shook.

Otakatay opened his eyes, and before she could pull away he grabbed her hand and pressed it into the wound.

His face contorted, and he let out what sounded to her like a warrior's cry before he passed out.

The smell of burning flesh filled her nostrils, and her stomach reeled. She swallowed past the bile in her throat and pushed the knife into his shoulder. The skin around the blade bubbled, and she closed her eyes. She inhaled before removing the knife and opening her eyes. The skin was red and rigid over the hole. She took the whiskey-doused cloth and laid it against the closed wound. *I have to do this one more time. Oh, dear God.*

He watched helplessly as his brother Little Eagle struggled to carry a bucket of rocks down the narrow path to the opening of the tunnel. He was six, tiny for his age, and not strong enough for this kind of labor. Throughout the dark, wet mountain deep holes were used for discipline, and digging. Little Eagle was edging his way around one that had been blasted yesterday. It was a fresh hole, and it was deep.

He wanted to go to him, to help his brother. He struggled, trying to loosen the ropes tied around his feet and wrists. He was his protector, his shadow. He yanked on the rope again.

He stopped hammering and watched Little Eagle take careful steps around another hole.

A loud crack echoed throughout the cave, and he didn't have to turn to see what it was. The leather whip the guard held flew high in the air and snapped.

He flinched.

"Get back to work," the man yelled.

He couldn't take his eyes of off his brother until he'd passed the hole—until he was safe. The whip lashed out biting into his flesh. He dug his teeth into his bottom lip and refused to look away.

Little Eagle glanced up at him, and he watched in horror as his brother lost his balance. The heavy bucket pulled him toward the hole. In an instant he was gone.

"Noooo," He screamed, and grasped at the air around him. He tried to yank free from the rope that tied him to the others, but he didn't move.

Otakatay woke to Nora pressing a damp cloth to his forehead. The dream was so vivid, so real it was as if he were there in the mountain all over again and saw his brother fall.

"You had a bad dream," she said. "Are you okay?"

He didn't answer. He didn't know what to say. If only it was a dream and not true. If only he'd been there to help him—to save him. He closed his eyes. He was a failure. Sorrow filled him, flooding his senses, and he couldn't see past the shame he felt to look at Nora's face.

He took her hand from his forehead and moved it onto the bed.

No longer a boy, he was an assassin with a vengeance. He killed to keep a promise. It was what kept him sane all these years. He pushed rational thoughts from his mind and brought forth the animal he'd come to know. The beast, who craved blood, thirsted for money and valor. He snarled and growled plotting revenge on those who'd done him wrong.

He looked into Nora's blue eyes. She shouldn't be near him—in the same room as a killer who slaughtered so many.

"Otakatay, are you okay?"

Concern etched her pretty face, and he closed off any feelings he might have for her. He needed to go. He needed to leave here and kill the man who had shot him last night. *Two times. I was shot twice.* He inspected his bare chest.

The sun shone through the bedroom window, bright and welcoming. He didn't know if it was morning or afternoon. The single thought that plagued his mind was where the other bullet had entered. He was sure it had gone into his chest, but when he searched his chest all he saw were old scars.

"I was shot twice."

He watched as her eyes darted about the room. She was nervous. The warrior within him came alert, and he scrutinized her every move.

"I was shot two times. Where is the other wound?"

"I think you need to rest." She tried to stand, but he grabbed her wrist. "Sit."

She slumped back down.

"Where was I shot besides my shoulder?"

"Umm. You were...uh...you were shot once."

He didn't believe her. He remembered a burning pain in his chest, the first place he'd been hit. The shoulder had been the second.

"No, I was shot here." He placed his palm over the center of his chest. The room dipped. He shook his head and focused on Nora.

Her face was white, and she chewed on her lip. She knew something, and he was about to get it out of her.

"Why is there no hole in my chest?"

He shook his head, battling the darkness that wanted to overcome him.

"You must be mistaken. You were shot once."

"You're one of them. You're the witkowin."

She was silent.

"I know I was shot here." He patted his chest. "Tell me what happened, now." His tone changed from calm to intense, a predator stalking his prey.

"You need to rest."

"You need to tell me what the hell is going on. Why is there no damn hole in my chest when I know I was shot there?"

The pain in his shoulder radiated down his arm causing his fingers to ache. He blinked trying to focus on her face, but his eyes wanted to close. He felt her hand on his forehead as her soothing voice faded into blackness.

CHAPTER TWENTY

Nora sat on the edge of the bed and watched as Otakatay's broad chest rose and fell in even cadence. He remembered the gunshot to his chest. *And I almost blurted out that I healed him.* She frowned. *Idiot.* Pa had drilled into her head to be careful, to keep the power her hands held to herself. The reason she'd been confined to four walls and a yard. And she didn't listen, yet again.

Otakatay had come to warn her last night. *Did he know who wanted to kill me?* She remembered the night Pa died. The sheriff still had no leads. What if the person who killed Pa wanted her dead also? Pa had no enemies, other than Elwood Calhoun, but almost everyone disliked the rich miner.

She crossed him off her list of potential murderers immediately and eyed Otakatay lying on the bed. Would he harm her if he knew? Could he have been the one who killed Pa? He had come to the cabin that night. *And thank goodness he did. I'd have burned my hands beyond repair.* He may be rough around the edges, but something told her he didn't kill Pa.

But one question remained. Did Otakatay know who did? She pressed her lips together. He was a bounty hunter after all, he hunted killers. She smoothed his thick black hair between her fingers. He knew who wanted her dead, so he had to know who killed Pa, and she was determined to find out who it was. She took the cloth from the basin, wrung it out and laid it gently on his forehead.

He desperately wanted her to see the horrible man he was, but when she observed him all she saw was sadness—broken and ragged. He held some sort of spell over her, and she wanted nothing more than to help him become whole again.

She sensed he battled with something evil, and she'd watched several times as he tried to harness whatever demon thrashed about inside of him. He bore marks upon his entire upper body, and pain melded with sorrow as she wondered how he ever survived such an ordeal.

Were those scars the reason he held such hatred for the white man? Had her people done this to him? With the tip of her finger, she traced a long scar from the rippled muscles on his stomach all the way up to his neck disappearing into the pillow he lay on.

She swallowed. Every muscle on his body was defined, and she stared in awe. She rubbed her legs together, as unfamiliar sensations pulsed in her most private place. She'd never seen anything like him. He was perfect. Her face heated as she covered him with a thin blanket. She needed some air.

She took his pants, shirt and boots into the kitchen. She needed wash water and the well was outside. *Someone wants you dead.* She peeked out the window and saw Jed working. She said a silent prayer, set her jaw and yanked the bucket from the counter.

She bolted outside. On her way to the well she picked up the other bucket to fill also. Jed waved to her. She smiled, and her lips quivered with uncertainty. She had to act normal. She couldn't go around acting leery of everyone. People would think she was crazy.

She set the buckets of water on the porch and scanned the yard, the street and the forest behind the cabin. There was no sign of Pal, and she worried he'd been hurt or worse yet, killed. She refrained from calling out his name and went inside instead. The wooden lock slid into place with a dull thud. She went to work washing Otakatay's clothes and scrubbing the floor. A knock on the door startled her. She peeked out the window and saw Seth standing there.

"Afternoon, Seth."

"Miss Nora."

The boy shifted from one foot to the other. "I found the bounty hunter's horse behind your cabin last night, and I took him to the Livery."

"Thank you."

"I know he's hurt. I heard the shots. But I won't tell anyone he's here."

She didn't know what to say. Seth had never spoken more than a sentence to her in the time she'd known him. She was a good judge of character, and Seth was genuine, he'd keep her secret.

She smiled. "I appreciate your help."

He nodded. "I'll feed and groom his horse until he's better." He tipped his hat and walked away.

He was a kind boy, and she was relieved to know he was there if she needed him.

Nora put another log onto the fire. The air still held a chill in the evenings, and she'd slipped into one of Pa's old sweaters to keep warm. Otakatay had slept the whole day, and the last time she checked on him he was still out. His skin was no longer warm, he'd been right to burn the wounds closed. Her stomach pitched remembering the sickening smell of burning flesh. She didn't want to do that ever again. Thank goodness he was on the mend and as she laid the thick quilt over top of him, she sighed.

The large pot of chicken soup simmered on the stove for hours, and she couldn't wait to taste it with the homemade bread Jess had left her. She pulled the kitchen curtain to the side and looked again for Pal, but there was still no sign of him.

Taking the ladle from the pot, she dumped a hearty portion into a bowl, and laid it outside on the porch. If Pal did come back during the night, he'd have something to eat. The gesture did little to ease the tension in her back. Where had he gone? She took one last look before closing the door for the night.

The cabin floor glistened, and no one would've guessed Otakatay had bled all over it last night. She crept into the bedroom and sat in the chair by the bed. She was exhausted and couldn't help yawning and stretching her tired muscles. Nora pulled the leather tie from her braid and placed it on the bedside table. She picked up her brush. The porcupine quills on the ivory handle massaged her scalp, and she closed her eyes.

"You're marked."

She jumped and fumbled to keep from dropping the brush, before placing it on her lap. Her eyes met his dark ones, and she smiled. "Oh, this?" She pulled back her hair to reveal the rose colored skin. "It's just a birth mark."

He frowned.

She almost went to him when he sat up and cringed from the pain. She couldn't help staring at his large muscles as they bunched and flexed before her. He reached for the glass of water beside the bed and took a sip.

"You bathed me?"

"Well, I…uh. Yes."

"Where are my clothes?"

He wasn't angry, and she realized it was the first time she'd seen a softer side to him.

"I washed them. They are hanging in the kitchen."

He nodded.

"I need to find Wakina."

"Oh, Seth came by earlier. Your horse is in the livery next door. You can go get him when you're well."

His dark eyes scanned the room, and she wondered how much he remembered of the last day and a half.

"I made soup. Are you hungry?"

"Yes."

She rushed into the kitchen and ladled a bowl for him, making sure to butter some bread, too.

"Here you go. Would you like me to feed you?"

"I'm not a damn cripple," he growled.

"I didn't mean—

"Are you not eating?" He positioned the bowl on his lap and dunked the bread into the soup.

"I didn't think—

He grunted.

She left and came back with her own bowl and bread. She shifted on the seat as he watched her sip from the spoon. His mouth twitched as he held the bowl to his lips and drank the soup.

"Do you frown often?" she asked, curious about the life he'd led before she'd met him.

He grunted again.

"Do you ever smile?"

"There is no reason to."

He put the empty bowl on the table beside the bed.

"Sure there is. Every time I hear a bird sing, I smile."

"That's because you are a little girl."

She straightened.

"I'll have you know I am nineteen years old. That hardly classifies me as a little girl."

He shrugged.

"How old are you?"

"Older than you, wicicala."

"What does that mean?"

"Young girl." He smirked.

She clamped her mouth shut. What was his problem? Why was he being so hard to get along with?

"That's your opinion."

He grunted again.

She put her bowl next to his, crossed her arms and glared at him.

"You are weak."

"I am many things, but I am not weak and I am not a *wicicaly* or whatever you call it."

"The truth lies within your eyes."

She bristled. "Pardon me, but who are you to judge?" She flung her arm at him. "You walk around like you're the damn reaper. Everyone who crosses your path is terrified of you." Her finger waggled in his face. "And so I'm clear, I don't care what you think."

"Yes, you do."

She blinked back tears and glared at him. She'd saved his life, healed him with her own hands and this is how he repaid her? She shook her head.

"You know nothing about me."

"I know someone wants you dead."

She could feel the color drain from her face, and her head spun.

"How do you know this?" she whispered.

She was unsure if she wanted to know, but the question had been asked, and she waited for his answer.

"He hired me to do it," he answered bluntly, and his black eyes roamed her face.

"But why?" *Did he know?*

"You tell me."

Get a hold of yourself. He can't be trusted. "I don't know why."

Otakatay's black eyes traveled the length of her body, stopped at her face, and she was sure he could read her mind.

"I'd say you do."

"I don't know what you're talking about."

She stood and reached for the bowls. He grabbed her wrist.

She gasped.

"I'm not going to kill you, Nora."

She believed him. He didn't lie, he had no reason to. If he wanted to kill her, he'd have done it by now.

"Thank you."

He pulled her closer until his lips were an inch from her own. His eyes never left hers, as he brought their lips together in a passionate kiss. The bowls fell from her hands onto the floor. All that seemed to matter was him, and the way he made her feel.

His tongue slid along her bottom lip, and she opened her mouth. He deepened the kiss and her body buzzed with excitement. He released her wrist and combed his fingers through her hair. Cupping her head, he pressed her closer to him.

The kiss seemed to go on forever, and she ached for his touch. Her hands caressed his chest and the muscles tightened. He pushed her from him, panting, and frowned.

Nora's cheeks flushed. She straightened her skirt, picked up the broken bowls and, without saying a word left the room.

Otakatay shifted on the bed. He wanted her, and damn it he needed to get a hold of himself before he lost control. She was in danger, and he was the enemy. He cringed when he lifted his shoulder. He wasn't going to kill her—he couldn't, but it didn't mean he should go off and seduce her. Shit, he'd been too long without a woman.

The girl knew why she was hunted. He'd seen it in her eyes. She didn't trust him, and he didn't know why that bothered him. Hell, he was a reaper like she'd said. He had no feelings, there wasn't a kind bone left within his body. Except when he was with her, he struggled to remain the man he'd trained himself to be. He grasped at the horrible things he'd done, so he could justify keeping her at a distance.

He could hear her banging dishes around. She was kind, soft and sweet. Not something to be mixed with his hate hardened bitter self. He needed to leave, to get the hell away from her. He sat up, and a searing pain stabbed his shoulder. He cradled the limb in his good arm.

He'd come here to warn her, to take her with him somewhere safe. He couldn't leave. Not until he killed the bastard that shot him. Not until she was no longer in danger. Anger consumed him, and he ground his teeth. The wasichu shot him, he'd put money on it. He ran his hand through his long hair. Nora was a girl—a girl in danger. She'd die if he didn't help her.

Shit. He owed her nothing. Yet, he couldn't walk away without knowing she was safe. He didn't like her. He simply wanted her body and nothing else. Satisfied that he held no feelings other than wanting to bed the black-haired beauty, he sat back against the pillow.

His shoulder hurt like hell, and he wished he still had his medicine bag. The Slippery Elm was good for burns and cuts. He'd given it to Nora the night she'd burned her hands, and he hadn't seen it since. He glanced out the window. He'd seen the plant in the forest and was regretting not taking some of the sticky bark. It took two days to dry and be ground into powder. Two days he didn't have.

He flexed his shoulder. The muscle was tight and sore. He removed the white bandage she had wrapped around it and examined the rippled and deformed flesh. His shoulder didn't stand out at all against the rest of his scars. The skin around the burn was red, but there was no infection, and he took the bandage, dunked it into the basin of water beside the bed and blotted the burn.

He held his arm up, grinding his teeth through the pain in his shoulder. Otakatay's forehead bubbled with sweat, and his stomach convulsed from the stress he put on the injured arm, but he continued to exercise the muscle. The eagle feather fell into his eyes. He thinned his lips. He hadn't forgotten his promise. It had taken him so long to get here. To realize that what he had was enough for now. He'd been driven by revenge and hatred. He should've completed the promise years before.

CHAPTER TWENTY-ONE

Elwood sat with his foot elevated on the mahogany desk. Ten stitches below the toes and five more on the bottom of his foot. The bruised foot still throbbed, and he'd been dulling the pain with whiskey since the previous night. The damn dog would pay, and he'd make sure it was painful.

He hoped to have Nora with him when he returned to the mine, but the little bitch wanted nothing to do with him. The fact that she was all alone with no one to protect her sweetened his plan to take her as his wife. But now he realized that she wasn't going to come willingly.

He swirled the alcohol in his glass, spilling some over the sides to run down his fingers. He was resigned to making her his wife the old-fashioned way. He smiled. Oh what fun that would be. Visions of her on his bed naked with terror filled eyes flooded his mind, and he grew hard thinking about it. Yes, he'd devise a plan. If he could get her here and ruin her reputation, everything would fall into place. Soon she'd be overflowing with his seed and so ashamed she'd be begging him to marry her.

"Boss, the boy is giving us trouble again." Red stood in the doorway his hair disheveled and a cut below his bottom lip.

He downed the rest of the whiskey and snatched the braided leather belt hanging on the hook by the door. The leather rope gave him the power he needed to run the mine and the filthy brats that worked for him.

The door to Joe's room stood ajar, and Elwood could hear Levi yelling at the boy.

"What in hell is going on?" He limped closer to them.

"I'm tryin' to get the boy tied to his post, and he ain't cooperatin'," Levi said, out of breath and harried.

Joe stood in the corner of the room. Tears ran from his eyes and into the dirt smeared on his cheeks. He pointed a colt .45 at Levi.

"Where in hell did he get a gun?" Elwood demanded.

"I was tryin' to get him tied up, and he pulled it from my belt," Levi whined.

Elwood scowled at Red unsure if he should hit him or the boy first. "Joe, you put that gun down now, you hear?"

He shook his blonde head. "No, Pa. No. No. No."

The boy would get it once he got the damn gun from him. "Please, Son, hand over the gun."

"I don't want to be tied up, tied up. I don't like it, like it." He cried. "I want June-bug, June-bug."

"June lives in town. Joe, remember the deal we have. No seeing her if you don't obey."

Joe shook his head again and waved the gun around the room. Everyone dived out of the way, and Elwood had to keep from lashing out at the kid as pain sliced through his foot. He needed to get the gun from the boy and quick. "Okay, Joe. I won't tie you up. I promise."

Joe stopped crying, and a big smile spread across his face.

The mind of a simple child perplexed him.

Joe laid the gun on the bed.

"You little bastard." Levi threw his hand back and slapped Joe across the face sending him into the wall. The sticks fell from his armpits as he slid to the floor, clutching his cheek and whimpering.

"Levi, Red, I want you to go into town and get the girl. Bring her here unharmed."

"Yes, boss," Levi said.

"On your way out, check on the others. Make sure everyone is doing what they're told. I'm in no mood for trouble."

Both men nodded and left.

Elwood closed the door and, with his other hand, released the rope with a loud snap. He smiled when Joe jumped. Careful of his injured foot, he walked toward him. The damn kid wouldn't cross him again, not after tonight.

CHAPTER TWENTY-TWO

He laid the dead rabbit on the table outside their house. Little Eagle sat beside him, a thin blanket wrapped around his narrow shoulders. Their mother had been dead two weeks, and their father hadn't returned. Left to fend for themselves, he had vowed to take care of his brother. There had been nothing left to eat in the shack after a few days, so he loaded the shotgun, and together they hunted for meat.

As the days passed, he prayed that their father never came back. He hated him, and because he took Ina from them forever, he wanted to kill him. He'd watch over Little Eagle. They didn't need anyone but each other, and together they'd make it.

He skinned the rabbit as a shiny black wagon bounced along the rutted road leading to their home. His father sat with another white man, on the seat up front. Buck Morgan had no friends, his father was a weasel, and he knew something wasn't right.

He tucked the blade beneath his sleeve and stood. He reached for Little Eagle, and with one arm pulled him close. He watched through hate-filled eyes as their father staggered down from the wagon and walked crookedly toward them. The air carried his familiar scent of sweat, unwashed clothes and alcohol.

He stepped back, taking his brother with him, and peered around his father's ripped and stained shirt to see the other man as he came closer. He couldn't help but gawk, and he forgot all about his father, when he saw the man's fancy suit. He'd never seen anything like him, or his shiny black buggy.

"Ina, Ina," Little Eagle cried into the back of his shirt as he hid behind him.

He reached back and patted the top of his brother's head.

"Un ohiti ke," he whispered. "Be brave."

The white man walked toward them.

He squeezed the knife and cupped his arm around Little Eagle to protect him. No one would harm his brother. He glared up at the well-dressed man and hissed, baring his teeth.

"What is this? Is your son part animal?" the man asked.

"He thinks he's tough, but once you knock him around a bit, he's like the rest of 'em half breeds. A coward," his father said, laughing before he took another drink from his bottle.

"What about the little one? Can he do the same amount of work?"

"I won't even charge ya for him. You can have him for free."

He studied his father then the other man. What did the man want? He took a step backward, pushing his brother with him toward the door. They wouldn't take Little Eagle, he'd protect him with his life. The rich man motioned to two large men behind him.

"Slim, Bob."

Slim had light hair, and Bob stringy and on top of his head, none at all. He hadn't even seen them he'd been so distracted by the rich man and his father.

He took another step back. Little Eagle whimpered into his shirt, and he wished there was something he could do to ease his fear. Large hands shoved him out of the way and yanked Little Eagle up into the air. Ear-splitting screams burst from his mouth. He watched helpless as Slim smacked Little Eagle on the side of the head.

He shouted, using the war cry his mother taught him, and ran up onto the tree stump catapulting himself into the air toward the man that held his brother. He slid the knife from his sleeve and into his hand, driving it into Slim's back. He yanked the blade from the flesh and swiped it across Slim's forearm.

The man dropped Little Eagle, and he dove for his brother, he had to protect him. He was struck from behind. Dark spots danced in front of him as he fell to the ground with a thud. The back of his head throbbed, and his arms hung to the sides, no longer able to fight. Two large hands picked him up and threw him into the back of the pretty black wagon. Little Eagle snuggled close burying himself into his neck and cried for Ina as it drove away.

Nora woke to Otakatay mumbling in Lakota. There was little light in the room, and she figured it was past midnight. She lit the lamp and pulled her tired muscles from the sofa and into the bedroom. She could see that he wasn't awake and knew without coming closer he was having another dream. She watched his face contort and twist. His arms jerked, and she went to him afraid he'd hurt himself more if she didn't wake him.

She put the lamp on the table and shook him.

"Otakatay, please wake up."

He stilled beneath her hand.

"You're dreaming. Wake up."

He opened his eyes and closed them again. "Leave."

She sat down in the chair and picked up the yarn and needles from the basket.

"Are you deaf? Leave." His tone left no room for challenge.

"No."

"No?"

Without looking at him, she said, "Yes, no."

"I don't want you here. Go away."

"I'm staying. Now if you'd like to go back to sleep, feel free. Or you can continue to pout. I don't care which you choose."

He grunted, said a few words she didn't understand, and she was sure she didn't want to, as he kicked his feet out from the quilt.

Minutes passed before she glanced up at him. He scowled at her.

"Tell me where you're from."

"Hell."

"Oh, nonsense. Where are your father and mother?"

"Dead and," he paused, "dead."

She stopped knitting and put the needles on her lap. "I'm so sorry. I didn't mean to bring up horrible memories for you."

He grunted again. "Buck Morgan wasn't worth the shit in the outhouse."

She didn't know what to say. He practically spat the words from his mouth as if they were poison. "He must've been an awful person for you to say that."

"Awful is too kind a word."

What had his father done to cause such hard feelings to come from his own son?

"How did he die?"

"I killed him."

"Oh."

She was silent while she debated her next question. Curiosity and the profound feelings she had for him all but shoved the words from her mouth. "Why did you kill him?"

"He was a snake who thought of himself and not his wife or two sons."

"You have a brother?"

He closed his mouth and held it shut, thinning his full lips. She met his eyes, and saw such anguish, such despair. How could she have been so daft? It was obvious that something had happened to his brother as well. The sheer magnitude of what he felt was reflected on his face. Pain and torment twisted his features and almost sent her fleeing the room to sob in a corner.

"Otakatay, I'm so sorry." She placed her hand over his.

He focused on her face, and she smiled.

"I cannot change the past."

She nodded thinking of Pa and how she'd love nothing more than to go back, and have him here once more. Life was not so easy, loved ones died. She wove the needle around the yarn and through the hole. She had no idea what she was making, and in truth it didn't matter. The hobby gave her something to do while she sat with Otakatay.

"When did your mother pass?" she asked, hoping to ease some of his pain by allowing him to talk about it.

"I was eleven winters."

"Was she sick?"

"My father killed her."

Wide eyed and mouth open, the shock of what he'd said was too much. She cleared her throat. She wanted to hold him and cry for all the horrible things he'd seen, all the unthinkable things that had happened to him. She didn't know where he'd gotten those scars, but she'd guess it was from when he was young. She couldn't imagine anyone inflicting that amount of torment on him now and living afterward.

"Is this where you were born?"

She glanced up from her knitting, taken aback by his question. He'd never asked about her past, she didn't think he cared.

"No, we moved here last year." She smiled sadly. "I've lived in every town from here to Texas." She took his silence to mean that he wanted to know more, and she continued. "Pa was always moving. He never liked to be somewhere too long. We were like gypsies, travelling from one place to the next. It was wonderful. I have fond memories of it." She had to keep from making a face as she lied, but there was no way she could tell him the truth. She didn't trust him.

"A simple yes or no would've worked."

Well, that didn't last long. Did he have a kind bone in his body? "Sorry I took up your valuable time," she huffed, and went back to knitting. She jerked the needle from the yarn. "You'd think you had somewhere to go."

"I do."

She glanced at him. "And where is that?"

"I need to kill the man who shot me."

He spoke in such matter-of-fact tones that, if it weren't for the gravity of what he'd said, she'd have burst out laughing.

"I see."

"Good. Now get my clothes."

"You are not going anywhere until your shoulder is healed."

He raised a brow.

"What good are you with one arm?"

"Want me to show you?" His dark eyes wandered her body.

She didn't miss the heated look he gave her, and it didn't take long to figure out what he meant.

She cleared her throat, shifted on her seat and went back to her knitting.

He swung his legs over the end of the bed, and she couldn't help but peek through her lashes as the blanket slid down his broad chest to rest on his lap. He yawned and stood, allowing the blanket to fall to the floor.

She buried her head in her hands. "What are you doing?"

"Stretching."

"Please, cover yourself." She waved her arm while still hiding her face.

He chuckled but didn't pick up the blanket.

He laughed? She opened her fingers enough for one eye to peek through. *Yup, he's naked, and damn it he was laughing.*

"Tsk, tsk, Wicicala."

"I am not a little girl." She shot up off the chair—her knitting fell to the floor. "I'm a grown woman."

He stepped toward her, and his chest skimmed her breasts.

"Prove it."

Without thinking, she ran her hand through his hair and pulled him toward her. She smashed her lips onto his in a feverish kiss. *No turning back now.* She thrust her tongue into his mouth and pressed her breasts up against his muscled chest. A low moan came from his throat, and he wrapped his arm around her waist lifting her from the ground.

She couldn't contain herself and ran her finger nails down his chest. He straightened, and she sensed his embarrassment. Not willing to end their embrace, she nipped at his bottom lip and was surprised when her hips rubbed against his groin. What was he doing to her? *I turn into a harlot in his arms.* But she felt whole and safe there. He sank into her and slowly pulled his lips from hers.

Nora's heart beat as fast as a wild mustang galloping across the prairies, and her breaths came in short puffs. Her breasts pulsed, and she yearned for more of him. She placed her hands on his chest.

He removed them, bringing them to her sides.

"They don't bother me," she whispered.

He coughed.

"They bother me." He picked up the blanket, and wrapping it around his middle he left the room.

She knew he didn't want her to follow, so she sat down in the chair. *I kissed him.* She touched her lips, still wet from his. She cared for him. Her stomach flipped, and she peeked at the doorway.

He aroused sensations within her she'd never felt before, making her hungry for his touch. How did this happen? She barely knew him. But as she licked her lips, remembering their kiss, warmth spread over her to linger in her most private place.

Otakatay peered out the window. He couldn't see a damn thing it was so dark. He needed to get out of this cabin. Being near Nora was no good, and he needed to stay on the path he'd set out for himself. He pulled the blanket tight around his waist. The little twit had actually risen to his challenge. He'd been playing with her, trying to get her to ask him to leave, and instead she'd surprised him with a kiss. An unbelievable kiss, one he'd think of over and over again for the rest of his life. He didn't need these distractions, especially the one that had just happened.

He rubbed his chest. He was shot here he knew it. He remembered the piercing pain when the bullet struck him. But where had the wound gone? He knew she was keeping that bit of information from him, and he figured it was because she was scared. A part of him wanted to know, to demand the information from her, while the other was intent on leaving and killing the son of a bitch who shot him.

He needed to finish this. *Wahi—I am coming.* The time had come, to become the venomous bounty hunter once again. He'd stalk his prey and use his knife to end lives. He made a fist. His shoulder was still sore, but he had to go. He had to place some distance between himself and Nora.

Tomorrow he'd leave and make sure she was in no more danger from the wasichu. As hard as it was for him to admit it, he liked the girl. She annoyed the hell out of him, and she talked endlessly, but she was soft and kind. He owed it to her to make sure she was safe, and he'd enjoy killing the white eyes.

He raised his arm and ground his teeth together. He embraced the sting in his muscle while he rotated his shoulder. The flesh burned, but he needed to work the arm so he could depend on it when needed. A paralyzed limb was no good in battle, and he continued to push the muscles as he moved his shoulder.

He glanced down at his chest and the unharmed skin. Aside from his scars, there wasn't even a mark that indicated a bullet had gone through. *Am I going crazy? I was shot here. I know it.* There was no way it could've disappeared so quickly. And why was he in no pain? He inhaled. It was as though it had never happened.

Too much for him to comprehend, he pulled the blanket up and over his shoulders. The room was chilly, and he placed another log onto the glowing embers. Nora knew what had happened the night he was shot. She was withholding where the other bullet struck him, but why? Was she afraid he'd kill her if he knew? *I told her I wouldn't.* She didn't know who hired him to kill the women like her, the ones with the witch-like tendencies. He scoffed. He never believed they held the power the wasichu had spouted of. The large bounty the wasichu paid for each scalp was why he did the work. He closed his eyes, and he'd never forget it.

The need for revenge pushed him to end lives and in return take what was owed. He had to finish the jobs, all of them, because he needed the money. He had to keep his promise. As it was he'd waited too long, been gone too many years. The guilt pushed aside any other emotions and lay heavy inside his stomach. He was a monster, and he had to end what he'd started.

He longed for peace. For a night filled with nothing but sleep. To rid himself of the demons that clawed their way through his soul and lashed out at the beast he'd become. He wished for a day he could laugh without a stab of blame piercing his chest. A moment he could embrace all that he'd done and start fresh—a clean slate.

There were times he'd fallen to his knees, the memories too much, the blood too vivid, the silence too loud, and he'd apologized—begged for their forgiveness only to be shadowed by the killer he was. The hunter who needed no condolence but the sound of justice as it screamed in his ears.

He pressed his face into his hands and rubbed his tired eyes. *It is who I am, what I've become.* He planned and plotted, and now it was time to end it. Now it was time to kill.

CHAPTER TWENTY-THREE

Nora waited for the door to close before she rushed to the window and watched Otakatay walk across the lawn. He woke while the chickadees sang, and the orange rays of dawn filtered through the windows of the cabin. Without even tasting the breakfast she'd put out, he'd left to saddle Wakina and find the man who shot him. There was no mention of him returning, only that he'd let her know when it was safe for her to venture out.

She shivered. Who shot him and wanted her dead? And how did they know of the powers she had? She couldn't see Jess saying anything to anyone about the day she healed her, and Joe, well she had faith in his promise, too. *Then who was it?*

Mr. Sutherland's face came to mind and his peculiar behaviour the other night. Her brows knitted together. He was a bit strange, but she didn't know him well enough to point a finger at him as the one who wanted her dead. She'd been in his store a few times before selling her mother's jewelry. He was quiet, and she figured that was because Willimena took over most conversations with her loud voice and overbearing mannerisms. She shook her head. He didn't seem the type to hire a bounty on women with a birthmark and a gift.

She wished her mother was still alive. She needed to ask her how she lived with such a secret. How she was able to heal and not be concerned with what people thought. Nora had been judged her whole life, if not by the people she healed, then by her own father. Pa's fear grew into resentment and then shame, until he couldn't be in the same room as her.

He preached to her about the Salem Witch trials back in 1692. How hundreds of people were persecuted without just cause. Husbands watched their wives hang from the gallows or burn at the stake. Many of the accused died within the filthy prisons.

He told the stories to her over and over again, trying to strike fear into her. But with the passing of decades people forgot about the deaths, and their concern turned toward the Indians and the need to place them on reservations. There was hardly any talk now of those who were different—of witches, or magic. But Pa still pushed her to be quiet about her gift, to never use it.

She'd shoved his concern aside, thinking he was being over protective. She never thought someone would want her dead and go far enough to hire a bounty hunter like Otakatay to kill her. Most people were kind after they were healed, thankful even. Yes, there were some who chased her, and some who wanted her for their own use, but there were so few she never heeded Pa's warnings.

She sighed and rubbed her hands together. She watched Otakatay walk inside the livery, and the ache in her chest intensified when he disappeared from her view. She saved his life, helped him when no one else could, and he'd tossed her aside as if she were nothing.

Sure, he said thank you, but she wanted more. She wanted, *love?* She frowned. He was not the kind who cared for someone like her. She couldn't deny that she had feelings for him, but the depth of her emotions even she couldn't see. *I kissed him for goodness sakes.* But was it love, or curiosity? She didn't know. He was a puzzle to her, and she yearned to put him back together.

Maybe it was her healing instinct that pushed her to want to help him. She watched while he fought nightmares. She'd seen his eyes cloud with anger and bitterness. And she hadn't missed the softness escape in fleeting moments before it was quickly hidden, tucked down far inside of him.

The empty room echoed the loneliness she felt, and she wrapped her arms around her middle for comfort. She took one last look out the window before she sat down at the table to eat the fried ham and toast she'd made earlier.

Nora was scrubbing the last plate, when a knock at the door startled her. She froze. Her hands remained in the soapy dish water as she waited, unsure of what she should do. If Pal were here he'd let her know who was there. Even though she'd only had the dog for a few weeks, she missed his companionship. She thought of him often and wondered where he was, and if he was okay.

Another knock.

"C'mon girl, I ain't standin' out here all damn day," Jess hollered.

She laughed and rushed to open the door.

"Bout bloody time." A bright smile spread across her wrinkled face.

"Hello, Jess. It's nice to see you."

She almost hugged her she was so thankful it wasn't the faceless man there to kill her.

"What brings you to town today?" she asked, stepping aside to allow her in.

"It's the first day of summer. Town celebrates it every year." She took off her hat and held it at her side. "There's always a picnic with games and later on a dance. I thought you'd want to go."

"Oh, I don't think—" she stammered. *Otakatay said to stay in the house. Not to venture out.*

"You're comin'. You need to get out of this blasted cabin."

She hadn't left the cabin in a while, and a few hours outside wouldn't hurt. She glanced out the window. It was close to lunchtime so surely no one would kill her in front of the whole town in broad daylight. Her cheeks heated. *Don't do it. Stay inside.* She folded her hands together and squeezed. Jess would be with her, it wasn't like she was going out alone. She inhaled and plastered a smile on her face.

"Let me grab my shawl."

It was a short walk to the lawn between the church and the school house. Tables were set with roasted chicken, ham, salad, bread and an array of delicious desserts. Even though she'd eaten breakfast an hour ago, Nora's mouth watered from the smells wafting toward her.

The whole town had shown up, and she smiled while she watched a potato sack race between the adults and kids. To her left was a baseball game, and to her right, four gentlemen were gearing up to play horseshoes. She tipped her face to the warm sun. Today she'd relax and enjoy Jess's company.

They zigzagged in between the blankets spread on the lawn until they found an empty spot near the school. She plopped down and smiled at Jess. The tension in her neck eased, and she set all apprehensions aside so she could enjoy the day.

Otakatay watched the town from the top of the hill. He ran his hand along Wakina's soft mane, glad he was okay. The young boy Seth had found Wakina wandering behind Nora's cabin the night he was shot and brought him to the livery to stay safe and be fed. He was grateful for the boy's fast thinking and caring nature. If not for him, Wakina could've wandered off or been taken by some wasichu.

He focused on the festivities below and tightened his grip on the reins. The town was unaware that a killer lurked amongst them or, he smirked, that one was watching. Tonight he'd kill the white man. He'd make sure Nora was safe, and then he'd carry on with his promise.

He forced himself not to glance at Nora's cabin. It was a warm day, and he wiped the sweat off his forehead. He hoped the girl listened to him and stayed inside despite the fun being had outdoors. She was safe as long as she didn't open the door. He felt bad for leaving her alone, especially with the white man hunting her, but he had no choice if he wanted to keep her safe.

Nora was different. There was no doubt about that. She was pushy, nosey, and irritating as hell, but something about her pulled at him. The first time they met he'd been drawn to her. There was something unexplainable in the way she held herself, watched him and even spoke. She radiated happy feelings, and it took everything within him not to succumb to the bright smile and warm exterior. The two days he stayed with her almost killed him.

He'd held himself at a distance for fear of being sucked into her smile and gentle attitude. He was none of those things. He stared up into the mountains. *Soon, I will rectify the wrong done.* He'd wasted enough time planning his revenge. Precious days had gone by while he lay in bed with a wounded shoulder. He'd been injured before and never stayed in bed longer than a day. He'd lost valuable time—time needed to finish what he'd started.

After he killed the wasichu, he'd leave the girl and all the soft memories she struck within him, and never return. Soon her face would disappear from his mind, and she'd be nothing more than a mere whisper, barely heard inside his heart. He tapped his heels into Wakina's sides and made his way back to the forest to wait for nightfall.

Nora spun around the street in Mr. Thompson's arms while the band played a lively tune. At first she'd been unsure about dancing with her father's old boss. He was married. His wife's rounded belly was ready to burst any day, but Mrs. Thompson smiled approvingly.

She hadn't laughed this much since she was little and Pa used to tell her funny stories by the campfire. Her cheeks ached as Jed swung her around. She lost her footing, and he slowed their pace and waited for her to catch up. She giggled as they took one more turn around the makeshift dance floor before the song ended, and they were both breathless.

The sun was low in the sky, and men hurried to light the lamps before darkness fell. The line up of young suitors waiting to dance with her seemed to be longer than when she left to dance with Jed. She placed a hand to her chest. She didn't have the energy for another dance. Not one of the men in the line even resembled Otakatay, and she couldn't help the disappointment that settled in her throat.

"I need to rest. I will come back shortly," she said to the waiting men.

A large hand gripped her arm, and before she could turn around, the doctor swung her into a waltz.

"Good evening, Doctor."

She smiled up at him and saw the horrible expression upon his face. His eyes narrowed to slits of green that cut into her, and she shivered. *What was going on?* He worked his jaw, as she was assaulted by the vigorous puffs blowing from his nose.

The sound of his breathing grew louder as his hold on her tightened. She stiffened in his embrace and tried to pull away, but he jerked her closer. He was surprisingly strong. She took a deep breath and tried not to concentrate on the hammering inside her chest. Something was wrong, terribly wrong. She tried again to pull from his grip, but she couldn't move.

"Doctor Spencer, please let me go."

He glared down at her.

She watched as his eyes glazed and he laughed. It was an unforgettable sound, clipped and giddy at the same time.

"I know what you are," he said, and she was sure he'd gone mad the way his eyes flashed with fury.

"I don't know what you're talking about."

She wiggled trying to pull herself from him. People danced around them, and she didn't know if she should scream or finish the dance.

"You're evil."

Before she could answer, he pulled her into the center of the floor and shouted. "Nora Rushton is a witch."

Nora's heart stopped right there. The music ceased, and in a matter of seconds all eyes were on her and the doctor. *Oh no. God help me.* She licked her lips and tried to swallow past the dryness in her throat. She searched the crowd for Jess and let out a breath when the old woman ambled forward.

"What in tarnation are you talkin' about, Doc? Nora's a nice girl," Jess said.

"This is not something you accuse a kind woman like Nora of," Jed said.

The doctor yanked on her braid pulling it free from the leather strings. She watched as the brown strip fell to the ground, silently mourning its loss. He pulled at her hair loosening the braid until her black tresses hung down over her shoulders and back. He jerked her close, pulled the hair above her left ear and revealed the birthmark.

"See this?" he asked the crowd. "This is the mark they all have. That's how you know they're one of them. It's the mark of the devil."

"What's this all about, Frank? Nora's never done anything to deserve such harsh accusations." Sheriff Reid stepped forward. "Lots of people have birthmarks."

The doctor's fingers dug into her arm, and she bit her lip to keep from crying out. Her lungs burned, and she tried to take a breath but couldn't. People swayed before her as she tried to scan the faces in front of her. The townspeople demanded he let her go, and she dropped her shoulders, releasing some of the tension. She took a step toward Jed and his wife, but was jerked back by the hair.

Jess pulled her Colt. "You let that girl go, Doc, or you'll be spittin' lead for a week."

"I know what she is. You should all fear her," he screamed.

Nora yelped from the snap of pain in her head as he pulled her hair again.

"What proof do you have to support these claims?" Jed asked.

When the sheriff took a step toward them, the doctor raised his gun and shot Jess. Nora's heart lodged in her throat, and her stomach dipped. In the distance she heard the women and children screaming, but all she cared about was getting to Jess, helping her.

Out of the corner of her eye she saw the sheriff dive for the doctor, and the moment his grip loosened on her arm she yanked it free. With one swift motion Nora dived for Jess, blood poured from her side. The *click* from other guns rang in her ears, but she didn't turn to see if someone was aiming at her. She needed to concentrate. She needed to save her friend's life. Without thinking of the consequences, she placed her hot hands over her friend's wound.

Nora's head spun as she clenched her muscles, feeling Jess's pain climb up her arms and slam into her side. She gasped while her ribs screamed in agony. Unable to stay upright, the pain too much, she hunched over and pressed her hands into the flesh. Nora's throat burned, and her vision blurred as she demanded the torn edges of skin close together.

She blinked. *Do not pass out.* Spasms shot across her chest and into her back, and she swayed to the side. Sharp talons ripped through her insides, stealing her breath and rocking her back onto her heels. She couldn't take the pain any longer and was about to remove her hands when she felt the wound close beneath them.

She fell to the side, laying on the dirt road and wheezed. Her hands shook restlessly, and she had no energy left to even lift them. Nora's stomach lurched. She turned her head and vomited until there was nothing left.

Every muscle in her body trembled, and her arms tingled, numb from the healing. A deafening silence surrounded her, and before she could remember where she was, before she could think of an explanation, rough hands jerked her to her feet.

"I told you. I told you all. She is a witch," Doctor Spencer shouted.

"He's telling the truth. We've seen it," a woman's voice called from somewhere in the crowd.

"She works for the devil," another shouted.

"I say we hang her. Tonight. Now," Doctor Spencer said.

Women screamed, children cried, men aimed their guns.

"Kill the witch," a woman in the crowd yelled.

The townspeople went hysterical and shouted for her life.

"She's all possessed, like," another yelled.

"Devil woman!" they chanted.

Nora's legs wobbled beneath her as each insult hit her like a bullet and punctured her tough exterior. She was so weak there was no way she could fight them all off. A tear slid down her cheek, and she had nothing left within her to even wipe it away. *Otakatay.* She didn't know why she silently called for him, but she closed her eyes and pictured his face. She sucked in gulps of air in an effort to calm herself and harness the fear as it ran rampant inside her. The doctor pulled her through the crowd as they spat and cussed at her.

"You damn fools she's not evil," Jess called from somewhere.

"Hang her, too. She's been touched by the girl," a man she'd never seen before yelled, and the crowd shouted as two men grabbed Jess and hauled her to a waiting tree with two ropes tossed over a high branch.

Pa had been right all along. He'd been right. It didn't matter that she saved Jess's life, she was different and they were afraid of her. There was no one to protect her, no one to come to her aid, and now Jess would pay the price for being her friend.

"Please," she begged, as they dragged her to the tree. "Please this is wrong. Take me. Do not hurt Jess." But her pleas fell on deaf ears as they screamed for them to be hung.

She dug her feet into the ground as they pulled her toward the waiting ropes. Crazed people, ones she'd spoken to this afternoon, pulled her hair and ripped her dress. She spotted Fred and Willimena Sutherland standing away from the crowd, fear etched on both their faces. They were afraid of her, and she felt sorry for them. A woman reached through the crowd and scratched her, cutting her cheek. She placed her forearm over her face to try and shield herself from the angry crowd.

Two horses waited under the hanging ropes, and before she was lifted onto one, someone tied her wrists behind her back. Colors blurred before her, and she prayed she'd pass out. She didn't want to be conscious when they slipped the noose around her neck. She didn't want to feel the rope tighten around her throat as the air was sucked out of her lungs forever.

A gunshot rang out, and she flinched. The sheriff rode up on a black horse, his hand held high as smoke billowed from the barrel of his gun.

"There will be no hanging." He waved the gun at the crowd and women shrieked, clutching their children close. "Let them go. We will do this the right way when the judge comes through next week."

"You saw what she is. She's dangerous. What if she casts a spell? She could kill us all," the doctor shouted. "Your children, your wives, we're all in danger. She's capable of anything. Look at the power she holds. She's evil, and we invite that here if we don't hang her!"

The crowd fired up again, demanding Nora's life. She watched horrified as the sheriff put his gun down, defeat written all over his aged face. He looked into her eyes, and she read the apology within them. The two men holding Jess tossed her onto the horse beside Nora. She couldn't stop the tears as they fell from her eyes.

"You better hope I die, cause if I don't I'll be shovin' the barrel of my 22 up your ass, you rotten son of a bitch," Jess said to the man placing the noose around her neck.

"Let her go, she's done nothing wrong," Nora begged.

They ignored her, and the crowd chanted, "Kill the witch."

She turned to Jess, her face wet with tears. "I'm so sorry."

"Darlin', don't be sorry. I'll be seein' my Marcus soon."

"This is wrong. You're innocent," she sobbed.

"Hush now. You be strong. Don't let these bastards see your tears. Then they've won. Hold your chin up."

Nora took a deep breath and willed the tears to stop. She turned toward the crowd and glared.

"That's my girl." Jess looked down at the two men beside her. "You damn heathens can rot in hell." She glanced up at Nora. "I love ya, girly." She winked before the horse shot out from under her, and she dropped.

Nora screamed as she watched her friend wiggle on the rope. She sucked in a sob as the doctor placed the rope around her neck. She struggled, and he smacked her across the face. *Otakatay, Otakatay.* She chanted his name in her mind and closed her eyes.

"You all must die. Every last one of you. Like the bitch that killed my wife," the doctor sneered.

"I am not that woman. Please, can't you see? I cannot harm anyone. I can only help them. My hands only heal."

"She said the same thing, she begged for her child, for her daughter. I would've killed the damn kid too but the bitch hid her."

"Who are you talking about?"

"The woman who stole my life," he stared at her, and she didn't miss the hollow look, "She was supposed to stop the bleeding, she was supposed to save my son. Instead she killed them."

"What was her name? What was her name?" she screamed.

He didn't answer, only tightened the noose around her neck.

Nora struggled against the thick rope. "Please, please tell me what her name was."

"Hannah." He slapped the horse, and Nora fell.

CHAPTER TWENTY-FOUR

Otakatay didn't have much time. He'd been in town to kill the wasichu when he heard the riot and went to investigate. Thank goodness he did. The horse under Nora had fled, and his heart stopped when he saw her dangling from a noose.

He let out a shrill war cry, and Wakina galloped into the centre of the crowd. He aimed his shotgun at the rope and fired. Relieved when it split and Nora fell to the ground. He glanced at the other woman swinging from the tree, when he heard the gun cock behind him. Out of the corner of his eye, he saw a man raise his gun. Otakatay turned and threw his knife into the man's chest, knocking him backward.

He leaned to the right in his saddle, his hair almost touching the ground, as Wakina cantered through the crowd. People ran in every direction.

"The witch has brought evil upon us with this Savage! Run," screamed a woman to his left.

If they only knew how close to the truth she really was. He yanked his knife from the man's chest and threw it at another man intending to fire his gun at him. The knife pierced his neck before he fell to the ground.

Otakatay jumped from his horse and ran toward the doctor who had his hands around Nora's throat. He ripped him from her and punched him in the stomach. He grabbed the knife from his back and smiled at the surprise in the wasichu's eyes.

"Thought you killed me?"

The doctor went for his gun, and Otakatay sprang forward, knocking him over. They rolled on the ground as the wasichu's fists pummeled his face. Each blow fueled his rage.

He growled and drove his elbow into the doctor's throat, stealing his air as he kicked beneath him. He glanced at Nora. She wasn't moving. He needed to get to her. He glared down at the man beneath him.

"Tonight you die," he said and without a second thought, he sliced his throat.

Blood soaked the front of the doctor's clean white shirt as life faded from his eyes.

He stood leaving the evil man to his fate, and went to Nora.

The street was empty except for the Sheriff, and he ignored the lawman as he knelt beside her. He placed his head to her chest and blew a sigh of relief when he heard her heart. Dirt smeared into the blood on her cheeks, blending with scratches on her face and arms. She'd taken a beating. He'd watched from the trees while the people tried to inflict wounds on her pretty face. Anger filled him, and he clenched his jaw.

He peered up at the old woman swinging from the rope. He straddled Wakina and cut the rope, taking the weight of the woman in his arms. Nora saved her life only to have them hang her any way. He still couldn't understand what he'd seen. How she'd done it. He closed the woman's eyes and placed her gently on the ground.

The sheriff cleared his throat, and Otakatay faced him.

"I will take care of her," he said motioning to Jess's body.

The lawman should've stopped the hanging, but he'd not been strong enough to go against the frantic crowd. Otakatay had seen the defeat written all over his aged face. The sheriff had watched as they strung the women up and never did a damn thing. He failed as a lawman, and Otakatay had no respect for him.

He opened and closed his hands, squeezing them until they hurt. He wanted to lash out at the old man, inflict pain on him, pain like Nora had felt. But the guilt of what he allowed to happen today was worse than any flesh wound he'd receive. The sheriff would replay this night over and over in his head for the rest of his life.

Otakatay went to Nora. The skin on her neck was red and swollen where the rope had bit in. She'd need some salve to heal the burn marks. *She'd need more than that.* He grazed the side of her face with his finger. She didn't deserve to be treated like this. She was kind, soft and sweet. She was white, the same color as they were, and yet they turned on her as though she were a killer, a murderer, *a breed.*

He lifted her into his arms and faced the sheriff.

"Go," the man said with sadness in his eyes when he glanced at Nora. "Take her somewhere safe."

Otakatay nodded.

The sheriff held out his arms, and he was reluctant to hand her over. Not after the man did nothing to save her. The monster within Otakatay shadowed his face, casting any illusions aside that he was agreeable.

The sheriff took a step back.

He walked toward Wakina, who knelt so he could get on without putting Nora down. He didn't spare the sheriff another glance, just kicked his heels into the horse's side and sped off into the forest.

Otakatay travelled the better part of the night to the cave nestled in the side of the mountain. After he laid her on the ground and covered her with his blanket, he made a fire to keep them warm. She hadn't stirred since he rescued her, and he wondered if she was ever going to wake up. He placed his head on her chest. The beat was stronger than before, and he exhaled.

He doubted she'd be able to talk for a few days, because of the noose. He cringed. He knew what it felt like to have a rope around his neck—to be tied up as if you were a dog.

He poked the fire with a branch and watched as the orange flames licked the air. He was so close to finalizing his plan. To seeing retribution for the years of suffering he and the others had gone through.

Little Eagle.

He stroked the feather in his hair. He'd never forgive himself for what had happened. He was supposed to keep him safe. Despair crawled through his veins to circle his heart and squeeze. There was no way he could take it back. No way to save him from the fall. He hung his head.

He escaped when the others hadn't, and he'd promised to return, to come back and save them. He ran his hand down his face. But he'd been gone so long. Would they remember? Would they still hope he'd return? He didn't know, and with each passing day he grew more restless.

He needed land and the money to buy it. They'd have nowhere to go, and he wanted to bring them somewhere safe. After years of killing outlaws, he'd built up a substantial amount of cash, but it was nowhere near the amount he required for his plan to work. For a while he thought all hope was lost, until he came upon the white man searching for someone to kill the witkowan.

He gazed out into the darkness and sighed. Desperation pushed him to do the things he'd done. The nightmares reminded him of the vengeance he carried and gave him the will to go forward. There was no choice but to throw aside the person he once was. He chose another name, one that was fitting to the beast he'd become, and he embraced the evil that it brought.

He forced himself not to care, not to love, but instead only to hate and to kill. He looked at Nora. To kill ones like her. He couldn't take back what he'd done. He couldn't forgive himself for it either. The wrongs he'd committed, and the lives he'd left behind haunted him. Blame and remorse filled him, and he gnashed his teeth together. Misery pooled inside his lungs, drowning him, and he sucked in a painful breath.

Nora stirred.

He wondered if the power she held was real. *It had to be.* He watched the old woman rise after being shot. He tried to wrap his mind around how she'd done it. How she was able to close the wound as if it hadn't been there.

He glanced down at his chest. He'd known all along she'd saved his life, but didn't understand it. He still couldn't. How was it possible? A low whimper grabbed his attention, and he watched as she slowly sat up. She was in pain, and he poured water from his canteen into the metal cup. He placed the cup on a rock beside the fire to heat.

"What happened?" she asked her voice no more than a whisper. She brought her hand to her throat.

"Your voice will return. Try not to talk."

The water boiled, and he sprinkled some of the ground witch hazel into the cup. The bark was good for many ailments, including a sore, inflamed throat. He wrapped a red bandana around the cup and handed it to her.

"Drink this. It will help."

"Jess?"

He didn't answer her right away. The old woman didn't make it. He'd saved Nora instead.

"She is gone."

She nodded and bit her lip.

"Drink."

She took the cup, smelled the drink and made a face at the awful scent.

"It works." He pulled some pemmican from his sack.

She hesitated, but the pain must've been too much because she took a long drink, and her body trembled from the horrible taste.

"What happened?"

"Don't talk," he growled a scowl on his face.

"Please tell me."

He ignored her, hoping she'd stay silent.

"Otakatay—

He brought his finger to his lips. "Shush."

"How did you find me?"

He rolled his eyes. He should've known she'd not listen and be quiet. Hell, she never shut up.

He groaned. "I shot the rope."

"You were there?"

He nodded.

"You saw what happened?"

He nodded again. How was it that he could be quiet, but she couldn't?

"Did you see? Did you see everything?"

He knew what she was getting at, but if she wanted to talk and not listen to him, he'd bait her a bit.

"I did. You're a witch."

Nora's eyes grew wide, and he watched amused as her mouth worked but nothing came out.

Finally, she is quiet.

"I am not a witch."

Well, that didn't last long. "I'd say you are by what I saw."

"I am not," her voice cracked, and she looked away. "I cannot confide in you."

"I saved your life. I'd say you can."

She was silent for some time, and he knew by the way her brow furrowed she was contemplating what he'd said.

"You owe it to me to explain."

Blue eyes watched him from across the fire, and he was sure he'd never seen anything as beautiful. He sat up taller and ignored the hammering of his heart.

"I am a healer."

"What's the difference?"

"There is a huge difference." She tried to shout, but it came out raspy and broken. She took another sip from the cup and shuddered.

It was awful stuff, but it worked.

"I am not a witch. I cannot cast spells or hurt people. I only have the ability to heal them."

He narrowed his eyes.

"I speak the truth."

He believed her, but it still didn't make sense.

"How do you do it?"

"My hands hold the power."

"You can heal anything?"

"No. I cannot heal the mind."

He nodded.

"Only flesh wounds?"

"Yes, and ones you cannot see, the ones inside."

He'd seen it with his own eyes. Hell, it was done to him and he still couldn't figure it out.

"You healed me?"

"Yes," she said with a loud sigh.

"So I was shot in the chest?"

"You would've died."

"Why didn't you let me?"

"Because I…" she averted her eyes, "because I could help."

He thought she wanted to say something else but changed her mind at the last minute.

"Why didn't you save your father?"

Nora's face changed immediately. Remorse shadowed her eyes, and she blinked away the tears he'd seen there.

"He didn't want me to."

He wasn't expecting her to say that. He took a bite of the pemmican he'd been holding, not because he was hungry, but for something to do. The space between them seemed to close in, and he moved back.

"Why not?"

"Because of me, we had to move from town to town all the time." She hung her head, and he had to lean in to hear her next words.

"He resented me for it."

Otakatay understood resentment, he understood the anger that came along with it, but what he didn't get was how anyone could resent her. She wasn't evil or horrible. She didn't hurt people. She healed them. She may be annoying, couldn't follow instructions even when her life depended on it, and she never shut the hell up, but those weren't reasons to hate her.

As far as he could see, her father was an imbecile. Hate came from deep within and if not careful it could consume a person, make them do things they never thought possible. *I would know.*

"Your father was an ass."

She shook her head.

"No, he had his reasons, and I didn't make it easy on him. But…" She stopped.

He waited.

"But I wish he'd have let me save him. I miss him so much."

One tear slid down her cheek, and he wanted to wipe it away, but held himself still instead.

"Drink." He motioned to the cup and was thankful that she listened and took a sip.

Nora's body trembled. The drink Otakatay had given her was horrible, and with each sip she had to concentrate so she didn't throw up all over the place. Her throat hurt so bad she was sure she'd never talk the same again. Her tongue was swollen, and the scratches on her neck pulsed. A cool cloth would help, but there didn't seem to be any water in the cave other than what was in her cup. She grazed her fingers over the hot skin on her neck and was surprised when he handed her one of his shirts.

"Wrap this around your neck. It will help until I can find more witch hazel for your cuts."

"Is that what I am drinking?"

He nodded.

"It relieves the swelling."

She took the shirt from him and wound it around her neck. Visions of last night crammed her mind. The noose, the crowd, the people she'd seen and conversed with that day, clamouring for her death. They attacked her, pulled her hair and ripped her dress.

She shook her head. She'd always be different, and she'd have to hide because of it. She thought of her mother. The doctor had killed Hannah Rushton years ago. He'd stolen from Nora a mother's love and warm embrace. He took from her father the chance to say goodbye and gave him a life filled with loneliness.

Anger twisted around her spine, and she straightened. She wanted to see the doctor pay for all that he'd done. She wanted him to feel the same pain her mother did hanging from the rope. The fear and revulsion of those who once were your friends, but found out you were different and called for your life. She peeked at Otakatay across the fire.

"What happened to the doctor?"

He glanced up at her, and she didn't miss the indignation as it shot from his eyes. "I killed him."

Relief spread over her, and she lifted her lips. "Thank you."

He shrugged.

She sighed.

"Are you hungry?"

He shifted his weight from left to right.

She sensed he needed to leave, and so she nodded.

He grunted and pulled his knife from the leather holder on his shin.

"Stay," he said and before she could reply he was gone.

Nora sighed and placed the cup down beside her. She was not drinking anymore. Another sip and she'd be heaving in the bushes. She thought of Jess and the last time she'd seen her. She closed her eyes as images of her friend dangling from a rope filtered through her mind.

She couldn't hide from the guilt as it slammed into her, and she let the tears fall. Jess always made her smile, and she'd cherish the little time they had together. She wiped her cheeks. Jess would curse her out for carrying on so, for being weak. She could hear her now. "Damn, girl, quit your cry babying." Jess would sure give heaven a new meaning. Nora smiled.

"You are with your Marcus," she whispered. "But I will miss you."

She moved closer to the fire. Her dress wasn't good for anything but the rag pile now. Ripped and stained, she wished she could take it off and burn it. She studied the cave Otakatay had brought her to. She didn't know where she was. He'd saved her, and each time she thought of him her heart swelled with warmth.

She was resigned to the fact that she had feelings for him. There had been something there the first time she saw him in the forest, and he threatened to kill her. But the time she'd spent with him had opened up a wave of feelings she didn't think existed, or at least she'd never felt before.

Last night she wanted to see his face in the line of men waiting to dance with her. When the town attacked her, she'd called out for him. And when there was nothing left to do but accept her fate, she closed her eyes and pictured his face. *Is it love that I feel?* She had no clue. She'd never been in love before.

She was sure of one thing and that was Otakatay. He'd been there when she burned her hands, tenderly spreading salve on them. He rescued her, risked his life to save her own, and for that she was thankful. But what she felt for him was more than mere appreciation. He was a Bounty Hunter, and he'd killed innocent women, but she knew in her heart he was not that man.

She saw within his eyes a sorrow, a misery so bleak that it broke her heart. When he kissed her, the world seemed to stop and all she could think of was him. She yearned for his touch, his eyes upon her, his scarce smiles.

She stared out into the forest. Dawn was approaching and the sun shone through the trees, bright and warm. *I love him.* It came as no surprise now that she'd accepted it, yet she didn't know what to do with her feelings.

All she'd ever wanted was someone to share her love with—someone to rely on, and to build dreams with. She couldn't tell him how she felt for fear he'd cast her aside. Otakatay never showed her any emotion other than when they kissed, and she'd been too caught up in her own feelings to watch for his.

She rubbed the edges of the soft shirt wrapped around her neck. It was deerskin, and she wondered where he'd gotten it. She inhaled the scent of leather and smoke embedded into the fabric. *Otakatay.*

She closed her eyes.

"What are you doing?"

He startled her, and she jumped, almost burning herself on the fire.

Black eyes stared down at her. He held the shot gun in one hand, and a skinned rabbit in the other.

"You cleaned it already?"

He shrugged.

"I didn't think you'd want to watch."

How did he know? She loved animals and knew their purpose, but she couldn't watch one be slaughtered.

He tied the rabbit to a long stick, added two more logs onto the fire and sat down beside her.

She inched away from the animal and fidgeted with her dress.

"You feel sorry for the rabbit?" he asked, amused.

She nodded.

"We need to eat."

"I know that," she snapped, "but why couldn't we eat berries or that stuff you were chewing on earlier?"

He grunted.

"Pemmican takes a long time to make, and berries won't fill you."

"What's in the pemmican?"

"Boiled fat, dried strips of pounded meat and some berries."

She made a face. It didn't sound appealing.

He shook his head, reached into his sack, pulled out a piece and handed it to her.

She lifted it to her nose and inhaled. The meat smelled musty. She closed her eyes and took a bite. She tasted the fat right away, but the berries added a sweet flavor, and she took another bite. It was delicious.

"You made this?"

"No, I trade for it on the reservations."

"Oh, I see."

She chewed on the dried meat enjoying every piece.

"Otakatay, did you ever live on a reservation?"

He shook his head.

"How come?" She didn't agree with what the government had done. They'd forced all the natives onto reserved land. The way she saw it, they stole their way of life. The government took their pride and smashed it.

"I am half white. I choose where I want to live."

The pemmican no longer appealed to her, and she put it on her lap.

He grasped his knife, and she saw the scars on his forearm, the same ones that marked his back and chest.

"How did you get those?"

He froze, and she watched as his eyes flickered with anger. She was sure he was going to lash out at her. She braced herself for the fight.

"A coward gave them to me," he sneered. "He believes in nothing but torturing the weak to gain riches."

"How awful." Nora's chest ached, and she laid her hand over his.

He tensed, but didn't pull away.

It wasn't pity she felt for him, but a deep sadness for the suffering he'd gone through. She ran her hand along his arm, pushed the sleeve up and revealed two nasty tracks. Nora's hands heated. She refrained, he wouldn't want her to.

She didn't care that he was full of marks, or that he was an Indian. She loved him. Her finger traced a long scar. How could someone do this to another person? Her eyes watered. What reason could they possibly have? She leaned over and touched her lips to a scar.

"Otakatay."

His forearm tightened but he didn't pull away. She ran her lips over the beveled and deformed skin, tasting her own tears. She wanted to weep for the agony of what he must've felt. He placed his hand in her hair, brushing the locks with his fingers.

She sat up and gazed into his eyes, the dark depths softened, and he rubbed his thumb across her cheek, wiping away a tear. At that moment she knew the love she felt for him was real, and he pulled her to him. She couldn't stop the swell of emotions as they burst from her and lit up her soul.

A whisper of a breath sat between their lips as he lowered his mouth onto hers in a feathery kiss. Supple lips melded with hers, and all she could think about was him and this moment. The kiss stole her senses, her fears—her heart. He'd been there when no one else had. He'd saved her, protected her.

Otakatay.

The fire crackled, the rabbit forgotten. He leaned into her, until she lay on the ground, and he hovered over her. Not once pulling their lips away. He deepened the kiss, tasting her, and she hummed beneath him. Nora's breasts tingled, while the spot between her legs heated and pulsed. She wanted him.

He unwound the shirt from her neck, while his other hand still cradled her head. He trailed kisses down her chin and onto her neck, stopping at the swollen spots to lick them. She ran her hand through his hair and onto his back. The muscles bunched, and she pressed him to her.

She didn't want this moment to end. She wanted to stay in his arms forever. His hand cupped her breast, and she arched her back. He was so tender, so gentle. She hadn't seen this side of him, and she smiled, knowing it was there all along.

He undid the buttons on her dress and massaged her bare breast with his hand, pinching the nipple. Oh, she was going to come undone. She could feel the hardness of his groin press into her. She needed to touch him. Feel his flesh beneath her palms—against her breasts. She tugged at the front of his shirt and was relieved when the buttons flew off.

She kissed his cheek, his neck and her hands rubbed the muscles on his back. She could feel the scars, there were so many.

He pulled away and was on his feet before she knew what had happened.

"Otakatay?" She sat up, holding her dress closed.

"Damn it. What are you doing to me?" The dark look she'd seen so many times before filled his eyes and cut into her.

"I... I thought—

"You thought what?" He pulled the burned beyond eating rabbit from the fire and threw it aside. "I am no good for you."

"Yes, you are." She stood and went to him.

He shoved her aside.

"No. I'm not. I am a killer, damn it."

He stood on the other side of the fire. His chest rose and fell. Rejection punched her hard in the stomach, and she wrapped her arms around her torso.

"I know what you are, and you're not that person, Otakatay."

His face changed. She watched as he masked off the man she'd just kissed, and brought forth the animal she'd seen in him on their first encounter. She took a step back.

"You're afraid, and you should be. I am a monster. I've killed women like you."

"But... but I love you," she whispered.

He grunted.

Nora's bottom lip quivered. He didn't want her not even a little bit, and she couldn't control the pain as it leaked from her eyes.

"Tomorrow, I will take you somewhere safe."

She hung her head, unable to meet his glare.

He snatched up his shotgun and left.

CHAPTER TWENTY-FIVE

Elwood paced the length of his office. The damn bastards were causing more problems. He hung the leather coil back on the hook. Blood had turned the tightly braided rawhide red. Bits of flesh still hung from it, and he smiled. He'd had to set a few of them straight tonight, and he'd beaten one so badly he didn't think the filthy Navajo would make it through the night. He'd have to replace him and soon.

Over the last year they'd been dropping like flies, some by his hand or his men's, and some from sickness. He'd told Levi and Red to toss the bodies in a pit on the other side of the mountains leaving them for the bears and cats that roamed the hills. He couldn't be bothered with digging graves. Once they were dead they were of no use to him.

Last month one of the savages found a fresh vein of coal. It brought a welcome change from the half-empty carts he'd seen lately, and he wanted more of it. He enforced longer shifts and less sleep. Those brats didn't need to rest; they were young and should be able to work a whole damn day without tiring.

He'd had to set a few straight about the rules again tonight. The tall one decided to fight, and Elwood made an example of him. He demanded respect and fear from the lowlifes. He owned them and when they forgot that, he had a way of reminding them.

He opened the drawer and pulled out a bottle of whiskey. Not bothering with a glass, he took a long swig. The liquor scalded his throat and set fire to his stomach. He glanced out the window while taking another drink. Levi and Red hadn't come back from town with Nora, and he was growing impatient. He ran his finger nails along the top of his desk, making a scratch-like sound. He wanted Nora. He'd wanted her for a long time, and he was getting damn tired of waiting for the little imp to change her mind.

He was a handsome man and could have any woman he wanted. But he wanted Nora, and damn it, he'd get her one way or the other. He'd given her flowers and jewelry. He'd asked her to dinner, but her father had said no, and dumped the gifts in the garbage. He even got rid of Jack Rushton, and she still wanted nothing to do with him.

He clenched his fist and groaned. The killing was supposed to fix everything. Nora's father was a drunk. He thought that with Jack out of the way, Nora would succumb to his charms. But she'd still denied his requests. Now there was no one left to protect her, and he'd have his way with her. She'd be his wife, the perfect trophy to perch on his arm. And when he tired of her, he'd cast her to the hills, too.

A loud knock on the door echoed throughout the room.

"Come in," he called.

Levi and Red sauntered in, their hair a mess and their clothes soiled. Both needed a bath and shave, but he had other things on his mind and didn't give a damn if they wanted to look like hell.

"Where's the girl?" he asked peering around them.

"Well, we went to town like you asked, and..." Levi glanced at Red.

"The townspeople were gonna hang her," Red finished.

"What? Why?"

"They were callin' her a witch. They hung that old Jess Chandler too," Levi said.

Jess's death was a welcome surprise. He'd battled the old crow for years to get her land, and now he'd have it.

"Where is Nora now? Did they kill her?"

He stood. He still had his stitches, but his foot didn't ail him as much as before, and he could walk without limping.

"Nah, but you ain't gonna like what we have to tell ya."

"Well, get on with it you fools."

"Some Indian rode in and saved her. Shot up the place too," Red said.

"Indian?" Elwood whispered. "Who?"

"He looked an awful lot like Hawk."

Elwood hadn't heard the name for almost ten years. The defiant half-breed had escaped killing his brother and two of his men. He hated that kid and wondered when he'd return. He knew the dirty Indian would want revenge for the beatings Elwood had given him and for what happened to his brother. How did Hawk know Nora? And how long had the renegade been in Willow Creek without Elwood or his men noticing?

Nora was his. He slammed his fist onto the desk.

"Find her. They can't be far."

Chapter Twenty-Six

Otakatay rummaged through his sack and pulled out the slippery elm. He'd found more after he left Nora's cabin two days ago. He'd take her to Denver when she woke. He figured that was the safest place for her to be. It was a city and no one would know her there. Denver was three days ride east, and he'd have to put his plans on hold. He couldn't be near her any longer.

He glanced at her, wrapped in his blanket fast asleep. Even now he was too close to her. He needed some distance from the desires she aroused within him. She'd become a distraction, one that he didn't need right now.

He shook his head. He'd been gone too long already, and he felt the weight of the time that had passed like a ton of rocks on top of his shoulders. He was so close even now, and yet Nora's safety stood in the way. He sighed. He'd have to wait another few days.

He yearned for the moment when he'd take his knife and put an end to the nightmares, when he could look at his reflection without cowering away in disgust. Was it even possible to know a night without reliving the past, a day where his soul could see beyond the evil desires within him? He didn't know, and he refused to allow himself a glimmer of hope.

He picked up the wooden bowl and grinder. With vehemence he ground the bark into a powder. His body buzzed for retaliation—for blood. *Soon I will have my revenge.* He dumped the powder into the leather sack and placed it on the ground.

Nora pushed herself up and rubbed the sleep from her eyes.

He concentrated on putting his things away and pulled the knife from the sheath on his back. Her beauty usually caught him off guard, but today he refused to look at her.

"Hello," she said.

He noticed her voice wasn't as bad as last night. He grunted.

She shifted and covered her legs with the long skirt. The rose-colored dress was torn. Dirt smeared the front. She had nothing else to wear. The fact that he cared about her dress, and he'd have to buy her a new one before they got to Denver, pissed him off. He was getting soft, and he couldn't have that. He flexed his arms. He was vengeance, fear, *a breed*, worth nothing more than flies on shit. And he'd do right to remember that.

She combed her fingers through her hair. The black strands hung to her waist in a blanket of long waves, and he was sure he'd never seen anything more mesmerizing.

She smiled, and he looked away. *What the hell am I doing?* He puffed out his chest. *I will not care for her. I will not.*

Light filled the cave, and she scanned the area. His bow and arrows, two shotguns and a knife were propped up against a wall.

"What's all that?" she asked.

"Weapons."

"I know that. Why do you have so many of them?"

"I am a bounty hunter. My job is to kill."

"Yes, so you've said." She scowled at him. "Can you shoot that?"

She pointed to the bow and arrows.

"Yes."

Why did she need to talk? He was trying to ignore her, and she wouldn't shut up. He glanced at the red bandana he'd used earlier to hold the hot cup and saw a second use for the cloth.

"Where did you learn?"

His Ina had taught him, but after years of being locked up and beaten, he'd had to retrain himself.

"I've always known."

She stared at him, and he recognized the pity in her eyes.

He sat up taller, and glanced at the bandana again. The idea had become very appealing. He worked his hands open and closed. His chest burned with anger. He didn't want her pity.

He didn't want anything from her. She thought she loved him. Hell, she was naive. He was not the type to love. He swept his hand through his hair. She had no idea who or what he was. He had no time for little girls with fantasies and professions of love. He wanted to spit, he was so disgusted. He took his knife and ran it across the whetstone.

"Are you angry with me?" She braided her hair.

He ignored her. Maybe if he didn't talk to her, she'd stop gazing at him with those innocent eyes of hers. Otherwise he'd be forced to use the bandana.

She finished her braid.

"Otakatay, have I done something to anger you? Please, I don't want what happened last night—

"Last night was a mistake."

She was quiet.

"You're a wicicala," he growled, "with little girl dreams."

Sparks flew from the blade while he sharpened it.

"I am not a little girl."

"So you've said. But when I look at you, that is all I see."

"Really?" She narrowed her eyes. "That's not what happened last night."

He grunted.

"You touched me with such gentleness. I know you're not the beast you proclaim to be."

He scowled, and his features faded revealing dark deadly corners.

"I've slashed the throats of women like you."

She went to stand, and he held up his hand to stop her.

"I know that, but I believe you had your reasons."

"I did it for money. I took their lives for paper!" He slipped his knife back inside the sheath on his back. "And I would've killed you, too."

"Why didn't you?" She threw his blanket from her and got to her feet. "Why, Otakatay, didn't you kill me?"

He spun from her. He knew why. He'd seen her face, gazed into her eyes. He didn't want to tell her. He called upon the revulsion, animosity and vile bitterness that lay dormant inside of him. He brought it forward and spun around. The knife he'd just put away, was cradled within his hand.

She stood still.

"Do not push me," he snarled.

"You're not going to kill me. You saved my life."

He ground his teeth together and clenched his jaw.

"You have feelings for me. Admit it." She tipped her chin and stood in front of him.

Before she could step back, he grabbed hold of her hair. He wrenched on it, placing the knife to her throat. "If there came a time when I allowed myself to care for someone, she would not be white," he said through clenched teeth.

He pushed her from him and picked up his rifle.

"Be ready to leave in an hour."

Nora watched him go. His cold words echoed in her mind and chilled her heart. A bottle of whiskey on an open wound would sting less. How could she think someone like him could care for someone like her, a little girl?

She winced. All he saw when he stared at her was a child. She was different. She was white and according to him no better than a snake. With every insult he'd flung her way, a tear fell from her lashes. *Where will I go now?* He was taking her to the city, and she was reluctant to go. She wanted to stay with him but knew he'd take her willing or not.

She had no one now. Pa and Jess were gone, and she couldn't go back to Willow Creek. She'd have to start anew, and whether she liked it or not, that meant without Otakatay. She wiped her wet cheeks. *I have to stand on my two feet.* She swallowed back the sob and took a shaky breath. She'd get along fine. She had to. All she ever wanted was freedom, and after Otakatay dropped her in Denver, she'd have plenty.

The love she felt for him was real, and she'd draw on those emotions to get her through the next few months. A part of her wanted to make him see how much she cared, show him her love. *How do you show a blind man the sun?*

There was no other place she felt safe than in the circle of his arms. Even though the times he held her were brief, those were the times she'd felt passion and a sense of belonging. Until he was able to drive out the demons he battled, he'd never accept her or the love she was offering. *Oh, Otakatay why won't you let me love you?*

She picked up the blanket and peered out into the forest. She needed to get out of the cave, to go for a walk. She glanced down at her attire. A good washing may help the soiled dress, and she wanted to wipe the dirt from her cheeks and neck. She'd see if there was a stream nearby, a dip would do her some good.

Tall trees stood all around her, and she stopped to gaze at the beautiful landscape before her. She followed the path as it wound down the steep hill. Not familiar with the narrow trail, she wasn't prepared for the sharp turn and almost fell over the edge of the cliff. She placed a hand to her chest. *That was close.*

She reached the bottom and glanced up at the huge hill. Would she be able to find her way back? She paused when she heard the birds singing overhead. She smiled. She studied the path, copying it to her mind and headed in the direction the birds had flown.

It wasn't long before the forest opened into a peaceful meadow. Green and purple stalks of lilacs swayed in the light breeze and surrounded the lake. Nora plucked a flower and inhaled its sweet scent. She sat down by the water's edge and slipped off her boots. She lay back, resting her head on her arms and closed her eyes.

"Well, well, look who we found."

She hadn't been at the meadow more than ten minutes when she heard the slimy voice behind her, and sensed the danger it brought.

"I'd say the boss is gonna be pleased."

She picked up her boots and slowly stood. The hairs on her neck rose. She gulped. *Keep calm.* Nora spun around and collided with two men. She recognized them right away as the men who worked for Elwood.

"What is it you want?" she asked trying to keep her composure.

"We've found it," said Red.

Great. She scanned the meadow. There was nowhere to go. She smiled at them.

"Sorry, gentleman but I have to go." She tried to go around them.

"I don't think so," Levi said, and she dodged his large hands as he lunged for her.

The men stood on either side of her. *Could I make it to the cave?* She didn't think so. She gripped her boots tightly in her hands. There was no way she was going with them. She'd have to run. *It's now or never.* In one swift movement she swung her arms out clipping both men with her boots, and ran like hell.

The boots weighed her down, so she threw them to the side. She looked back and seeing them in hot pursuit, she picked up her pace. Nora's heart thudded in her throat as she burst from the meadow into the forest. The hard earth pierced her bare feet, but she didn't have time to stop. She could hear them behind her and they were getting closer. *Where was the path? Where was Otakatay?*

She jumped over a fallen log and kept going. Branches caught in her hair, pulling the strands from the braid, and she swatted at them. When she turned to see how far away they were, she tripped on a root and went tumbling head over feet. A jolt of pain burst from her ankle, and she cracked her head on something hard. She tried to get up, to grab onto something for support, but the trees would not stop spinning around her. Nora's middle pitched. She waved her arms hoping she'd connect with a branch, when someone yanked hard on her braid.

She screamed through clenched teeth.

"Got her," Red yelled.

Levi came through the trees. An eerie smile spread across his pockmarked face, and Nora shrank away from him. He pinched her cheeks together and squeezed until she felt teeth cut the inside of her mouth. He placed his wet lips onto hers.

She punched his wide chest and shook her head.

"Boss ain't gonna like that, Levi."

He pulled away, and Nora spat in his face.

"Do not touch me again," she hissed.

Red hugged her from behind, securing her arms.

"What the boss don't know won't hurt him. Besides, we had to chase her."

Levi wiped his face with his sleeve and puckered his lips for another kiss.

She waited until he was close enough then hauled off and kicked him in the groin.

"Son of a bitch," Levi screamed and fell to the ground.

She struggled to pull her arms from Red's grasp, but the brute held her to him. She was so busy trying to fight Red she didn't see Levi until she felt the burn when he slapped her across the face. Black dots danced in front of her. She opened her mouth to call for Otakatay, but was struck with another blow. The light faded to nothing.

Nora woke slung over the back of a horse, her wrists tied together. The uneven steps did nothing for her turning stomach, and she swallowed back the urge to puke. Her head hurt so bad she was sure someone had taken a log to it. She opened and closed her mouth feeling the puffy lip. She turned her head to see where they were heading and saw smoke billowing from a large hole in the mountain. She blinked and scanned the area. She was at the mine. Elwood's mine.

Damn it.

The mine was a fair size, and as they drew closer she was shocked at what she saw. For a wealthy man, Elwood did nothing to keep up the place. Dilapidated buildings littered the property along with broken rail carts and hundreds of rocks scattered all over.

She pushed herself up onto her elbows, ignoring the pain in her head and stared at four Indian boys. They stood on either side of two wagons sorting rocks from their buckets. Another boy carrying a bucket, walked out of a hole on the mountain. She watched, horrified, while he struggled to get it to the wagons.

There were no men here. An uneasy feeling crept over her, and she scanned the area again. All she saw working were boys, and all of them native. She looked up at the hill. Two man-sized holes were shored with wood to allow the boys to walk through, but it was the tiny tunnels inside the mountain that concerned her. She wondered how many boys were forced to go inside and crawl around the dark, dank caves.

She shuddered. *The poor darlings.*

She remembered what Joe had said. Elwood put him in a cave when he was bad. These were children. How could Elwood treat them like this?

A young boy, no more than seven, came running down the mountain. His clothes were ripped and soiled. He was screaming, and she saw the tears run down his hollow cheeks. She sucked in a breath as a man burst from a wooden structure a few feet from the small hole in the mountain and chased after him. It wasn't long before he had the boy by the neck and raised his hand to the child. Nora squeezed her eyes closed.

The others stopped their work, and Nora noticed their legs were tied together. These boys were slaves—prisoners. Elwood treated them like he did his dog. Thank goodness she'd healed Pal. She hoped he was still okay.

She squinted to get a better look at the boys. Slash marks covered the skin on their arms. Her eyes misted, and she pushed her head into the horse's side to stop the tears.

When she was pulled from the horse a piercing pain shot up her leg and throbbed in her ankle. She wobbled, and stood without putting any pressure on the sore limb. She steadied herself by reaching out to grab hold of the horse beside her. The sun shone bright, and she held her other hand up to block the powerful rays.

"Nora, darling," Elwood called as he walked down the verandah of a massive house.

So this is where all the money went. The house was built with logs and boasted large wood poles holding up a covered porch. Four long windows stared back at her from the front. The home was beautiful, but left an awful taste in her mouth when she considered how he treated the young boys. She peered around him for Joe. Where was he? She hadn't seen the boy at all and prayed he was all right.

"I'm glad to see you're unharmed after the horrible incident that happened in town." He kissed her cheek.

She yanked her face away.

"Why have you brought me here?"

"Why I want to marry you, of course."

"I've told you before. I will not marry you."

"Yes, but there is nowhere for you to go."

"I will be fine. Now please untie my hands."

She thrust her arms out in front of him.

"All in good time."

He smiled, and she wanted to slap him.

"I am not staying here and I will not marry you."

"There's no one else to protect you."

"Where is Joe?"

She heard Levi and Red snicker behind her, and her throat grew thick. *God, please let Joe be okay.*

"The boy is no concern of yours."

"What have you done with him?"

"Don't trouble yourself with thoughts of Joe."

"Where is he? I want to see him." Nora struggled against Levi's hold and yelled, "Joe, Joe."

Elwood backhanded her. "You will see Joe when I say so."

She tasted blood, but she wouldn't succumb to Elwood's demands. "You bastard. You abuse young boys to work at your mine."

He raised his hands and clapped three times.

"Well done. I knew you weren't as stupid as your drunken father."

She stiffened. Pa didn't deserve his insults. She lunged forward, but Levi had a hold of her arms and jerked her back.

"Why are you doing this? Those are children."

"Yes, yes they are, and they serve a purpose at my mine."

"What purpose is that?"

"Nora, you are so naive. Do you know how much money it would cost me to hire men? I'd have never gotten to be as wealthy as I am now if I'd had men working for me."

"You treat them like slaves. You're a snake." She tried to yank her wrists free, wanting to scratch his eyes out.

"Precisely, my dear, and I intend to keep doing so."

"You have no idea what you've done. Otakatay will come looking for me." She didn't think he would, he wanted to get rid of her, but she needed to scare Elwood.

"Is this the renegade who rescued you from hanging?"

"Yes, and he'll gut you like the pig you are for taking me, too." *He is probably well on his way and glad I am gone.*

Elwood's face changed from handsome to ugly and rigid. He stepped toward her, yanking her braid so her neck craned to the side. "This renegade, did he have you?"

She wanted nothing more than to be that close to Otakatay, but he'd pushed her aside. "Yes," she lied.

"You little bitch."

Elwood's eyes narrowed and his bottom lip curled. He raised his hand and slapped her across the face.

Tears filled her eyes and her cheek ached, but she refused to show any hint of defeat. *I will not cower.* Blood trickled down her chin, and she left it there meeting his crazed eyes instead.

"You gave yourself to a savage, a lowlife, but would not come to me?" he bellowed.

"I am not attracted to someone who beats children."

He brought his mouth down upon hers in a rough kiss.

She twisted away from him, but couldn't go far with Levi holding her.

"I'd never lay with you."

"Oh, Nora, you will. But first I must use you to lure in your dear Indian."

He took hold of her tied wrists and tugged her toward the center of the mine.

Fear slammed into her, knocking the air from her lungs. She hunched over, muscles cramped and her legs shook. Elwood had lost all sense, and he no longer resembled the well dressed man she knew. He gave her a chilling glare as his lips moved but nothing came out.

"He will come for me, and he will kill you," she lied again. "Otakatay will make you pay for what you've done."

"He will come, but he will die."

She dug her heels into the ground and almost came undone from the sharp stabs in her ankle and the bottoms of her feet. She knew without looking at them, they were cut and bleeding. Why did she take her boots off? She tried to jerk her wrists from him.

"He's a bounty hunter. There will be nowhere you can hide that he can't find you."

Elwood stopped and whirled toward her.

"Do you love him?"

She glared at him and remained silent.

"Do you love him?" he screamed, shaking her arms.

"Yes."

"And he loves you?"

Oh, she wished he did. She tipped her chin.

"Perfect."

He yanked on her wrists again and she hobbled, trying not to put weight on her injured ankle. They came to a thick pole anchored into the ground in the center of the mine. Blood smeared the wood, and long slash marks covered the entire surface.

He whipped the boys here.

Elwood untied her arms, wound them around the pole and tied them back together.

She looked up. The pole was so tall there was no way she'd be able to get loose. Defeat swelled in her stomach, and she tried to ease the heaviness with slow breaths.

"Now we wait for your beloved to come," Elwood whispered close in her ear. "You see, dear Nora, I know your Indian well, and I have a score to settle with him."

The scars on his back, the deformed skin on his arms and chest, oh dear God, he'd been here. Otakatay had been here.

"He doesn't love me. I lied. He will not come for me. He used me. He hates me." She spoke the truth, and the words hurt worse than any slap Elwood could give her.

"I think he will."

He motioned for Levi, and the man handed Elwood a blue strip of cloth. He jammed it into her mouth and tied it tight behind her head.

Nora screamed into the cloth.

"I can't have you giving my plan away. Levi, you watch her." He kissed her forehead before he left.

CHAPTER TWENTY-SEVEN

Otakatay stood in the meadow and stared down at Nora's boots. When he arrived back at the cave and discovered she was gone, he went searching for her. He traced her tracks to the clearing by the lake, when he saw four other footprints. Unease crept up his neck and squeezed as he assessed the rest of the area.

He didn't like the way the prints pushed into the ground. The front of the foot was deeper than the back, as if they anticipated she would run and they'd have to chase her. The size of both prints told him they belonged to men.

He studied the area some more and spotted the broken branches on the lilacs. He went to investigate and noticed more hanging twigs. She'd come through here. He followed her trail back into the forest, to an uprooted tree stump. Dirt was strewn around, and a petite hand print was embedded into the ground. *Nora.*

Four drops of blood lay next to it. She tried to fight them off, but she was no match for their size. She was in trouble, and he needed to find her. Wild rage trampled over him like a herd of mustangs.

The sun dipped behind a cloud and cast shadows from the trees onto the forest floor as he led Wakina up the hill. The trail they left wasn't hard to follow, and he got the impression they'd done it on purpose. He ground his teeth together. His fingers curled around the reins and squeezed. He'd enjoy killing the bastards.

As the trail veered north and climbed up the mountain, recognition flowed over him like lava. He touched the feather in his hair. *I promise.* He examined the familiar cliffs and hills. Dread, thick and moist, covered his skin. He'd been waiting for this day and braced himself for the battle to come.

He clicked his tongue, and Wakina continued to climb the trail.

He didn't know how Nora knew the mine owner, or if the bastard had seen them together and was acting on revenge, but he'd find a way to get her back, even if it meant trading his life for hers. His body hummed as he imagined the impact of what the night would hold.

Vengeance, untamed and barbaric raced through his veins. He yearned to release the rage, the hate. He was thirsty for tainted black blood, and only one person could quench that need. Elwood Calhoun, the rotten son of a bitch. He was next to the devil when it came to wickedness, and Otakatay was determined to send him straight to hell.

He mourned every day for those he'd left behind. They were boys—sold by their own for a petty bottle of whiskey, or a few coins. Shunned, the boys were tossed aside, never loved or cared for. Anger stirred in his stomach, and he bit back the curses he wanted to let fly.

Visions fogged his mind, and he tried to blink them away. But as he drew closer to the mine his senses tuned in, and he couldn't stop the images as they invaded his soul. His nostrils flared, and he smelled the rancid beef that had been slapped on the ground in front of him. The pain from not eating for days forced him to put the green meat into his mouth. His belly lurched. He heard the trickle of water running down the rocks, and the wretched moans of the others starving or being beaten. He wished he could go and help them.

He remembered the weight of their dead bodies as he carried the little ones, the weak ones and the ones his age to the edge of the cliff. He felt the tears fall from his eyes when he begged Elwood Calhoun to spare Little Eagle, to take him instead. His ears rang with the snap of the leather whip, the laughter that followed and the pain that was yet to come. He heard it all, felt it all, and his insides burned with anger—with retaliation.

Tonight he'd finish what he'd waited so long to accomplish. He'd kill Elwood Calhoun. He'd release the boys and bring them home. He ran his hand down Wakina's long mane. He'd save Nora. Chances were he wouldn't make it out alive, but he promised them, and damn it now was the time for him to own up to it.

Nora had been sitting on the ground for half the day, and she was sure her face was bright red from the hot sun beating down upon her. Sweat beaded in between her breasts, and the fly-away strands from her hair clung to her forehead and cheeks.

Her nose itched, and she tried to nestle her chin into her shoulder and relieve the irritating tickle, but all she did was cause a jolt of pain to shoot up her neck. The bandana in her mouth tasted of sweat and pig, and she'd tried several times to push it out with her tongue. The stench-filled cloth was loosening, but it was still too tight.

She glared at Levi. He tipped his chair back onto two legs, slumped against the rickety fence. He was snoring loud enough to wake the dead. How he could stand this heat, she didn't know, but if she didn't get some water quick she was going to burst into flames.

She cleared her throat and was about to call out to him when another idea came to mind. She slid down onto her back and stretched, pulling at the rope around her wrists, she kicked the chair out from underneath him. The brute fell to the ground with a startled curse and rolled two times before he stopped.

She tried to hide her smile, but changed her mind and grinned at him through the bandanna. Even though it wasn't much, she tipped her chin and gave him a cool stare.

"You little wench," he spat. Dust flew from both his hands as he scrambled to his feet and charged straight at her.

She pulled herself back into a seated position as he pounced on top of her. Large hands wrapped around her throat, crushing her windpipe. She kicked her feet but wasn't strong enough to heave him off her. Black dots danced in front of her as she tried not to pass out. A gunshot split the hot afternoon air. The hands left her throat, and she sucked in fresh air.

"Levi, you touch her again and I'll put lead in your ass," Elwood said as he sauntered over.

The man glared at her, and she couldn't help but shiver. His empty, wooden eyes told her he wouldn't think twice about killing her. She gave him a nasty look, not willing to show defeat.

Elwood knelt beside her and removed the bandana. "Now, Nora, if you're a good girl, I will let you live after all of this."

"Go to hell," she hissed.

He laughed. "Ahh, you will be a fun one in bed." He traced his finger down her cheek. "And soon I will find out."

She jerked her face away and struggled against the pole, trying to loosen the ropes tied around her wrists. "I need some water."

Elwood motioned to Levi, and he dunked a tin cup into the bucket.

Nora's mouth watered.

Levi stood over her, filled his mouth with the water, smirked and spat it all over her.

She tucked her chin into her chest and prayed for the strength to go up against Elwood and his men.

"Thank you," she said curtly and turned toward Elwood. "You're wasting your time. Otakatay won't come. He doesn't care about me."

Elwood observed the hills and forest surrounding the mine. "He'll come, and I'll be waiting." He left her and headed toward the boys separating the rocks into carts.

She watched as he picked up a few, his face contorted with anger, spit flew from his mouth while he yelled at them to work faster. The boys never lifted their heads to make eye contact with him, and she noticed they flinched with each movement he made. She wished she could help them. Her hands heated, wanting to mend the open cuts she'd seen on their arms and legs. The warmth in her palms intensified, and she curled her fingers into a fist to stop the trembling.

Otakatay had lived here. He'd been Elwood's slave. It all made perfect sense now. She thought of Pal, how he was like a wild beast, attacking just for the taste of blood. Otakatay was no different. He killed for money, for a reason she didn't know, or was too oblivious to see.

There had to be an explanation. A fresh start maybe? She shook her head. That didn't seem to fit either. He could start over anytime, but he chose to hunt women like her. Doctor Spencer must've paid a handsome reward for the healers because it was the money that drove him to kill the women in the first place. If he killed for satisfaction, she'd be dead by now. But why did he need all that money? And why hadn't he come back to kill Elwood?

She surveyed the hills. There were five guards and Elwood. No one else was here. Otakatay could kill them all, and Elwood wouldn't know what hit him. So why hadn't he done it? Why was he hell-bent on travelling the continent searching for healers when the man who caused him such anguish was a few miles up the mountain from Willow Creek?

A loud slap permeated the air, and Nora snapped her head around to see where it had come from. A guard hovered above one of the boys at the rock station. The boy stooped over and clutched his cheek. She couldn't see his face for the long black hair hiding his features, so she twisted around to get a better look.

The boy glanced up, his hair falling to the side, and his eyes locked with hers. The truth unravelled like a ball of yarn. Chest tight, she bit her lower lip and held back the sob wanting to burst from her mouth. The money was for these boys—to help them.

Otakatay had tried to make her believe he was a monster, when all he ever wanted was to rescue these kids. She couldn't control the misery as it filled her eyes. How had she been so blind?

Hours had passed, and she was glad to see the sun settle in behind the mountains. Pain sliced through her shoulders, and she rotated them to ease the stiff joints. A flicker of color caught her eye, and she counted fifteen boys as they came out of the hole in the mountain.

Their ankles were chained together, and the clanking of metal links echoed toward her. Two men as dirty and unkempt as the boys walked alongside them. They were led to a building with missing planks and half a roof twenty yards from where she was tied. One by one the boys filed inside, while the men stood outside the doors.

As she scanned the surroundings for more children, she spotted another hole, no bigger than three feet high by two feet wide, in the side of the mountain. A portly guard sat outside of it. It wasn't long before more boys piled out of there, too. Some carried buckets, while the others carried a hammer and stake.

From what she could see, these boys were younger than the first ones, no older than six or seven. She inhaled, and her chest ached. Oh, dear God she wanted to help them. She jerked her arms, trying to get free. The rope bit into her flesh tearing the skin from her wrists.

The younger boys stared at her as they were ushered toward the same building as the others. Hope flashed in their eyes for a mere second before they realized she was tied up, a hostage like them. She couldn't bear to look into their eyes. No liveliness or youthful mischief swirled within the dark depths. All that stared back at her were empty, sad, desolate eyes of children forgotten. Boys that were tossed aside and not a second thought to anyone.

Her vision blurred, and she looked away, unable to see the torn and ratty clothes hanging from their bony, food deprived bodies. She couldn't gaze upon their broken and cut skin, the scars from so many beatings. And God help her, she couldn't see the despair clouding their eyes when they stared at her, knowing she couldn't do a damn thing to help them.

Hot rage bubbled and spit from her eyes as she glared at Elwood. Never in her nineteen years had she wanted to harm someone as much as she wanted to punish Elwood Calhoun for what he was doing to these boys.

She thought of Willow Creek. The townspeople assumed he was a rich miner with a simple son. They pitied him, gave him the best suite at the hotel, ordered in the finest whiskey while he was there. She was so disgusted she wanted to scream. They had no idea what he was doing up here on the mountain. How for years he'd tortured and beaten these young boys for his coal.

If she got out of here alive, she'd make sure those people knew what they'd harbored all these years. She'd make them feel the shame, helplessness and guilt she felt as this very moment.

There was a commotion by the door to the bunkhouse. She watched horrified as a little boy, no more than six came loose from his chains and ran toward her. She struggled with the rope around her wrists, wanting to reach out to him.

Tears soaked his dirty cheeks, and he yelled something in another language. Skinny arms wrapped around her neck as he burrowed himself within the curve of her hip and chest. Loud sorrowful sobs shook his little body, and she wished she could hold him in her arms. Her tears fell onto his knotty, unwashed hair.

"Shush, baby, it's okay," she crooned, rocking him from side to side as best she could. Nora's chest ached, and she didn't think she'd ever breathe the same again. The agonizing cries from the youngster tore at her soul, and she vowed to help him and the others. She'd find a way to rescue them.

The stocky guard yanked the boy from her chest and smiled down at her showing four rotten teeth. A high pitched scream came from the youngster as his arms and feet kicked the air.

"Leave him be," she yelled.

The man ignored her, walked past Elwood and threw the boy inside the building. He shut the door behind him.

"You bastard." She squirmed against the pole. "How can you do this to these children, they're innocent."

"I own them. Bought them fair and square," Elwood said nonchalantly.

"They're babies, missing their mothers."

He spun sadistic flat eyes toward her. "Some of their mothers sold them. So before you go and get all high and mighty, you may remember that I am doing these brats a favor. Half of them would be dead by now if it wasn't for me."

"But why them, they're so tiny and—

"Exactly! I can blast smaller holes, and these heathens can crawl in them. Less dynamite means more money."

"Yes, but men are a lot stronger than children."

He shrugged. "Maybe, but I'd have to pay them."

"So all of this is for the money. You're killing children for money?"

"They are Indians, and not worth shit. I'd save an outlaw before I'd help one of these lowlifes."

"Why do you hate them? What have they done to you?"

"They're thieves," he yelled. "Heartless killers who say they live off the land and then rape and murder our people." His arms flung out, and he glowered at the shack. "When I was twelve, those bastards slaughtered every man and woman on the wagon train we were on. They took my sister, and if we hadn't run, my brother and I would've died also."

Nora stared into eyes that bore hate of the vilest kind.

"Those dirty skinned Injuns," he pointed at the shack, "will pay for that day."

Elwood was a man who begrudged a whole race because of something a few had done.

"They are only boys. They have done nothing to you."

"Those boys will grow to be men, and kill our people. I plan to rid the territory of the red man, one filthy brat at a time."

Nora thought back to the boys she saw earlier. None of them looked older than fourteen. "What do you do when they get older?"

"Why kill them, of course."

"You're insane," she screamed, "I cannot wait for the day when you pay for all you've done."

He eyed her for a long while before he burst out laughing.

"My men are well trained. No one will touch me, not even your dirty Indian."

"I wouldn't be so sure. Otakatay is a killer, a hunter and he will show you no mercy."

"He won't make it past the shack." Elwood pointed to the building the boys were in.

Nora peered around him, and her breath caught in her throat when she saw three guards laying dynamite around the structure.

"You're going to kill those boys?"

"If your savage tries to release them, I will light the fuse."

"They are just children. Please, you can't do that. Please."

He shrugged. "I will find more on the reservations to replace them."

"I'll do whatever you want." She was on her knees. "I'll marry you, lay with you. Please, please take me instead."

"Now you beg for me to have you." Fire shot from his eyes. "You'd do it all to save them?"

"Anything. I will do anything. Please, don't hurt those boys."

"You're pathetic." He slapped her hard across the face. "Your skin is white. Yet you talk as if those brats are yours." He bent down until his face was almost touching hers and pinched her cheeks together. "I will have you no matter what. And then I will kill you too."

She didn't know what else to say. She yanked her face from his grip and wrestled with the ropes around her wrists. She needed to get free to save them, to save Otakatay.

Elwood pulled the bandana back over her mouth. He kissed her on the forehead and laughed all the way to the house.

She screamed through the cloth lodged between her teeth and kicked her legs out. How was she going to warn Otakatay? How was she going to rescue the boys? She lay limp against the pole, helpless. Bile crawled up her throat, and she swallowed past the angst—the utter disappointment of not being able to do something. She stared through tear-filled eyes at the shack.

God help us all.

CHAPTER TWENTY-EIGHT

Otakatay stood among the corpses and skeletons. He'd gone to the open gravesite to pay his respects to those who hadn't survived long enough to see him return. He'd stood on the cliff high above the bodies, but needing to be closer, he climbed down the mountain.

There he saw Yellow Knee. He was a fresh body among the dead, and Otakatay ignored the sob lingering in his throat. The boy had been eight when he'd escaped and promised to return. Now, he'd never know freedom. He'd never breathe fresh air that wasn't tainted with rotten meat, vile bodies, and coal. He'd never taste the glory of independence. Otakatay had been too late for the young man. He'd failed him.

The pressure of what he'd done sank onto his shoulders, and he fell to his knees. The bow tied to his back cut into his skin, and he left it there. He hung his head. Remorse stirred in his gut, raw and spoiled. Guilt pressed into his back, curving it, as he moaned from deep within his soul.

Anguish clouded his vision, and he couldn't contain the sob as it burst from his clenched teeth. Tears overflowed onto his cheeks and chin. He placed his hand on Yellow Knee's cold one.

"I am sorry." He looked at the bones of the dead around him, "I am so very sorry."

He sat with Yellow Knee for the better part of an hour, before he carried the boy into the forest. There, he found a clearing, and laid him down on the ground. He pulled a bow from his pack and rested it gently on Yellow Knee's chest, he was a warrior. He couldn't let the mountain cat or any other animal feast on the child's body, so he gathered rocks to place around and over the boy.

"Wakan Tanan kici un—May the Great Spirit bless you." He placed the last rock over him and left.

Otakatay waited until it was dark and decided to come into the mine from the north side, where the graves had been. If Elwood and his men were watching for him, this would be the last place they'd guess he'd come from. He edged along the mountain until he could make out the house and other buildings below.

Three fires burned around the mine, lighting the area. He scanned the ground for any sign of Nora and stopped when he saw something move. He spotted the rose-colored dress immediately. She was tied to the whipping pole in the middle of the yard.

Rage rippled through him, and he flexed his hands. Had Elwood whipped her? He squinted to get a better look, but she was too far away. The miner would know great pain if he so much as touched one hair on her head. She hadn't moved. Her hands were tied to the pole, and her body slumped to the side. Time was running out.

He scrutinized the rest of the mine. He counted four men, two on either side of the shack, one by Nora, and one twenty feet below him. Quietly, he aimed his arrow at the man closest to him. He pulled the string back, paused, held his breath, and let go. He listened as the arrow whistled through the trees and struck its mark.

He jumped over a fallen log and took off down the hill toward the man. The arrow protruded from the man's back, and he was on the ground moaning in pain. Otakatay pulled his knife and placed it between his teeth. He rolled the guard over, and drove the blade into his heart.

One

He wiped the blood onto his denims and inched closer to the other buildings. He moved with ease, blending into his surroundings. He crouched within the bushes beside the shack, cupped his hand and hooted. The guard looked up into the trees. With great skill, he came from behind slit the man's throat and carried him into the forest. He left him there for the bears and the crows.

Two

The hinges on the wooden door creaked as he opened it. He stepped inside and tripped on something. He leaned over to get a closer look.

"Son of a bitch."

Elwood had laid dynamite around the building. He was going to kill the boys. He needed to get them out of here and fast. There was enough dynamite to kill them all and bring the building down on top of them. He turned toward the sleeping boys. He curled his lip. The mine owner would die tonight.

He stepped over the dynamite and waited until his eyes adjusted to the dark room. The stench invaded his senses, and he pushed all thoughts of the past from his mind. He needed to help the boys before all hell broke loose.

I promised.

Bodies were strewn all over the dirt floor fast asleep. Many were missing and had died since he'd been here. Shame settled in his gut. He searched the sleeping faces for any familiar ones and recognized a few. The rest had been too young when he'd escaped.

He knelt and woke an older boy. The smell from his unwashed body made Otakatay's eyes water.

The child opened his eyes and sat up.

"Do you speak English?" Otakatay whispered.

He nodded.

"Do you remember me?"

The boy's brown eyes narrowed, and he tilted his head to the side. "Cetan?"

Otakatay smiled. "Yes, it is me, Cetan."

The boy leapt into his arms.

He didn't care if the boy smelled. He wrapped his arms around him and squeezed. He'd take him and the others home. "What is your name?"

"Shinte Galeska—Spotted Tail."

"I need your help. You have to wake the others while I take care of the guard out front."

The boy nodded and scrambled to do as he was told.

Otakatay crept toward the door. The guard was directly on the other side. He paused, determining the best way to overtake him, when one of the boys began to cry. The door swung open, and he stepped back into the shadows.

The guard charged forward, whip in hand.

Otakatay lunged from the wall, knocking the man to the ground. He hadn't noticed how solid the guard was until his large chunky fists pummeled Otakatay's face. He could feel blood drip from a cut above his left eye. The blade of the knife poked into his leg, and he struggled to get it. The guard was a head taller than him and fifty pounds heavier.

He looked back at the boys and took a hard punch to the chin that snapped his neck back. He whirled around to face his attacker. Another blow to the jaw crushed his teeth together and sent painful vibrations up the side of his face. They wrestled with each other on the ground, and Otakatay was on the bottom. He glanced at the boys again. They were standing against the wall, watching the fight. Some were crying.

I promised.

Otakatay growled. He spat the blood from his mouth and heaved the giant off of his body. With panther-like skills he jumped on top of him, pulled his arm back and drove his elbow into the guard's nose, breaking it. Blood sprayed everywhere, and he hammered his fists into the man's face until he no longer fought back. The guard was out cold, or dead, and he didn't give a damn which it was. He huffed, as his chest rose and fell in uneven cadence. He wiped the blood from his mouth, and gathered the boys so he could usher them into the forest.

Halfway across the shack, a flicker of light eliminated the room. Fear knocked the air from his lungs. The guard had pulled himself to the open door, struck a match and was lighting the dynamite.

"Run! Run!"

Nora sat up. She could've sworn she heard Otakatay. A loud boom echoed throughout the mine as the darkness lit up with orange and red. Hot air blew across her face as the building the boys were in exploded.

"What the hell?" Levi said from behind her.

Oh, no. Not the children. She thrashed against the ropes as a black cloud rose into the sky. Every muscle in her tired body screamed in pain. The shack had been blown to bits. Charred wood and ashes floated in the black sky. She tried to hold on and fight back the tears, but the shock of it all was too much, and she sobbed into the bandana lodged in her mouth.

"What the bloody hell happened?" Elwood shouted, as he ran toward them, Red in tow.

"Not sure. It just exploded."

Nora laid her head on a rock as harsh sobs shook her body. She tried to suck in a breath that wasn't paired with an excruciating pain in her chest, but it was no use. Her shoulders ached, and her hands went numb. Nothing mattered anymore. Otakatay and the boys had died.

"They must've seen the Indian. Why else would they blow the building?" Levi said.

Elwood marched toward the burning wreckage. He picked up a piece of wood, and hollered out in pain. It was hot, and he dropped it, dancing around holding his hand.

He deserved more than a burned hand. He deserved to die. She glared at him.

The debris from the shack had fallen in large chunks where the building once was. There was no way anyone could sift through the mess until everything cooled off.

Levi fell to the ground beside her, an arrow wedged in his chest.

Elwood fired his gun into the forest around them. He ran toward them. "Where did it come from?"

"I don't know. It's that savage. He isn't dead. He's here." With one arm, he dragged himself to the fence and slumped against the pole. Blood flowed from the wound on his chest.

Elwood broke the arrow off and tossed the stick aside. He handed Levi a gun. "Shoot at anything that moves."

Levi nodded as sweat formed on his forehead, and he turned a pasty shade of gray.

Another arrow whizzed by, hitting Red in the throat.

She wasn't sure if he died right then or from the next arrow that struck him directly in the heart. She scrambled to the side, but she wasn't fast enough and his bloody body landed on her legs, pinning her to the ground.

"We're going to die," Levi whined. He waved the gun out in front of him and shot into the trees.

"No, we're not." Elwood pushed Red off of her legs and untied the rope that held her to the whipping pole. He tied her wrists in front of her and hauled Nora to her feet.

Nora's arms and legs were weak, and she stumbled as she tried to stand.

"Stand up, damn it." He lugged her up.

The bandana, moist from her tears and saliva, had stretched. She pushed it out of her mouth with her tongue. "Let go of me you rotten bastard."

She jerked her arms back, trying to loosen his grip.

He cuffed her with the butt end of his gun.

Pain vibrated up her cheek bone, buckling her knees and sent vomit up the back of her throat. She swallowed so she didn't throw up. He wrenched on her hair, and she stood.

Otakatay.

"If your lover shoots another damn arrow, I will kill you."

"Go to hell." She spat in his face.

He growled and punched her hard in the jaw.

Nora fell to the ground, the dirt floor swayed beneath her, and her vision blurred.

Elwood pulled her up again. He clamped his right arm around her waist and held her arms pinned to her sides.

"Hawk," he shouted into the forest. "Hawk, you low-life half-breed. Show yourself. Come down and face me."

Elwood was hysterical. He muttered to himself words she couldn't understand, and his left eye twitched while his head ticked to the side.

"Get your gun ready," he said to Levi.

The man bobbed his head up and down, while he aimed the short barrel at the trees in the distance.

Hours passed, and Otakatay still hadn't come through the forest. The first rays of light began to crest over the mountain as dawn approached. Elwood sat in a chair with Nora on the ground in front of him. She glanced at Levi. He hadn't moved in over an hour, and she wondered if he'd passed out or died.

Where was Otakatay? Had he left her here to fend for herself? Had he freed the children before the shack exploded and forgotten all about her? She didn't think he'd do such a thing, but the throbbing in her jaw and cheek had her second guessing him. She was exhausted, her muscles sore and tender. Every time she moved pain sliced across her arms and legs.

Over the last few hours she'd listened to Elwood mumble and convulse behind her. He'd gone crazy. He'd shoot at anything that moved and had reloaded his .42 several times since sitting in the chair.

The trees rustled in the distance, and she narrowed her eyes to get a better look. Elwood heard it too and fired at the bushes.

"You are wasting valuable bullets."

Nora spun to see Otakatay standing ten feet from her, his shot gun aimed at them. A purple bruise covered his right cheek, and a nasty cut over his left eye was caked with dry blood.

He was here all along.

Elwood stood and hauled her with him. He pointed his gun at Otakatay, and then changed his mind holding the barrel to Nora's temple instead.

"Levi, Levi," he yelled.

"Your friend is dead," Otakatay said.

Nora sensed the danger, as it oozed from his body, and she shivered. He resembled the killer she'd seen in the woods weeks before. The hunter and Elwood was his prey.

"If you shoot, I pull the trigger and kill the bitch."

"She is not mine. I don't give a damn what you do with her."

His words stung worse than any cut she'd ever received. Unable to look at him, she averted her eyes to the ground.

"Yes, she is. You rescued her from hanging. She said you've had her," Elwood sneered.

Otakatay laughed. "Those are fantasies of a little girl." His black eyes scrutinized her attire. "I would never sleep with a white woman."

"You're a liar. You've always been a liar," Elwood screamed. The sound reminded her of a cat in heat.

Otakatay cocked his shot gun and the click seemed loud enough to wake the dead. "Where is he?"

"I should've killed you back then," Elwood tightened his grip on her.

"Where is he?"

"He is dead."

Regret flickered across his black eyes, and he blinked.

Elwood fired his gun, and Otakatay dropped to the ground.

"No," she screamed, yanking herself from Elwood's hold. She ran to Otakatay and fell onto her knees beside him. Blood soaked his shirt above his forearm. He'd been shot in the lower shoulder. *Thank God.* Her hands heated and shook.

Elwood stood over them, his gun aimed at Otakatay.

"You will have to shoot me first," she said and sprawled across his chest.

Otakatay ignored the pain in his arm. He bit back the smile lingering at the corners of his mouth after Nora lay on top of him. She was quite the fighter, and he was proud of her. As he waited for the guard to die and dawn to approach, he'd watched her.

Elwood had hit her several times, and her pretty face showed the signs of his fists. She didn't cower from him, instead lifted her pert chin and challenged him, making the mine owner go even more insane.

He sensed Elwood standing over him now, about a foot from his legs. Nora was still stretched out on top of him.

"You stupid bitch." Elwood grabbed her hair, pulling so hard that she screamed out.

Otakatay flexed his muscles.

Elwood stood with his arm around her throat and aimed the gun at him.

Quick as a bolt of lightning, he kicked his leg out and tripped Elwood, sending both him and Nora to the ground as a shot went off.

He was on his feet, knife in hand, when he saw blood ooze from Nora's leg. Within minutes the front of her dress was soaked, and her bruised face lost all color. He let out a violent howl, and lunged at Elwood knocking him backward.

"I will enjoy this," he said between clenched teeth, and he pressed the blade into Elwood's throat.

A bone-chilling growl came from nearby. Otakatay twisted and was face to face with a black wolf.

"Attack, Savage. Attack," Elwood shouted, squirming beneath Otakatay.

The dog bared his fangs and growled as saliva dripped from his mouth. Black eyes narrowed in on Elwood, and he snarled, licking his teeth. The black hair on his back stood straight up, and he pawed at the ground.

Otakatay slid carefully off of Elwood, sensing the dog wanted nothing to do with him.

He went to Nora. She was passed out from the loss of blood. He ripped the bottom of her dress and tied it around her thigh to stop the bleeding. He pressed his head to her chest and was glad to hear the strong beats.

He smoothed the dark strands of hair away from her face and kissed her forehead. She'd fought for him. She was willing to give her life for him. He observed her tied wrists, the skin red and swollen, her bruised cheeks and pink lips. She never cared that he was a half-breed, that he'd killed women like her, or that he'd said hurtful things to her. She still cast her body over his injured one, willing to take a bullet for him.

He'd been wrong all along. She was his match. She was his woman, and he loved her. He lifted her into his arms, bit back a curse from the stinging in his arm and carried her toward the house.

The sharp growl from the wolf as he bit into flesh and Elwood's loud screams faded into nothing, and Otakatay never turned around.

He kicked open the door and walked through the well-furnished home into the kitchen. He laid Nora on top of an oiled wooden table. A bucket of water sat on the counter. He dunked the cloth in and squeezed out any excess moisture. He pulled her skirt up and cleaned the wound. The bleeding had stopped, so he left her side to build a fire in the hearth.

When the flames had grown hot enough, he heated the knife until the tip was bright orange. He bit down hard and dug the blade into the wounded flesh, searching for the slug. He blew out a relieved sigh when, less than a minute later, he pulled the lead ball from her leg.

She stirred, and he needed to get moving before she woke. He heated the blade again and without hesitation, he pushed it onto the hole, burning it closed.

Nora tossed her head from side to side and cried out while reaching for her leg. He didn't know what to say to ease the pain as she whimpered beside him, so he pulled her close and held her instead.

He brought his forehead to Nora's and whispered, "Techihila mitawin." He gazed into her sea-blue eyes and knew his heart would never beat the same again. "I love you, my woman," he repeated in English.

She gazed up at him, and her eyes watered.

"Nora, Nora," Joe called from behind them.

Otakatay helped her sit up.

"Joe, thank God you're okay," she said.

Otakatay released her and pivoted toward Joe. *It can't be.*

The boy had been beaten, his white shirt was ripped and blood stained. A frayed rope bound his wrists. He leaned into one stick, and Otakatay's chest ached when he stared at Joe's deformed legs. *Elwood said he was dead.* His stomach lurched, and his throat worked as he tried to swallow. Tears filled his eyes, and he held out his hand.

Joe took a step and recognition danced within his own eyes. "Cetan? Hawk, Hawk?"

He'd waited years to hear those words, and before he could catch himself, before he could reign in his emotions, a loud sob burst from his lips. In two strides he reached Joe and hugged him tight.

"How I've missed you."

"Hawk, Hawk. You came back," Joe cried.

"I will never leave you again. I promise."

Nora cleared her throat, confusion written all over her beautiful bruised face, and he went to her.

"I'd like you to meet my brother, Little Eagle."

She smiled as tears shone in her eyes.

He stared at her. Nora amazed him. She was in pain, and yet she was smiling. He left her to search the kitchen for clean bandages and found some strips of cloth in one of the drawers. He pulled the leather pouch from his pocket and rubbed the slippery elm onto the burn before wrapping it tight.

Nora flinched, but did not cry out. The love he felt for her brought more tears to his eyes.

Joe stood beside him, as Otakatay lifted Nora from the table, cradling her in his arms. Together they walked out of the house and watched as the boys ran from the forest shouting, "Hawk, Hawk."

Nora pulled his chin toward her. "I love you."

He smiled and touched his lips to hers.

Epilogue

One year later

Nora stood on the porch and peered out at the land surrounding her home. It had taken them six months to get things in order on the ranch. The addition to the house was complete. The day Hawk rescued the boys, her life changed forever.

She smiled.

Sheriff Reid, Fred Sutherland and a few others from Willow Creek had shown up at the mine that awful day. They'd seen the smoke from the explosion and wanted to make sure everything was all right. The men were ashamed and mortified at what Elwood had done. They promised Hawk, Nora and the boys a place within Willow Creek. Most of the townspeople were welcoming, with apologies and tearful hugs when they saw the boys.

Sheriff Reid handed Nora the deed to Jess's ranch. Happy to have somewhere to go and pleased to be continuing Jess and Marcus's dream, Nora took the deed and wrote Hawk's name alongside hers. They owned it together. With the reward money Hawk had acquired they purchased more livestock and built onto the home for the boys.

"Our little one is hungry," Hawk said from behind her.

She faced him and smiled.

He held their daughter, Morning Star, bundled in the crook of his arm. At two months old, she was all her father. Black hair and tanned skin, but she did have Nora's blue eyes, and behind her left ear, folded in the crease, she too was branded.

She was beautiful, and some days Nora sat staring at her for hours.

"You cannot feed her?" she teased, as she ran her fingers along the top of the baby's head.

He smiled, and she knew she'd never tire of seeing his face light up with joy.

"No, I cannot." He kissed the top of Morning Stars head and placed her into Nora's arms. "I don't remember, Wife, if I've told you yet today how much I love you?" he whispered into her ear.

Nora smiled. "Yes, my husband, you have, twice this morning. But I cannot remember if you've shown me."

His black eyes twinkled, and he kissed her neck, allowing her a taste of what was to come. "I will make sure to show you tonight."

She shivered in anticipation of their love making.

He laughed and wrapped his arms around her. "Wastelakapi—Beloved."

She tipped her head and kissed his chin. She knew the name he called her, and each time he said it she melted.

Since moving to the ranch, her husband had changed. No longer angry and bitter, he now had a different purpose—raising the boys and being a husband and father. His happiness overflowed onto her, and together they built a home filled with love and laughter.

"Hawk, Hawk. Come quick," Little Eagle called from the field.

He chuckled. "I must go and see what my brother wants."

"We'll sit and watch from here," she said.

He looked down at her, the passion and love vivid in the dark depths. He kissed her slowly, lingering a moment, before he ran down the steps toward his brother.

Nora's heart swelled while she watched her husband place his arm around Little Eagle and talk with him. He never tired of him, or his questions. Otakatay had found peace with his brother. She watched as Raven and White Bear sauntered over, and Hawk messed their hair affectionately. He'd taken the boys from the mine and given them a home.

Once a week, she taught them lessons from the school books she'd acquired by mail. She enjoyed the time she spent with them. Over the months Nora grew so close to each boy that they called her Mother. She loved each one as if he were her own.

Hawk was intent on showing them the Lakota way, but encouraged the white man's as well. He wanted them to be fluent in both worlds. He trained them to work with the horses. He showed them how to brand cattle and till the land surrounding their home. He taught them to take pride in what they had.

He worked long hours tending the livestock and the fields with the boys, and she missed him during the day. She counted the hours to when the house was quiet and everyone was asleep. In the privacy of their room, he'd take her in his arms and between tender kisses, he'd whisper in Lakota how much he loved her.

"Nora, Nora, Nora," Little Eagle shouted.

Pride filled her as she watched her brother-in-law run across the field without his sticks, his knees no longer deformed. She'd healed his legs a month after they'd come to the ranch.

"What is it, Little Eagle?"

It had taken her awhile to get used to his new name, but now she only saw him as such.

"A butterfly, a butterfly." He ran up the steps and stopped in front of her and Morning Star. Loud breaths came from his smiling lips as he opened his hand to reveal a squished orange and black butterfly.

"Oh, honey, I think the butterfly is dead."

His eyes watered, and his bottom lip trembled.

"It's okay, there are plenty more," she said and pointed to a yellow one flying around the oak tree in the yard. "Why don't you see if you can't find me another one?"

"Okay, okay." He dropped the butterfly onto the porch and took off into the field.

Nora picked up the pretty insect and sat back down in the rocking chair. She nestled Morning Star close and placed the butterfly on top of the blanket.

A dimpled hand reached out and touched the black-tipped wings.

The wings fluttered, and Nora smiled as the butterfly flew away.

Keep reading for a note from Kat and a sneak peek from
Blood Curse, *Book 2 in the Branded Trilogy.*

MESSAGE FROM THE AUTHOR

Dear Reader,

This story is very dear to me because of the emotions both main characters go through. Otakatay has been cast aside from his own people. He's grown up a slave where he fed his hate for white people and those around him. He trusted no one and relied on no one. There was never anyone there to give him guidance or to show him kindness.

Nora leads a very similar life in regards to her emotions. All she wants is the love of her father, who resents her for the gift she was born with. But Otakatay and Nora both took different paths in how they dealt with these situations. She has not allowed her father to alter her way of thinking. She doesn't care what color you are, if you're rich or poor. Everyone is equal to her, everyone deserves a chance. But she is still judged. She is still an outcast, who has experienced hatred at its worst.

When I see the way our world is, full of hate and anger, I cringe. I watch people, myself included judge others by the way they look, or how they behave. The old adage "Walk a mile in someone else's shoes" fill my head and bring me back to reality that I am no better than the next person.

It was love that healed Otakatay and saved Nora, and it is with love and empathy that we can look at those around us who are different and hold out our hand.

I hope you enjoyed *LAKOTA HONOR*.

Love,
Kat

BLOOD CURSE
BRANDED TRILOGY, BOOK 2

Appalachian Mountains, Virginia 1723

Pril Peddler lifted the green shawl from her trunk and wrapped it around her bare arms. The change in seasons brought a damp chill to the morning air, and the heavy woolen wrap kept her warm. She peeked at the small face, huddled under the blankets at the back of the wagon. The charm above the child swayed on the string Pril had hung it from. A dull ache hummed in her chest when she thought of the horrific loss her clan had been dealt.

The evil was near, and she'd need to work another spell to keep them safe. Late for counsel with her brother, Galius, she kissed the soft cheek of her daughter before heading to the door.

Hand up, she shaded her eyes from the bright sun as she stepped from the back of the vardo. She pulled the heavy burlap curtain down to close the opening and walked toward Galius.

"Your steps are light this morning, Sister. One would think you did not want to be heard," Galius said as he stirred the coffee beans inside the metal pot.

Tension twisted her gut. He was right. She did not want this counsel. She did not know what to say. She let the flicker of merriment in her brother's eyes wash over her, relaxing the muscles in her shoulders.

"My step is the same." She poked him with her finger, trying to ease her own nerves and his as well.

His lips lifted as if to smile, and she held her breath. It'd been weeks since he smiled. Pril's heart ached, and her lips trembled.

He held up the bubbling pot. "Would you like a cup?"

She inhaled the aroma of strong coffee beans and nodded, taking a seat on a wooden stump by the fire.

He handed her a cup and sat down across from her.

The wood crackled, and sparks jumped from the heat onto the ground in front of her. She tipped her chin, concentrating on what to say next. Ever since the murder of her niece, she'd not been able to hold a conversation with either of her brothers without offering apologies. This morning was no different. She could not look Galius in the eyes and see the anguish and sorrow within them.

The Monroes had come again.

They'd never be safe.

She blinked away the tears hovering against her thick lashes. Tsura was asleep in her wagon, while another was lost to them forever. The door of her brother's wagon creaked open, and Milosh's wife, Magda, stepped out. Black circles settled around her sunken eyes, and Pril felt the stab in her chest once more. Long brown hair fell untied down the woman's back. The black clothes, she'd put on weeks ago, hung on her body unchanged and wrinkled from sleep. Milosh came from behind their wagon, a jar of honey in his hand. Pril stood when Galius' large hand grabbed her wrist.

"They are not wanting to see you today, Sister."

She heard the regret in his voice, swallowed past the guilt in her own throat and nodded. Milosh hadn't spoken a single word to her since the death of his child. He blamed her, and it was clear so did Magda.

"I…I'm so sorry, Galius."

He didn't reply right away, and without seeing it, she knew he had wiped the tears from his eyes. "Alexandra's death is not your fault."

The words were spoken because they needed to be. Gypsies stayed together no matter what. They were family. There was no truth to his words, and Pril knew it.

"Are you going after them?" she asked.

"I hold no power. No spells flow from my lips. I am strong, yes, but they are stronger." He stared at her, his eyes pleading. "We need the pendant."

Guilt thickened her tongue. The gritty residue clung to her lips and tasted bitter.

The talisman had been in their family for generations, blessed by each new Chuvani. Vadoma had promised her the pendant before she died, but Pril never saw it, and there had been no time to search for the jewel when they fled.

"Without the pendant we cannot break the curse. We cannot protect our people."

She knew this. They all knew this, but no one had a clue as to where the talisman was. She'd tried to call an image forward, to make a finding spell, but nothing worked.

"We have lost one of our own. Our clan is frightened. They have lost faith. We cannot fight the Monroes. We have neither the numbers nor the skill." He took a long drink of his coffee. "And neither do you."

She glanced at him.

"I know you, Sister. You're planning to take Tsura."

Pril sighed. She did not know what else to do. The Monroes were coming for her child. Alexandra had died because of that. Milosh and Magda hated her.

"Running is not going to change anything."

"It will save lives. It will…help Milosh and Magda to heal."

"No, it will not. Running will get you and Tsura killed, and that is all."

"How can you look at me when you know what I've brought to our family, when you know that this is all because of me?"

Galius blew out a long breath that moved his thick beard from his lips. She watched, through tear filled eyes, as his bottom lip quivered.

"Vadoma put this burden on you. For that, we do not judge."

Their sister had died a vile death. She'd betrayed their clan and had been hung while being burned. Pril ached for her sister's guidance and counsel. She yearned to know that what she was doing was right.

"We had a plan, and up until Alexandra's death it worked. We will rethink and come up with something better—stronger."

The plan was simple. Dress the girls as boys, and the Monroes wouldn't find them. But someone had figured out Alexandra was a girl. Someone had told the Monroes. They came for her, stealing the precious child in the middle of the night. The morning two weeks before, as the clan frantically searched for her, a harrowing scream Pril would never forget echoed across the land. Milosh found his daughter's body by the river, her neck broken.

She raised a shaky hand to her mouth so she wouldn't let out the sob she held against her lips.

"I have enough for one more protection spell." She had lied. Her forehead ached because of it.

He glanced at her, his eyes showing no emotion. "You will concoct another."

"I cannot."

He frowned.

"The spell has the oil Vadoma blessed. Without it, Tsura is at the mercy of the Monroes, and so are we."

Galius pumped his large hands into tight fists. "Surly you can think of another?"

"I cannot. Vadoma placed the blood curse. It is only with the blessed oil that I am able to create the spell to keep danger away. The oil is almost gone."

He worked his jaw. "That gypsy whore—

She held up her hand to stop him from blaspheming their sister. It wasn't right. It brought evil to curse your own, and Pril would have none of it.

"Our sister had her reasons. Leave it be."

"Reasons? She betrayed us. Left us with a curse we cannot break and wealthy plantation owners hunting our very hides—killing our children!"

She hung her head unable to look at him. What could she say? He was right. Her very niece had died but thirteen days ago.

"Where is the book?"

Throat tight and dry, she refused to meet his gaze. The book held her mother's spells. Only she knew where it was, and unlike the pendant, she'd not lose it.

"I have it safely tucked away."

"Is there no spell for what we need?"

"The child is not of my blood. I cannot protect her, or the others, like she can."

Tsura was Vadoma's child, but Pril raised the girl as her own.

"And she is gone."

"Has been nigh on four years."

Galius' face softened. He placed his hand on her shoulder. "I need to speak with Milosh. We may have to move again, once he's healed." He gave her a light squeeze and walked away.

Pril watched through hooded lids as Galius moved toward Milosh. The two shook hands and embraced. She longed to be enfolded in Milosh's arms, forgiven of all her transgressions.

She wiped at the tear on her cheek. He'd not consider it, for he despised her. Magda placed her head on her husband's shoulder. Their love was strong, and she prayed it would get them through their grief.

She brought the cup to her lips and sipped the now cold coffee. Memories of a time, when life was simpler, brushed her mind. There were no worries. No threat of the Monroes hanging over them. They were free. Now, they never stayed in one town longer than a month. The Peddlers wandered the land, searching for a safe haven where they could raise their children.

The rustle from the other wagons brought her head up, and she watched as the rest of the clan rose for the day. Sisters Sabella and Sorina exited their vardo and smiled at her from across the yard. The two girls had joined them a few years ago, when the Monroes had attacked their family, burnt the wagons and killed most of them. Both unwed and beautiful, they were very good at creating new balms and potions to sell at the markets. Sorina enjoyed living with the clan, and she loved to visit with the others, while Sabella never spoke and preferred to remain alone.

She lifted her hand and waved. She liked the sisters and had shared dinner with them many times.

Her brothers knew the truth about Pril's child and had made a pact to never speak a word of it to anyone. She, on the other hand, was finding it difficult not to tell the others. Each time they hid the children, packed in the middle of the night, or took turns guarding the camp, she felt the stab of guilt twist in her heart.

"Mama?"

Pril turned, mug still in hand, and gazed at her daughter. Black corkscrew curls fell around her plump cheeks and clung to her pink lips. She wondered what her hair would look like grown out and knew, if the Monroes did not stop their relentless hunt, she'd never see the day.

There were days when Pril herself forgot, only ever seeing her child in long pants, cotton shirt and a cap. But in the evenings, when the moon was bright, she cherished the mother-and-daughter moments they had in their wagon. Pril told her daughter made up fairytales of Kings and Queens. She'd allow Tsura to play with her dolls and try on the lovely dresses Pril had secretly made for her.

She held out her hand and watched as Tsura ran to her. At four she didn't understand how to use her gifts, which sometimes resulted in accidents. But it wasn't the mishaps that had her worried. It was the mixture of good and evil, within the girl, that she feared.

"Oh, my sweet. What has you up and out of the vardo already?"

Tsura's green eyes locked with hers. "I had a bad dream."

Pril straightened. Dreams were the way her people saw the future, or the past. Tsura had them often. She took the girl's hand and led her back to their wagon. She smiled at those they passed on the way. Her shoulders straight, she remained the same not to draw anyone near. Once inside the wagon she closed the flap, and waited a few minutes before she sat on the bed beside her daughter.

"What did you see?" she asked.

"Blood, Mama. Lots of blood."

She squeezed the blanket on the bed to stop her hands from shaking. "Whose blood?"

The child shook her head, black curls bounced up and down. "I do not know."

Pril pulled her daughter close and kissed the top of her head. Tsura went very still, and her tiny body grew hot. She sat back and gently placed Tsura away from her. Past lessons had taught her well.

"Sweetheart, are you okay?"

Beads of sweat formed at Tsura's hairline, to drip down her forehead and cheeks.

She was careful not to touch her and placed a hand beside her daughter's instead. The heat from the girl's flesh warmed her hand, and the wagon grew hot.

"Tsura, look at mama."

Green eyes that showed a red rim around the color stared up at her. Pril wished she could do more to help her child. When Tsura got like this, Pril knew she couldn't control what her body was doing. She wanted nothing more than to help her daughter learn how to use her gifts. With Vadoma gone she would have to learn alongside Tsura.

"Mama?"

She smiled, watching as the redness left Tsura's cheeks. She reached out to sweep back the wet curls hanging in the girl's eyes.

"I'm sorry." Tsura hung her head.

She pulled the girl into a tight hug, her body still hot, but Pril didn't care. "You are learning," she said.

She felt the nod against her chest and squeezed her tighter. Thankful once more that she was safe. "What were your thoughts?"

"I was angry."

"How come?"

Green eyes peered through black lashes. "Because Alexandra's gone."

She ran her finger along her daughter's round cheek. She pushed aside the guilt pressing against her soul. "We are all very sad."

"I've seen the man who stole her."

Pril waited until her heart resumed its normal pace and asked, "You saw him?"

She nodded.

"What did he look like?"

"He was a negro."

That was odd. The Monroes always sent a well-dressed aristocrat to do their dirty work. Were they enlisting the help of their plantation workers now? That would explain why none of the Peddlers spotted the well-dressed killer. The Monroes had sent a slave.

"But, mama?"

"Yes, dearest?"

"The man did not kill her. He tried, but he could not do it."

"How did Alexandra die?"

"I do not know."

Pril pulled her close. If Alexandra hadn't been killed by the slave, then who had taken her life?

"And mama?" Tsura whispered. "They killed him."

Pril ran her palms down the front of her skirt as uneasiness settled deep within her, and the soup she'd eaten for dinner churned in her stomach.

The Monroes were near once more. She'd not done the protection spell over them all, the one she'd said countless times before, to protect Tsura and the others from harm. She used the oil on Tsura, thinking she'd concoct a different spell for the others—but she'd forgotten, and now Alexandra was gone.

She hung her head. *How could I have been so foolish? I am the reason my niece lies within the cold ground.* There was nothing she could do to stop the desolation as it crawled up her spine and curved her back. Life was precious—even more so when it was a young one. It was any wonder Milosh blamed her so. The shame covered her and blurred her sight as tears washed her cheeks. She'd been selfish when she should have rationed the oil and cast the spell—strengthened the charms.

She pulled the jars from the shelf. Rosemary, bark and the remnants of the oil her sister had blessed. The jar was empty, except for the thin layer that clung to the glass walls.

Pril did not receive the gifts her sister had. Vadoma had been the firstborn daughter to Imelda, the enchantress. Their mother had been very strong in her magick, aiding those in need with potions and spells. Pril held no such power. Her only gift was the counting of the spells. She could not move things, throw a beam or have seeing dreams. She was useless.

She blew out a breath and stared at the last of the oil. There was enough to strengthen the charm, but not cast a full protection spell. She'd known this when she used the oil for Tsura a month ago. But now that her niece was gone, the act of what she'd done came down upon her, weighing on her heavily. She leaned into the counter and pressed her fingers to her temple, massaging the strained blood vessels.

She took the jar and stepped outside into the darkness. The clan asleep for the night, she went to Mortimer, her Ox, tied behind the vardo.

"Hello, my friend." She stroked his rough fur. "I need but one drop this time."

The ox turned his head toward her and bowed.

She smiled.

"Good boy."

Quickly, she slid the needle along his neck enough to produce one drop of blood. She held the jar next to Mortimer's neck, watching as the blood ran into the glass mug and mixed with the oil. She dipped her finger into the mixture and ran it along the scratch.

"For the gift thou hast given, receive mine with love." She watched as the wound healed.

Inside the vardo, she stoked the fire in the small cook stove and placed an empty pot on the burner. She pinched the rosemary, a symbol of Vadoma, and dropped it into the jar of oil to swirl with the spice. She watched as it mixed together with the oil and blood. Next she took the bark from the forest and dropped it into the pot. The bark sparked. She poured the mixture of oil, blood and rosemary into the pot, listening as it bubbled and hissed.

"Protect mine child from the evil that hunts. Keep her spirit hidden to their wants."

The liquid evaporated into a cloud of smoke, and she watched as it drifted over the child to settle on top of her sleeping form.

BLOOD CURSE is available in a new 2018 edition!

ABOUT THE AUTHOR

Kat Flannery's love of history shows in her novels. She is an avid reader of historical, suspense, paranormal, and romance. She has her Certificate in Freelance and Business Writing.

A member of the National Romance Writers of America and Paranormal Romance Guild, Kat enjoys teaching writing classes and giving back to other aspiring authors. She also promotes other authors on her blog. She volunteers her time at the local library facilitating their writing group, and has taught writing classes there as well. She's been published in numerous periodicals throughout her career, and continues to write for blogs and online magazines.

Her debut novel CHASING CLOVERS has been an Amazon Top 100 Paid bestseller. LAKOTA HONOR and BLOOD CURSE (Branded Trilogy) are Kat's two award-winning novels and HAZARDOUS UNIONS is Kat's first novella. Kat is currently hard at work on her next series, THE MONTGOMERY SISTERS.

VISIT KAT AT: www.katflannerybooks.com
FIND HER ON FACEBOOK: Kat Flannery, author
FOLLOW HER ON TWITTER: @KatFlannery1
GOODREADS: www.goodreads.com/author/show/5284914.Kat_Flannery
GET KAT'S NEWSLETTER: http://eepurl.com/druxu9

24476197R00104

Made in the USA
Columbia, SC
28 August 2018